SINGLE MALT

AN AGENTS IRISH AND WHISKEY NOVEL

LAYLA REYNE

Single Malt

Cover Design: Cate Ashwood Designs

Cover Photography: Wander Aguiar Photography

1Ed Editing: Edits by Kristi, Deborah Nemeth

2Ed Editing: Adam Mongaya, Sandy Bennett

Second Edition

August 2023

E-Book ISBN: 978-1-962010-00-9

Paperback ISBN: 978-1-962010-01-6

Content Warnings: Explicit sex; explicit language; violence; off-page death of a former spouse; instances and/or discussion of homophobia.

ABOUT THIS BOOK

FBI agent Aidan "Irish" Talley had it all until a harrowing car crash left him with a heap of survivor's guilt and a hole in his heart where his happily ever after used to be. Aiming to fill the void, he returns to work—and to a new partner. Charming, smart, and athletic, Jamie is the last thing Aidan's bruised heart needs.

Cyber agent Jameson "Whiskey" Walker joined the Bureau three years ago and has pined for Aidan ever since. Working with the Irish expat is a fantasy and a challenge, one Jamie intends to win by earning the surly older agent's trust and respect.

Except there's no time for team building when a hack on a high-security biocontainment facility spirals into a larger terrorist threat. With targets on their backs, Aidan and Jamie are forced to trust each other as they're pushed to the explosive edge. Even then, it may not be enough to save the thousands of lives at stake, including their own.

Competent heroes, action-packed thrills, and high-stakes romance blend together in this adrenaline-fueled first book of three, now in its second edition with a new cover and formatting and extended content.

AUTHOR'S NOTE

Yes, whisk(e)y is spelled multiple ways in this book and series. This is intentional, not an error, and is based on current naming conventions for distilled spirits (and because I'm a whisk(e)y snob who wants it correct). For the uninitiated (and as a forever reminder for Kim):

Whiskey—with an 'e'— refers to grain spirits distilled in Ireland and the United States.

Whisky—with no 'e'— refers to grain spirits distilled in Scotland, Canada, Australia, or Japan.

So, for example: Jameson, the brand of grain spirit distilled in Ireland, is whiskey; and Macallan, the brand of grain spirit distilled in Scotland, is whisky.

I won't bore you with bourbon, rye, and all those distinctions. This should do you. Cheers!

To my KrnuL Panik:
For the countless hours of "Destiny," bottles of whisk(e)y, and years of love that made this dream possible

ONE

Tonight was a top-shelf whisky kind of night.

Cleared by the Bureau to return to work after an eight-month absence. Three-piece suit cleaned, pressed, and ready for his first day back. New partner and new assignment waiting for him. Aidan didn't know the identity of either yet, but that didn't matter. He needed something—*anything*—besides alcohol and playgroups to dull the crushing survivor's guilt.

Pushing aside half-empties in the kitchen cabinet he'd repurposed as a bar, he dug the Macallan 18 out of the back corner and set it on the granite countertop. He had just grabbed a crystal tumbler out of the adjacent cabinet when the doorbell rang. He pulled out a second glass, not altogether surprised by his late-night visitor. He left the glasses and scotch on the dining room table and crossed the living area to his door.

Checking the peephole, he confirmed his visitor's identity and swung the door open. "I wondered if you'd make the drive down tonight."

Melissa Cruz breezed past him, tossed her oversize Fendi bag on the couch, and toed off her studded Valentino sandals. "Least I could do, seeing as starting tomorrow you'll be making the drive up to San Francisco every day again." The offspring of a Black ballerina and a towering Cuban refugee-turned-restaurateur, his sister-in-law, and now boss, sashayed on model-long legs across the living room while pulling her thick fall of dark curls into a ponytail. Aidan had never met anyone as graceful, or as deadly.

"Please," he said, closing the door behind her. "I know you're just here to mooch my whisky."

"And you know I'd rather drink tequila." She pulled the cork out of the tall, slender bottle of scotch and sniffed, wrinkling her nose. "Gabe never could break you of this nasty habit."

Aidan pressed the heel of his hand to his stinging chest and swallowed hard, struggling for words. "Mel," he managed hoarsely.

"You ready for tomorrow?" she asked, obligingly changing the subject. She poured two fingers worth into each tumbler and held one out to him.

Taking the glass, he fell into the chair across the round wooden table from her. "I don't know, boss lady, am I?"

Mel had been promoted to Special Agent in Charge of the FBI's San Francisco field office two months ago. A well-deserved promotion to a position she had been gunning for since Academy. "Your medical and psych evaluations say so, but Dios sabe you're smart enough to fool just about anyone."

He took a swig of his drink, eyeing her over the rim of the glass. "Except you."

"Except me." She pinned him with her dark brown eyes,

full of sympathy and concern. "I hurt too, Aidan, same as you."

He drowned his rebuttal in another swallow of scotch. He loved Mel like a sister, and he didn't doubt her pain, but no way was it the same kind of agony he suffered every day. From the hole in his chest where his world used to be, to the pins in his arm that, with every move, reminded him of all he had lost. She'd lost her brother and a colleague, but he'd lost Gabe, his husband, and Tom Crane, his FBI partner for fifteen years.

"If you're not ready, you don't have to come back yet," Mel said. "Or at all for that matter. Between your trust fund and the inheritance from Gabe, you're set."

Aidan tossed back the rest of his whisky, letting the burn slide down this throat and fill his hollow chest with fleeting warmth. As much as he enjoyed spending extra time with his niece and goddaughter, Katie, he had finished his physical therapy, passed his psych evals, and was eager for the distraction of work. At forty-two, he still had plenty of agent years left in him.

"What've you got for me, SAC Cruz?" he asked, making his stance on work clear.

Mel emptied her drink and turned the glass over on the table. "You're off undercover work and long-term assignments. I want to keep an eye on you awhile longer."

"No argument here."

Gabe, an investment banker who'd worked all hours, hadn't minded Aidan's interminable absences. Now, though, with his family still tender after losing Gabe and almost losing him, Aidan didn't intend to disappear for weeks on end in the barrios chasing drug dealers or in grimy mob bars working over informants.

"Good." She tapped her manicured trigger finger against her glass, a tell that meant she was holding something back.

"What else?"

"I don't think it was an accident."

The same words he had ranted for a month after waking from his two-week coma, only his allegations had been born out of shock and denial. He couldn't cope after learning his husband and partner were dead. Eight months removed from that terrible night, he had progressed past pain and guilt-induced conspiracy theories, past angry finger-pointing at incompetent local detectives, to accept they had been in the wrong place at the wrong time. That he hadn't swerved fast enough out of the way of an oncoming SUV.

The entire time, Mel hadn't spoken a word to him about the accident, and now she was saying his grief-stricken notions had been right?

"What the hell?" He slammed back from the table, toppling his chair and surging to his feet. He kicked the chair out of the way and paced the narrow strip of hardwood floor between the table and wine racks. "Why are you telling me this now and not eight months ago? I twisted myself into knots for weeks thinking I'd missed some clue or that I should be out there catching the assholes responsible for their deaths. And fuck if I wasn't right."

She let him burn out his anger raging and pacing. Once he'd gathered himself, righted his chair, and sat back down, she rose and went to her bag on the couch. Returning with a small black flash drive and a red-striped restricted personnel file, she pushed the former across the table to him first. "This arrived for me on the day of my promotion."

He picked it up and turned it over in his hand. It was a generic model, something anyone could buy at any office supply store. "What's on it?"

"I don't know."

"You don't know?"

"The files are encrypted. It was delivered to my home, no return address. I tried opening it on my personal computer, but I can't get past the file directory."

"You didn't have our cyber team try to crack it?"

"Given the circumstances of its delivery and the attention I received with the promotion, I didn't want to risk it."

"Because you think this"—he held up the flash drive—"has something to do with the accident?"

"Every file on it is dated the day of the crash."

He dropped the jump drive as if he'd been burned. It bounced, end over end, to the center of the table. "So that's my next assignment? Uncover the truth behind the accident?"

"No, that's not your assignment."

He furrowed his brow. "I don't follow."

"This investigation"—she tapped the flash drive with her nail—"is off the books for now. Someone above me shut it down as soon as SFPD ruled it a hit-and-run. Until we know for certain it wasn't, and who and why the investigation was shuttered, we fly under the radar."

He nodded toward the personnel file. "Is that someone you suspect is involved?"

"No." She nudged the folder toward him. "This is your new assignment."

Opening the file, he read as far as the top line, which identified the department the file belonged to, and slammed it shut. "Cyber?" He shoved the folder back at her. "What the fuck?" He reached for the bottle of scotch and poured himself another double. He had agreed to no undercover work, expecting she would assign him to a local field team. Maybe legal or financial crimes, given his law and business degrees. Cyber had never crossed his mind. Sure, he was technically competent and logged an embarrassing mountain of hours playing *Destiny*, but he was no hacker, nor did he know how to track one. "Do you really think Cyber is the best use of my skills?" He glared across the table, willing Mel to change her mind.

"Your skills as an investigator and field agent are the very reason I'm putting you in Cyber. Your partner and mentee has the hacker end of things covered."

"And who are you partnering me with?" He slouched in his chair, downing half his whisky. A split second later, once her words sank in, he bolted to the edge of his seat. "Wait, did you say 'mentee'? Are you partnering me with a rook? That is the last thing—"

"Calm down. I'm partnering you with Walker."

"The Whiskey kid?"

Mel nodded and pushed the personnel file back in front of him. "Jamie's the best we've got in Cyber. He also shows promise as a field agent, though he hasn't been out there much in his three years since Academy. That's why I need you to mentor and assess him. He's committed to Cyber for two more years, so you'll work cybercrimes cases that take you out in the field."

"You'll never be able to put him undercover. His ugly mug was all over sports television when he played."

Mel raised a disbelieving brow. "Ugly?"

She had him dead to rights on that lie. Opening the file again and flipping past the cover sheet, Aidan stared down at the younger agent's headshot. Waves of light brown hair, piercing blue eyes, high cheekbones, and a wide, easy smile. *Ugly* wasn't a word anyone ever used to describe Jameson Walker, dubbed Whiskey by the national sports media given his first and last names. As a married man, though, *ugly* was what Aidan had told himself anytime the sinfully handsome two-time NCAA champion crossed his path.

"Fine." He pushed the file away and threw back the rest of his scotch. "The kid's never met a reporter or camera that didn't love him, which only reinforces my point. He's blown for UC work. Way too recognizable."

"That doesn't preclude him from all fieldwork." Frustration laced her voice. "He's got potential. You'll bring it out in him."

Aidan didn't want to rile Mel. He had been on the receiving end of her temper more than once. But he didn't see how a partnership with Walker would work. He had no interest in cybercrimes and no interest in being partnered with someone so goddamn attractive while he was still reeling from the losses of eight months ago.

He scrubbed his hands over his face and into his hair, clenching the freshly dyed blond strands. "Hermana, this is a bad idea, for so many reasons."

Standing, she rounded the table and rested a hip next to where he'd propped his elbows. Hands that could snap a man's neck wrapped gently around his wrists, tugging his hands from his hair and holding them in hers. "Trust me, hermano. It may not seem like it with your first case back, or the second, or even the third, but I'm giving you everything you need."

"Everything I need for what?"

Her fingers tightened around his. "To solve their murders."

Standing inside the cave door, Aidan tucked the file he carried under his arm and peeked through the server racks. Interior to the thirteenth floor with no view of the outside world, "the cave" was what everyone called the converted boardroom housing Cyber Division. A few other agents sat at their workstations along the back wall, but there was no sign of Walker.

Good.

Aidan needed the extra minutes to pull himself together. He'd caught maybe two hours of sleep last night. After Mel left, he'd booted up his personal laptop and plugged in the flash drive. He'd made it as far as the directory of files with the date that made his chest ache and got no further, though not for lack of trying. Realizing the encryption was beyond his skill level, he'd pinged a couple tech-savvy informants, and when they failed to get him through the wall, he'd messaged his *Destiny* buddies, hoping to find a hacker among the gamers. No such luck. By sunup, he'd been on his youngest sister's doorstep, laptop and doughnuts in hand, offering to get his niece ready for preschool if Grace would take a crack at the encrypted files. As head of IT at Talley Enterprises, she worked magic with computers, but in the two hours she had given him, she managed only one wave of the wand, cracking a file containing two bank account ledgers Aidan couldn't make heads or tails of.

A voice inside his head, one that sounded an awful lot like his boss and sister-in-law, reminded him the quickest path to solving the riddle of the flash drive was right through those server racks—or should have been. Last night, between bouts of beating his head against the wall, he had reviewed Jameson Walker's file. BS, with honors, in computer science from North Carolina, top of his crypto doctorate class at MIT, one of the Bureau's top Cyber agents in only three years. But Aidan was reticent to trust a thirty-year-old kid he hardly knew.

A kid who'd broken every road course record at Quantico, stripped the test car afterward, rebuilt it overnight, and broke his own record the next day, which was why Aidan had spent the better part of his first day back at work culling vehicular data from his accident reports and redacting all identifying information. Walker knew how cars moved. Would he see something in the tire tracks the SFPD detectives had missed? Would something in the way Aidan's Jaguar had crumpled lead them to the dark SUV that had never been found?

Before he started to spiral into the doubt and guilt that always colored his thoughts about that night, Aidan shook off the memories and straightened his tie. He was nervous enough as it was for a meeting with a man he'd passed in the hallway countless times. It wasn't just the jump drive in his pocket or Walker's good looks making him uneasy. He'd been partnered with Tom Crane right out of Quantico. They had learned the ropes together and built a solid foundation of trust that kept them at the top of the Bureau's clearance board. He and Tom had been a well-oiled machine for fifteen years. Aidan didn't think he'd ever be so professionally well-matched again—definitely not with a partner twelve years his junior and in a division where he had little experience. He didn't know how to be a mentor. He had never flown solo or been in one place long enough to take on that role. The pressure of doing so now was a responsibility he hadn't counted on when returning to work.

"No need to get gussied up for me."

Aidan startled at the deep Southern drawl behind him. Despite the other man's presence around the office and on television, Walker's North Carolina accent always threw him for a loop. Not something heard often in the Bay Area and one of the many reasons sportscasters and every secretary on the floor loved him. More disturbing, though, was the fact Aidan had been so lost in thought he hadn't heard Walker approach. Was he that out of practice or was the other agent that quiet on his feet, despite his six-foot-five shooting-guard frame? Banking the question for later, Aidan turned to face his new partner.

"Don't flatter yourself, Whiskey."

Grinning, Walker leaned his muscled shoulder against the doorjamb. "You're the one straightening his Windsor knot and playing with those shiny cuff links."

Aidan stopped his thumb from absently swiping over the gold and emerald clovers Gabe had given him on their wedding day. Tugging his jacket sleeves down, he gave Walker a discreet once-over, not letting his eyes linger more than professional courtesy allowed. Dusty, worn Chucks, battered Levi's, a gray Giants jersey hanging open over a snug black tee, revealing a sculpted torso and cut biceps. It took all of Aidan's considerable undercover work to hide the spark of desire rocketing through him. Eight months since his husband's death, ten years since he'd felt a flicker of interest in another person besides Gabe, and it was this one—his new partner, his mentee, a straight man by all accounts—who stoked those embers to life again.

"I'm sorry." Aidan shook off the disturbance. "Did I miss the casual-day memo?"

"Easy, Irish." Walker removed his baseball cap and ran a hand through his hair, ruffling the flattened waves. "Boys and Girls Club outing at the ballpark later this afternoon."

"Irish?"

Walker's blue eyes sparkled like he'd solved an impossible puzzle. "The cuff links, the brogue in your voice that slips sometimes . . ." He leaned forward and Aidan fought not to react to the heady tropical scent of his cologne. "And I've only ever seen eyes that color on natural redheads."

"What color is that?" Aidan asked, putting aside the fact Walker had seen through the disguise he had worn for three decades.

"Autumn," Walker answered, voice dropping an octave. "Like a pile of fall leaves back home, right after it rains. Dark brown swirled with brick red and flecks of gold."

Coffee with a dash of Goldschläger, Gabe used to say. But damn if Walker's description, spoken in that seductive drawl, didn't send another flare of desire scorching through him.

A flare instantly doused by guilt and propriety, compelling Aidan to snap, "Awfully poetic for a jock."

The sparkle in Walker's eyes died and all affability bled from his expression. Shouldering past him through the server racks, Walker lowered himself behind the messiest desk in the mini bullpen. On either side of two laptops, stacks of files teetered, pens lay uncapped, and empty soda cans rolled. He pushed aside a file heap, paid no mind to the papers he sent flying, and threw his heels up on the desk corner. "I don't think you came here to talk poetry, Agent Talley. What do you need from Cyber?"

Shit.

In his haste to shut down his own traitorous reactions, Aidan had swung too far the opposite direction. Walker was his partner, his mentee, and slinging insults would not earn his trust. Instituting damage control, he circled the desk and hitched a hip up on the opposite corner. "Mel didn't tell you?"

"Mel?"

"SAC Cruz."

Walker shook his head, and Aidan added another bottle of scotch to her IOU tally. "You've got a new partner."

"Who?" He dropped his legs and shot to his feet so fast Aidan barely had time to get out of the way. "Am I getting transferred out of Cyber?"

"No." Other agents were staring. Aidan waved them off and beckoned Walker to sit back down. "We'll be doing a bit of both. Mel wants you assessed for fieldwork."

"*We*?" Walker appeared adorably dumbfounded. "You're working Cyber now? But you and Agent Crane were this office's top field agents."

Aidan ignored the kick to his gut elicited by Walker's mention of his former partner and fell back on arrogance to hide his vulnerability. "You'll be learning from the best then."

"But I'm good with computers."

The hesitation and disappointment in Walker's tone surprised Aidan. Surely a guy his size, one who'd taken his fair share of bumps on the court, wasn't afraid of a little fieldwork. Aidan had also read the medical reports in Walker's file. The injury that had cut short his NBA rookie year was no longer an issue. In fact, if Aidan had read the report correctly, it had healed before the start of what would have been Walker's second season, if he'd returned. Something about his decision not to and his reluctance to leave the cave now set off Aidan's alarm bells. He would have to dig into that and determine if it was going to be an issue going forward. For now, though, he had more pressing matters to deal with.

"I hear you're also good with cars." He tossed the accident file on Walker's desk. "These are field reports from a hit-and-run. I want your read on them."

Walker pulled the file toward him and thumbed through its contents. "What are you looking for?"

"The other car, which was never found. Deductions you make about the accident—speed at impact, directionality, etcetera. Any discrepancies between your conclusions and the existing accident reports. I want a new set of eyes on this."

"I've got a few identity theft matters to wrap, and court testimony tomorrow and Friday for a piracy case. I can look at this over the weekend and have a report ready Monday. Will that work?" The coolness was still there in Walker's tone, but his eyes had warmed with a detective's hooked curiosity.

Aidan could work with that. He'd been married to a former athlete. Competition and achievement were powerful motivators for people like Gabe and Walker. "Monday it is." He deliberately infused his eyes and words with unconcealed challenge. "Impress me."

TWO

Pulling up at the top of the arc, Jamie let the ball fly, then sprinted beneath the basket, not doubting his aim for a second. Catching the ball as it fell through the net, he started back down the court—dribbling, spinning, and juking this way and that.

Layup, swish, catch, sprint to the other end of the court.

Repeat.

He'd been at it a half hour already, his usual early morning workout in the deserted YMCA a few blocks from the office. Sweat trickled from the ends of his hair down his temples, his jaw, and the center of his back beneath his jersey.

The physical exertion did nothing to silence Aidan's words from last week.

Not his parting "Impress me" shot.

The one earlier. "For a jock."

Days later, those words still stung.

Not that he wasn't used to them. Or the stunned expression when someone realized he was more than just a pretty-boy baller. It usually occurred when he spoke in complex computer science terminology that was unintelligible to the fool who'd two seconds ago thought themselves smarter than him. Those times, Jamie relished proving wrong the person who'd misjudged him. Last Wednesday, though, he had opened his mouth and, before thinking better of it, revealed more about his interest in his new partner than he should have. Nothing like being misjudged and shot down by the man he'd lusted after for three years.

How was he supposed to work with Aidan Talley?

Jamie had wanted Aidan since he'd first laid eyes on him. Blond hair that was always perfectly coiffed and expertly dyed, hiding, Jamie knew with one look at those eyes, fire beneath. A long, toned body capped by broad shoulders, showcasing the three-piece designer suits he seemed born to wear. Rough voice that concealed an Irish brogue Jamie heard hints of when Aidan and SAC Cruz thought no one was listening. The air of confidence and superior intellect that many deemed arrogance but was the very thing that turned Jamie on the most.

He had kept his distance, though. Aidan had been a happily married man, judging by the open displays of affection between him and Gabe at office functions. Seeing them together had been painful. Not because Jamie wanted Aidan and couldn't have him, nor because Aidan and his husband were a study in beautiful opposites. The one pale and freckled, six foot and lean-muscled; the other a hulking former defensive tackle with warm brown skin, cropped black curls, and dark eyes. No, it hurt because Jamie wanted to be that happy without the national media making a headline out of it.

Who was he kidding? He had killed that dream the day

he'd committed to play for one of the most storied programs in all of college sports.

"You know," came a rough, rumbling voice from the far end of the court. Aidan stood against the padded pole beneath the opposite basket, giving him the same poorly disguised once-over that had seared him before. "Watching you move like that, I'd never guess you'd suffered a career-ending injury."

Comments and speculation like that were the very reason Jamie worked out in a nondescript gym, never played in office leagues, and rarely joined neighborhood pickup games. He'd long ago tired of answering the "Why'd you quit?" question. He had his reasons. He would never tire of the game, though. His first conscious memory was from his second birthday when his dad had put a miniature basketball in his hands. The game would always be his first love. It might have also cursed him so that it was his only.

"No comment," he said, reciting the phrase he hated yet used more than any other.

Aidan raised his hands, gold and emerald cuff links sparkling in the morning rays sneaking through the gym's grimy windows. Yesterday's three-piece pinstripe had been traded for a charcoal one, paired with a starched white shirt and tie the same light blue color as Jamie's jersey. Only a shade or two off from the little blue bottle logo on the coffee cups Aidan held in his raised hands.

Saved from office sludge; thank God.

Trotting down the court, he took an easy shot from his natural two spot. The ball swished through the net and bounced at Aidan's feet. The other man pushed off the pole, shuffled the ball between his shiny oxfords until he got a toe beneath it, and flicked it up into Jamie's hands.

"Don't stop on my account," he said with a grin.

Jamie headed back down the court. "Add soccer to the list of Irish giveaways."

"Plenty of Americans play football now."

Jamie laughed despite his efforts to play it cool. "Keep 'em coming."

Layup, swish, catch.

Circling, he was surprised to see his partner sans jacket and vest, yanking his tie off over his head. "How'd the event at the ballpark go?" Aidan unclipped the clovers, set them on top of the folded jacket and vest on a bleacher, next to the coffees, and rolled up his sleeves.

"Great. The kids had a good time, and the players were very generous with their time."

"You played baseball too growing up, right?"

Jamie nodded, words having escaped him at the sight of Aidan stepping onto the court in four-figure loafers, hands splayed in a wordless gesture for the ball.

Expertly handling a bounce pass, Aidan wove the ball between his legs, spun and drove down the lane for a picture-perfect layup. "That's two. Leaving your man open." Jamie shook off the surprise and caught a chest pass from Aidan, who ran past him toward the other end of the court. "You ever cross paths with MadBum?"

Were they really going to do this? Play a pickup game with him in his sweaty college uniform and Aidan in dress clothes? By the look of his partner standing at the top of the opposite arc with his arms outstretched and bouncing on his toes, they were.

Game on.

"He was a few years behind me." Jamie dribbled and juked, testing Aidan's defensive moves. "Only ran into him once. Playoffs my senior year."

"He win?"

"Of course he won." Jamie pulled up from the wing and sank a three-pointer.

"Nice shot." Aidan gave him a grin that did odd things to Jamie's stomach. Distracted, Aidan got the jump on him and flew down the court, laughing. "Too easy."

Aidan was surprisingly good. Up and down the court, he played him close. Arms and hands reaching around to try and knock the ball loose, hips bumping, each contact sent an illicit thrill through Jamie. As if the sweat-soaked, see-through dress shirt and brogue-laced smack talk weren't enough, Aidan made him work for every shot and kept the score close.

"Twenty-one," Jamie said, half an hour later, after sailing the ball over Aidan's head to sink the game-winning jumper.

"Well played, kid." Aidan jogged beneath the basket and used his toe again to launch the ball into Jamie's hands.

"You played point?" Fast in transition, quick on his feet, and sure of hand, Aidan's skills and six-foot stature made point guard the obvious position.

"Woodside High Tigers," Aidan answered as they ambled over to the bleachers and collapsed on the bottom row. "Basketball in the winter, soccer year-round. Wasn't good enough to play either for Stanford, but I kept up both in intramural leagues."

"You're good." Jamie grabbed the water he had left two rows up, drank half, then offered the bottle to Aidan. "I was surprised you kept it that close."

Aidan drained the rest. "You're not the first six-and-a-half-footer I've played ball with."

Jamie froze, recalling the first time he had met Gabe Cruz, the rare case of someone taller than him. Caught up in the idea of working with Aidan, Jamie had lost all his manners and forgotten to express his condolences.

"Aidan, I'm—"

"It's Monday," he cut him off. "Give me your report."

"Here? Now? I thought you wanted it in writing."

"Not necessary. Tell me what you found."

So much for the report he had spent hours drafting. Shaking off the annoyance, Jamie snagged his coffee and took a quick sip, failing to suppress a small moan of delight. Even cold, it was better than any other coffee in San Francisco.

Something that looked an awful lot like heat flashed in Aidan's eyes, but he cleared his throat before Jamie could get a better read on it. "Today would be good."

Determined to prove he was more than a jock, Jamie launched into his debrief. He reported what he had learned. That the missing car's tire tracks and the dark paint on the red Jaguar's front right fender could only be from a late-model black Ford SUV; that shards of tinted glass mixed with shattered clear had led him to search traffic and ATM camera footage for a dark SUV with tinted windows in the surrounding area at the time of the accident; that he had found the vehicle and scrubbed the images until he got a clear shot of the VIN and plates, discovering the former scraped off and the latter stolen; that by triangulating and sequencing footage from where the SUV had been parked to where it collided with the Jag, he'd concluded someone had radioed ahead, let the SUV driver know when the sports car hit the Geary Expressway, and the SUV had rocketed off the blocks, taking deadly aim at the Jaguar. With each recited detail and corresponding conclusion, Aidan's face grew more and more pale.

Recalling the reports he'd reviewed, how every mention of victims or persons at the scene had been redacted, Jamie put it together in seconds. He picked up the other coffee cup and held it out to Aidan, an offer to cushion the blow. "Those reports were from your accident, weren't they?"

Taking the cup, Aidan turned his blank gaze on the court. Cold now, the liquid failed to bring any color to his blanched face. "You just confirmed it wasn't an accident."

"The cops ruled it otherwise? You left out their final conclusions."

"I didn't want to bias yours." Aidan set his cup aside and shifted to face him once more. "They ruled it a random hit-and-run. Said I didn't swerve out of the way fast enough."

"Bullshit," Jamie said, furious on Aidan's behalf. "That accident was not random and there was nothing you could have done to avoid it."

Aidan's tortured gaze drifted out over the court again. "You don't know that."

Jamie grasped his arm and waited for Aidan to return his attention. "Look, we're just getting to know each other, but you said it yourself, I'm good with cars. So trust me when I tell you there was nothing you or anyone else behind the wheel could have done to avoid that collision. Hell, even I couldn't have swerved fast enough, and I smoked everyone's ass on the road course, including my own." Jamie counted Aidan's short, surprised laugh a win. "We gonna continue investigating this?"

"Yeah." Aidan rose, and Jamie was doubly pleased to see some of the tension he had carried in with him gone. "Keep it off the books until we know more."

Jamie followed, getting to his feet and handing Aidan his suit jacket, vest, and cuff links. "I can set something up for us on a different channel, so to speak."

"I'm sure you can."

Aidan's wicked grin sent a shiver racing through Jamie. Thankfully, before he opened his mouth and said too much again, Aidan's cell rang. He stepped away, taking the call, and Jamie ducked into the locker room. Five minutes later, freshly showered and suited, he came back out on the court just as Aidan hung up.

"That was Cameron Byrne. He's here on a kidnap and rescue matter tied to one of my old cases. Sounds like we could use your cyber expertise. You want in?"

By the look in his autumn eyes, Aidan was asking about more than just the K&R case. Jamie answered both the spoken and unspoken question. "I'm in."

THREE

Absolution.

Something neither the doctors nor the detectives had been able to give Aidan for eight long months, and Jameson Walker gave it to him in five days. Aidan had known his "for a jock" comment was unfair; the kid's file proved as much. He'd had no doubt Walker would impress him. He hadn't expected him to upend his world, freeing him of the guilt that had plagued him since the night of the accident.

No, not an accident. Not a hit-and-run. A hit, plain and simple. Mel suspected it; Walker confirmed it. Now, all Aidan wanted to do was work with Walker to get to the bottom of it, but Cameron Byrne needed his assistance.

Byrne specialized in kidnap and rescue cases, particularly those involving children. With six nieces and nephews, and a seventh on the way, Aidan never ignored his calls for help, on the off—terrifying—chance he might need Byrne to return the favor one day. But the thirty-something Bostonian was not an easy man to work with. He played strictly by the rules, rarely cracked a smile, and had a dark temper to match his black eyes and hair. Aidan didn't expect Walker's laid-back manner and oozing charm to go over well with the surly Byrne.

Make that the second time he'd misjudged his new partner.

They walked into Byrne's war room, and Aidan moved to introduce them but stalled when Byrne's dark gaze snagged on Walker and his round face broke into a beaming grin. Aidan stood, frozen in surprise, as Walker brushed past him and greeted Byrne in a backslapping hug.

"Three years, Whiskey," Byrne said in his thick longshoreman's accent. "You don't call, you don't write."

"I called your sorry ass last week," Walker replied, smiling wide. "And you're the one who can't bother to stop by when you're in town."

Byrne laughed and patted Walker's cheek. "You got me there, brother."

He obviously meant it colloquially, but the way the two interacted reminded Aidan of the way he and his brother behaved. How far back did this bond between Walker and Byrne go? And why the fuck hadn't Walker mentioned this on their way over?

Forcing himself into motion, Aidan stepped forward and cleared his throat. "How do you two know each other?"

They stood side by side, arms slung over each other's shoulders. "This asshole"—Byrne tilted his head toward Walker—"broke my leg in a tourney game my junior year at BC. Stupid, earnest freshman that he was, he felt so guilty he offered to take my place in my dad's crew that summer."

"Your dad's *crew*?" Aidan asked. He couldn't mean Irish

mob. Aidan knew every face on that particular board and Cameron was nowhere on it.

"Deep sea fishing," Byrne answered. "I was mobile enough to cook and navigate and clean cabins, but I was no good on deck. Jamie filled in for me once the pretty Southern boy got his sea legs under him."

"Oh God." Walker clutched his stomach, equal parts groaning and laughing. "Don't remind me."

Byrne elbowed him in the ribs. "So much beef stew."

Walker threw out an arm, swatting at him. "You are the worst best friend ever."

Dodging the flailing limb, Byrne laughed and stepped forward with his hand outstretched. "Talley, it's good to see you, and thanks for agreeing to help."

Shaking his hand, Aidan struggled to come to terms with this alternate reality where Cameron Byrne laughed and Jameson Walker was his best friend. Was the world coming to an end? Could his partner charm snakes? Facing information overload, he clicked into professional gear and cut short the bizarre reunion. "What've you got for us?"

"This case isn't pretty, but you're just the two agents I need."

Byrne was right. It wasn't a pretty case. It was uglier than most, in fact. Over the next five days, Aidan drank his weight in coffee, hardly slept, and saw so many pictures of exploited children the coffee was all he could hold down. They were searching for a kidnapped preteen who'd turned up in a pornography reel accessed, via prison library computer, by a sex trafficker Aidan had collared two years ago. Aidan and Byrne pursued the ring the old-fashioned way—through muscle and interrogation—while Walker followed their electronic and financial trails.

Together, their efforts led to an abandoned Pescadero property near the coast. With SWAT teams behind them, they converged on the five-acre parcel, each taking one of the three dilapidated structures. Out of the Friday morning fog, they carried a dozen missing children to safety, filled two prison vans with handcuffed criminals, and confiscated enough hard drives and other electronics equipment to keep Walker busy for days.

Throughout the investigation, Walker improved Byrne's mood, and it was by far the best working experience Aidan had ever had with the K&R specialist, despite the wear and tear of the case, physically and emotionally. As with Byrne, Walker charmed every other agent and officer they came into contact with, and when it came to the takedown that morning, he followed orders to a T and secured his structure before either Aidan or Byrne cleared theirs.

Aidan was impressed, all right, and giving serious consideration to trusting Walker with the flash drive burning a hole in his pocket. It wasn't the same one Mel had given him. Instead, he'd copied onto a blank one the two financial records Grace had cracked and two more encrypted files of the same type and size, assuming they would also be bank records. He wanted to know if they led back to the detectives who'd swept his dead husband's and dead partner's murders under the rug. After Walker's work on Byrne's case, Aidan had no doubt his partner could follow this financial trail and, if he asked, decrypt the rest of the original drive's files. A test first, though.

But before they could get to that, Byrne wanted to have

drinks with them before catching his flight home. They had agreed to meet at a bar and grill near UN Plaza. Aidan pulled open the heavy wooden doors, pushed through the blue draft curtains, and scanned the crowded, cavernous space. Two- and four-top low tables to the left, all of them full; high-top tables in the middle, large groups standing around each; a big antique wooden bar to the right, three rows deep of people. Owner Sullivan Baxter was one of the two bartenders behind the bar, darting back and forth as he pulled bottles off the staggered shelves. When Sully spotted him, his eyes widened in surprise then warmed in greeting. He waved and pointed toward the far end of the bar.

Jacket and tie gone, sleeves rolled up, Walker stood with Byrne on one side and a stunning curly-haired brunette on the other. Aidan recognized her as Sully's wife and executive chef, Valentina. Rising on her toes, Tina whispered something in Walker's ear, and he laughed out loud. Every pair of female eyes in the crowded restaurant, along with a few male ones, turned to check him out. Fuck, he was gorgeous, and so very off-limits. As if sensing his presence, Walker glanced up at him, a wide smile splitting his handsome face. Aidan shoved aside every inappropriate thought that raced through his mind, unbuttoned his suit coat, and snagged the glass of Maker's Sully left for him at the end of the bar.

"Talley, it's about time," Byrne said as Aidan joined their group. "I've got to head out soon, and I'm not sure I can trust Jamie's virtue to this vixen." He gave Tina a wink.

Cameron Byrne drinking. Cameron Byrne winking. Definitely an alternate reality.

"Aidan, so good to see you." Tina stepped forward and kissed his cheek. "Ha sido de largo."

It had been too long. Eight months and fifteen days, to be exact. He, Gabe, and Tom had been on their way from here to Tom's place in the Outer Richmond the night of the accident.

Shaking off the dark thoughts, he returned Tina's embrace. "Good to see you too, hermosa."

"Gorgeous," she scoffed, then switched back to Spanish, complaining that he hadn't brought his gorgeous new partner to visit yet. Never mind that Tina was happily married. She enjoyed a good-looking man as much as Aidan did. "You always have the best luck."

"Not so lucky this time. The kid's my work partner, and he's straight."

She laughed at the same time Walker's empty glass hit the bar, hard, startling them both.

"Where are our manners?" Tina switched fluidly back to English. "Sorry about that. Bad habit of ours. Another round?"

Byrne nodded and she scurried behind the bar, calling to Sully for two whiskeys and a Dr. Pepper.

"So, Talley," Byrne said, "I gotta thank you and Cruz for getting Jamie out in the field. Waste of talent, him hiding behind that computer all day."

"Some would say it's a waste of talent he's not on the court."

Walker sighed. "I'm standing right here."

Byrne shrugged and paid him no mind, just like an older brother. "You can try having that argument with him. Speaking from experience, it won't get you anywhere. Besides, that was talent out in the field today too." He clapped his meaty hand on Walker's shoulder, giving it a squeeze. "You did good. Knew there was a reason I recruited you."

Walker's attractive, embarrassed blush gave way to an even more attractive smirk. "You mean it wasn't because I—"

"Jameson," Byrne growled, cutting him off and making them all laugh. Aidan would have to get that story out of Walker. Tina came back with their drinks, and after a little more ribbing, mostly at Walker's expense, Byrne downed his whiskey, shook Aidan's hand, and gave Walker another hug, holding him longer this time. "It was good to see you, brother," he said, loud enough for Walker to hear over the crowd, meaning Aidan heard too. "Even better to work with you. Proud of you, Jamie."

"Thanks, Cam. Tell Pops and the boys hello for me."

"They want to see you."

"How about I swing up next time I'm home?"

"It's a plan," Byrne said, before turning to Aidan. "You hold him to it."

He nodded. "Count on it."

Walker pushed through the crowd with Byrne to the door, and by the time he made his way back, Aidan had snagged two barstools. "So where's home now? Rockingham or Oak Island?"

Wide blue eyes shot to his. "You've read my file?"

"You haven't read mine?" Walker shook his head. "I'll have my assistant get it for you."

"That's not necessary."

"Don't you want to know who you're working with?"

"I know who I'm working with," he drawled, low and husky. It was as if Walker flirted without meaning to, like it was all part of the Southern charm he couldn't help but exude.

"So, you and Byrne," he deflected. "That's more than one summer at sea together."

"What do you mean?" Walker looked nervous all of a sudden.

"You two remind me of me and my brother. That kind of relationship takes time, not one summer together."

Walker relaxed and sipped his soda. "It was multiple summers, during undergrad and grad school when I was at MIT. That first year was the best haul Pop Byrne ever had. Called me his lucky charm and insisted I go out with them at least once each summer."

"Superstitious much?"

"Come on, Irish." Walker jostled his shoulder. "Your family runs a shipping empire. You of all people should know how superstitious sailors are."

Aidan side-eyed him. "So you have read my file?"

That mischievous smirk returned with a vengeance. "Not your FBI file . . ."

"I don't want to know." Aidan shook his head in reluctant surrender and downed the rest of his whiskey.

Once he stopped laughing, Walker angled toward him, one elbow resting on the bar. "Listen, I wanted to thank you for bringing me in on this one. It was great working with Cam." His gaze went to the glass of ice in his hand, and he added softly, "And with you."

Aidan removed the glass from his hand, drawing his gaze again. "Byrne's right. You did good, Whiskey. You impressed me." He smiled, earnest and true, and Aidan made his decision. Setting the glass on the bar, he reached inside his suit jacket, pulled out the flash drive, and slid it across the bar to Walker. "A reward, of sorts."

He picked it up and turned it over in his hand. "What's on it?"

"Files connected to our other investigation." Jamie's eyes darted back to his. "Bank account ledgers from a file my sister decrypted, plus two more encrypted files. Probably the same, given the type and size. I want to know what we're looking at exactly and who the accounts belong to."

"Maybe I should see if they lead back to the detectives who investigated your accident, seeing as they covered up a crime."

"I think that'd be a good place to start." Assured of his decision, Aidan withdrew his wallet, slid a fifty across the bar to Sully, and slipped off his stool. "Mom's babysitting my niece tonight. Friday ritual. I promised to swing by and read her a story before bed."

"Read her one for me too," Walker said with a sad smile. "After the week we've had . . ." Further evidence all that charm was one hundred percent genuine.

"I'll do that." Aidan buttoned his jacket. "I'm on lecture panels at Hastings with Mel Monday and Tuesday. Let's plan to debrief on Wednesday morning."

"Sounds good."

"You need a ride?"

Spinning on his stool, Walker rested his elbows behind him on the bar. "Think I'll stay here and enjoy the scenery a little while longer," he said, eyes roaming the crowd.

Aidan figured he knew who Walker was looking for. "You saw the ring on her finger, right?"

"Who?" Walker glanced back at him, doing an A-plus job of playing dumb.

Chuckling, Aidan turned to leave with a "Night, Whiskey," then stopped when Walker called his name.

"Thank you." Walker palmed the flash drive. "For trusting me with this."

"You earned it."

FOUR

Jamie stepped outside his Bernal Heights home, and his world narrowed to a single point ten feet down the sidewalk. The racket of the morning commute dimmed, the riotous mix of city odors faded, and all his attention focused on the gleaming black sports car parked at the curb.

And the man standing beside it.

When Aidan texted a half hour ago that he would pick him up on his way into the office, Jamie wasn't sure what to expect. His partner standing in the open door of an Aston Martin Vanquish Carbon Edition had been nowhere on the list. Two things of beauty first thing in the morning. Not a bad start to his day.

"We've got a meeting with Mel in twenty." Aidan tossed him the car keys. "She's got a new case for us."

That snapped Jamie out of his daze. Not the flying keys, nor the mention of a new case, but the ridiculous notion of driving from Bernal to UN Plaza, during rush hour, in anything less than thirty minutes.

"Did you get into narco's evidence stash over the weekend?" Jamie asked.

"Mel wants you assessed for fieldwork. I want to see these legendary driving skills."

"Those were closed courses."

"If you don't think you can handle it, I'll drive."

Jamie grinned. "Oh, I can handle it."

Growing up seven miles from a former racetrack, he had spent countless hours of his childhood watching cars race and racing a few of his own. He still had relatives in North Carolina who ran moonshine down the mountain in Christmas trees. He could drive with the best of them. San Francisco drivers, however, were far from the best.

"It's not me I'm worried about," he said. "It's the rest of the drivers in this city."

"Hey now . . ."

He speared Aidan with a you-know-I'm-right look.

"Okay, fine. Most Bay Area drivers belong in remedial driver's ed. What better way to assess your defensive driving skills?"

"It's your car." Jamie rounded the hood, waited for a car to pass, then opened the driver's-side door and slid in, surprised at the amount of legroom. He'd auditioned his share of sports cars and ended up with a Grand Cherokee SRT because it was the only sport vehicle he could comfortably fit in. He had never tried one of these, though. "It's roomy."

"It was Gabe's," Aidan replied curtly and slammed the passenger door shut.

Jamie mentally kicked himself for being a thoughtless jerk and started to apologize.

Aidan cut him off again, reaching across the console to punch the ignition button. "You need the blue lights?"

Jamie let the deflection slide, for now. "I don't *need* them, but if you don't want to attract a tail of black and whites, you might want to put them on."

"Fair point." Aidan tapped a button on the electronic console, activating what was obviously a custom feature on the Vanquish. "Every minute we sit here is a minute lost."

"You sure about this?"

"You break it, you bought it. I know you're good for it."

Yeah, he was good for it. The buyout of his NBA contract provided him with a nice little nest egg. He wouldn't need to tap it for this, though. He ran his left hand over the stretched leather steering wheel and used his right to knock the gearshift to manual.

Giving Aidan his most evil grin, he tapped the shifter paddles and revved the engine. "Start the timer, Irish."

He spotted an opening and gunned it, the car roaring to life before settling into a seductive purr. He dodged, swerved, cornered without brakes, feeling out the Vanquish's handling in case he never got the chance again. It was a thing of beauty, and he was in the zone, speeding across Cesar Chavez and into the Mission.

"All right, Whiskey," Aidan said, humor in his voice. "Time to come back to earth."

He stuck out his bottom lip and pouted. "But I like it here."

His partner laughed, the warm sound filling the inside of the car and Jamie's chest. He had missed Aidan the past few days. Granted, they had really only worked one full week together, but that one week, as harrowing as it had been, made up for their rocky beginning. Aside from Aidan's annoying habit of referring to him as "kid," he treated Jamie as a full-fledged partner, not a rookie mentee. He was included in meetings and decisions, and Cam and Aidan had trusted him to run all technical aspects of the operation last week. Working a case with two men he admired, he had proven his worth behind the computer and in the field, and in doing so, they had rescued those kids and saved God only knew how many more from falling into the ring's trap.

Jamie was starting to think this partnership with Aidan could work if he could rein in his desire. Aidan believing he was straight helped, but he would only be able to keep up that charade for so long. He thought for sure Cam would blow it. Hell, Tina had caught on within ten minutes of their meeting, but Aidan remained oblivious.

For now.

"Tell me what you found on the flash drive," Aidan said, bringing Jamie out of his thoughts and back into the car for another impromptu debrief.

"I started by cracking the other two files." He tapped his thumbs on the steering wheel, tamping down his tendency to gesture while explaining technical matters. With a quarter-of-a-million-dollar automobile at his fingertips, he kept his hands firmly on the wheel. "More bank ledgers, as you'd expected. The encryption was very sophisticated. I'd like to meet this sister of yours who cracked the first file."

"She's eight months pregnant and married to an army field surgeon bigger than you."

Jamie shrugged. "So?"

Aidan rolled his eyes, probably thinking he meant to hit on her. In reality, Jamie just wanted to better know the people who knew Aidan, hoping to gain more insight into his partner. Added bonus that she shared his interest in computers. He needed more friends like that. Not hangers-on who were only interested in his former fame or money and who'd sell him out to the tabloids for the right offer.

"Who'd the bank accounts trace back to?" Aidan asked, getting them back on track.

"Still working on that." He glanced over as disappointment flashed across Aidan's face. "They're offshore. I can't access them through official channels without a warrant."

"And unofficially?"

"I'm working on it. I did check travel records for the detectives on your case."

"Visits to nonextradition countries?"

"Not yet." Jamie swerved to miss a delivery truck that pulled out in front of them, earning a serenade of car horns. "They did, however, make trips to the Cayman Islands."

"Not exactly the number one vacation destination for cops."

"Not even in the top ten."

Aidan smiled. "And what is?"

"Psycho Donuts, Voodoo Doughnut . . ." He continued listing off famous doughnut shops as they sped through a yellow light across Mission, narrowly missing a Muni bus. Aidan's hand shot to the oh-shit handle above the passenger door, reminding Jamie of the other question he'd meant to ask. "The dates on those files . . ."

Aidan glanced out the window. "They're all dated that date."

"All?"

"I'll get you the rest," he said as Jamie pulled into the parking garage with two minutes to spare. Once parked, Aidan turned back to him, leaning forward and lowering his voice. "Mel will want us to prioritize whatever case she's got for us. We will, same as with Byrne."

It seemed unfair to ask Aidan to work any other cases when the most important one of his life hung over his head. If they could just tell Cruz . . .

"Mel knows," Aidan said, as if hearing his thoughts. "She's the one who gave me the flash drive. But for all our sakes, we continue to keep this investigation off the books and out of the office. Everything proceeds like normal. Got it?"

Jamie nodded. "I'll keep looking."

"I'm counting on it."

Last week with Cam had been a field case with cyber elements. The case SAC Cruz assigned them—a series of hacks at Galveston National Laboratory—was right in Jamie's wheelhouse and he couldn't be happier. The SAC down there, Gary Clark, was a friend of Cruz's, and he had called in a favor, requesting reinforcements for their overworked cyber teams. Practically bouncing on the edge of his seat by the time she dismissed them, Jamie couldn't wait to dive into the intrusion reports and catch the scent of their hacker. While he loved a good car chase, a hunt through ones and zeros was like no other high.

Recognizing his barely contained excitement, Aidan tasked him with reviewing the intrusion reports while he coordinated with GNL and the local field office. He wanted to get a read on the personnel situation at both and determine whether they would work the case from San Francisco or go to Texas. They worked until Janitorial kicked them out, and Jamie was back in the cave first thing in the morning. He only looked up, hours later, when the smell of food tickled his nose, and the increasingly familiar cadence of his partner's gait teased his ears.

"I'm guessing by that half-feral hacker look you haven't eaten yet?"

Jamie shook his head, and after a moment of indecision, Aidan sidestepped his cluttered desk in favor of the adjacent empty one. With each takeaway container Aidan unpacked, Jamie's eyes grew wider, and his mouth watered at the food truck bonanza laid out before him. Assorted bao and sliders, garlic noodles, deep fried bacon mac and cheese balls, bowls of curry, étouffée and jambalaya. "I wasn't sure what you liked." Aidan held a paper plate out to him.

Jamie ignored the offered plate and went straight for the carton of pork buns, gobbling one whole, then belatedly, and uselessly, waving a hand in front of his mouth to cool it off.

Aidan laughed. "Food's hot."

"No shit." He grabbed another bun and went through the same motions—the scorched roof of his mouth was worth it for the delectable taste and his partner's easy laughter. "Something to know about me," he said after washing it down with a sip of Dr. Pepper from the Big Gulp he had nursed all morning. "There ain't much in this world I won't eat."

"Good to know."

They piled their plates with bits of everything, Jamie sank into his chair, and Aidan claimed the one behind the empty desk. "You've had the new case file over a day now,"

Aidan said after a few minutes of stuffing their faces. "Give me the rundown."

Jamie pulled his eyes back from where they had rolled after taking a bite of the rich, hearty étouffée, and gathered himself. "Three reported cyber intrusions on the firewall for the biosafety level four labs at Galveston National Laboratory. Triggered the access control watchdog. No discernable pattern as to when the breaches occurred. First one was on Sunday at two in the morning, the second Monday afternoon at three, and the last at nine on Tuesday morning. The breaches lasted less than fifteen seconds each, but first responders were called to the scene, per GNL, University of Texas, and City of Galveston safety protocols. Everyone in the affected labs was quarantined and the building locked down until emergency hazmat teams gave the all clear. No additional breaches, so those first three attempts were probably knocks."

"What do you mean by *knocks*?"

He tapped his knuckles on his desk. "Knock, knock."

Aidan took a sip of his Thai iced tea. "Okay, I'll play along. Who's there?"

"Exactly. That's what our hacker wanted to know. Who's there?"

"They were checking the monitoring framework."

Jamie nodded. Finishing his étouffée, he moved on to the jambalaya and momentarily lost control of his eyeballs again. When they righted themselves, Aidan was watching him, equal parts amused and impatient. Best get his shit together. "They were probably also testing whether they could get through GNL's outer firewall to remotely flip access switches."

"Outer firewall?" Aidan asked. "The reports from the field office only mentioned one."

"Which is why on my way in this morning I had a chat with GNL's chief information security officer. The field office only requested logs for the firewall around the exterior access points. I've requested *all* the BSL-4 logs, including those for the internal access controls behind the air gap."

"Meaning they're on their own intranet?"

"Correct, Agent Talley. Not a Luddite after all."

Avoiding his gaze, Aidan pushed garlic noodles around on his plate with a pair of chopsticks. "Not just a jock after all." Before Jamie could contemplate the rush caused by his simple retraction, Aidan asked, "How is it you know so much about BSL-4 lab security?"

"A crypto classmate from MIT works at USAMRIID. I called him last night."

"Busy bee," Aidan said, pleased. "Tell me about these additional access controls."

Jamie shoveled several bites of rice, sausage, chicken, and shrimp into his mouth before setting the plate aside so he could talk with his hands. "GNL has multiple BSL-4 labs within the GNL building on UT Med's campus. Each lab spans four floors. There's an access keypad on each interior door and on the doors to the cabinets holding biological agents."

"A list of which was also missing from the case file."

"I noticed that too. A call to the field office was next on my agenda."

Aidan shook his head as he rose, dumping his plate into the trashcan at the end of Jamie's desk. "Let me make that one. I spoke to Gary earlier, but I need to get a better read on his agents, whether they're going to work with or against us and why they left gaps in the file."

Jamie tossed his plate and helped Aidan pack up the leftovers. "Maybe they're just overworked and haven't had time to do the follow-up."

"Maybe."

Aidan's cautious tone had Jamie leaning forward and lowering his voice. "You think we're investigating our own?"

"I'm reserving judgment until I get more facts."

"Well then, unless you want me on the call with Texas City, I'm going to keep digging through these reports."

Aidan flashed that wicked grin of his again. "I've got something else in mind."

Jamie got to drive the Vanquish again after all, this time to the SFPD firing range across town. Twenty-eight minutes, door-to-door, record time in Jamie's book, the Vanquish's tires spit gravel as he swung it into the parking lot. Glancing over, Aidan looked both impressed and green around the gills.

He recognized what Aidan was doing—putting him through the Academy paces. Firing range today, roadwork yesterday, stamina last week, though there were other ways besides a basketball game to test that last one. Equally sweaty and far more enjoyable. Jamie let the image of Aidan writhing naked beneath him carry him out of the car, past the front desk clerk who winked and slipped him her number, and into the shooting booth.

His happy thoughts withered, though, as he watched

Aidan drill fifteen rounds into the bull's-eye of the black-and-white silhouette. Aidan held and fired the Glock 22 like a natural, like he had done it a million times. Jamie practiced often, but before joining the FBI, he'd touched a firearm only a handful of times. Give him a car chase any day of the week.

Aidan pushed a button to swap the targets out and stepped back from the shooting table. "All right, kid," he said, voice tinny through the comm device inside the earmuffs. "Show me what you got."

Jamie held his breath as they squeezed past each other in the narrow booth and approached the shooting table. Assuming the stance he had learned in Academy, he raised his own service weapon and fired, hitting the target to the right of center mass.

"Nice try," Aidan said. "Now, back to our case."

Jamie glowered over his shoulder. "You brought me out here for one shot?"

"No, you've got fourteen rounds left in that mag. We're multitasking."

"And shouting." Even with the earpieces, they had to raise their voices.

"Yes, well, rules." Aidan waved dismissively at the earmuffs. "Now, who would normally have access to the BSL-4 labs?"

Another basic training test. In the field, there'd be more than him in a booth shooting targets, more than just Aidan buzzing about his consciousness. There'd be live targets, and he would be expected to assess and solve problems on the run. He needed to fire automatically, naturally, like Aidan. Recalling his training, he lifted his arms and fired while answering Aidan's question.

"Docs, med students, lab workers, building and network security. Anyone with an authorized key card. Those were not what triggered the breach. No unusual activity was logged on any of their cards."

"We're looking for an outsider, then."

"Maybe." Jamie sent the last bullet through the silhouette's bull's-eye and smiled over his shoulder.

"Should have made that shot the first time." Aidan flashed him the bird. "Next mag," he said, turning his finger upside down and flicking it in a get-back-to-business gesture. "Why *maybe*?"

Jamie punched the button for a new silhouette and loaded the next clip into his weapon. "As we discussed, the logs we have are only for the external firewall."

"So if it turns out the air-gapped firewall was also breached, there'd have to be someone on the inside who could access it."

"Unless there's an outside network or connection GNL and UT aren't aware of."

"How do we find that?"

Jamie emptied the clip as fast as he could, one round after another, aiming in the general vicinity of the silhouette's center mass, then slammed the gun down on the shooting table. Whipping off the earmuffs and tossing them next to the gun, he spun and explained, hands flying free. "We're looking for a similar signature to connect access to the outside hack and any potential inside hack."

Aidan eyes slid not so subtly to the discarded weapon. When Jamie didn't budge, he huffed, removed his own earmuffs, and leaned one shoulder against the glass enclosure, resigned for the moment. "What do you mean by *signature*?"

"Same IP address, even if it's a bogus one." Jamie ticked off the possibilities on his fingers. "Points of origin. Token the hacker left behind."

"Why would someone do that?"

"Think of our hacker like any normal perp. It depends on how good they are. A bad hacker, like a sloppy unsub, may leave evidence behind without realizing it."

Catching on, Aidan smiled that knowing smile that did weird things to Jamie's insides. "And some perps love the chase. They want to get caught, so they leave clues."

"Or, third option, they're just cocky little shits."

"Assuming *you're* on the cocky, skilled end of the spectrum, if you weren't on this side of the law, would you leave a token behind?"

"Oh yeah," Jamie drawled with a smirk of his own.

Aidan abruptly pushed off the wall, looking anywhere but directly at Jamie as he slipped past him, donned the earmuffs, and reloaded the gun. Was that a blush staining his partner's cheeks? Was it possible he affected Aidan as much as the other man affected him?

His own earmuffs back on, he waited for Aidan to send several shots through the tattered silhouette's bull's-eye before picking up another investigative thread. "Are we sticking with the bioterrorist motive the local field office posited?"

"That's the obvious answer." Aidan squeezed off a few more rounds. "Get your hands on a BSL-4 toxin, build a dirty bomb, kill a bunch of people."

"I've seen that movie too." That earned him a side eye. "Other ideas?"

"Going on your cocky-little-shit theory, I won't discount

hubris. Fame, glory, sex. Or maybe it's someone looking to make a few bucks."

"You think our hacker might try to sell it?"

Aidan nodded, and that feeling in Jamie's gut turned from the good kind of odd to the bad variety. This case was high stakes, not just Academy training with his attractive instructor.

"I've already set up alerts and contacted a few fences," Aidan said. "We'll know if anything connected hits the market."

"And I've got alerts on the network security system in case there's another breach."

Lowering the gun, Aidan removed the earmuffs and turned, resting back against the shooting table. "GNL security know you did that?"

"Nope, cocky little shit, right here." Jamie grinned, jutting two thumbs at himself.

Aidan shook his head and smiled indulgently. "Well, I think we've got another cocky hacker on the inside."

Jamie's smile died as he removed his ear protection. "Which means we have to go to Texas."

"Don't look so thrilled. What've you got against the Lone Star State?"

"We would have gone undefeated my senior year, if not for the Longhorns."

"You did make them pay for it in the Final Four."

"I did."

Aidan pushed off the table, handed Jamie his weapon, and brushed past him, rolling down his sleeves as he went. After grabbing his jacket from the hook outside the booth, he shrugged into it, adjusted his sleeves, and clipped in the cuff links.

Jamie tucked his weapon into its harness and pulled on his own jacket. "When do you want to leave? We could catch a red-eye out tonight."

"You said you had alerts in place for further intrusions?"

Jamie nodded.

"Assuming nothing comes up, we'll take the red-eye Saturday night. My niece's birthday is Saturday. Gabe and I . . ." He cast his eyes aside and paused to clear his throat. "We were her godparents. She doesn't understand why he's gone. I need to be there for her."

"Aidan—"

"Let's go."

Aidan turned for the exit and Jamie grabbed his arm, spinning him back around. "Dammit, Talley, let me say it, then you won't have to keep avoiding it."

"I've heard it enough already," he snapped, tortured gaze locked on Jamie's hand around his arm.

"Believe me, I know better than most." Between his father's death and his injury, Jamie had heard more than enough condolences.

"Then why?" Aidan asked, gaze still averted.

Jamie glided his hand down Aidan's jacket sleeve to the shirt cuff and sparking cuff link, straightening it. "Respect. Not for what you lost, but for what you had. And my Southern mother would kill me if I didn't."

Aidan looked up, one corner of his mouth slightly hitched. "How's she ever gonna know?"

"You weren't raised in the South. They always know."

Aidan raised his wrist, the afternoon sun catching the emerald clover. "Irish, as good as."

"Then shut up and let me say it."

Aidan pressed his lips together and nodded.

"I'm sorry, Aidan."

"Thank you." His autumn gaze held Jamie's several long seconds until Aidan held out his open palm. "I'm driving back."

Jamie dropped the keys in his hand. "By all means."

FIVE

Aidan sat at his office desk the next morning, scanning GNL's BSL-4 inventory. Ebola, hemorrhagic fever, anthrax, West Nile virus. The list went frighteningly on.

Galveston National Laboratory was a high-security national biocontainment laboratory, handling biosafety level two, three, and four pathogens. It was the largest such facility on any academic campus in the world. The only places on par with it in the US were Rocky Mountain Labs in Montana and the Centers for Disease Control in Atlanta. Those sites, however, were highly regulated and government-operated. GNL, by contrast, was situated in the middle of the University of Texas Medical Branch's campus—academic buildings to the front and back, a primary care hospital adjacent. The sheer number of civilians in the immediate vicinity of GNL on a daily basis—professors, students, patients, their families and visitors—was enough to give Aidan a headache.

"That's not a good face," Mel said from his open doorway.

He looked up from the list of doom. "Have you ever seen the inventory of a BSL-4 lab?"

"All the outbreak movies ever in one place?"

"Pretty much."

She sat in the visitor chair across from him, her gaze skating over his shoulder to the empty desk behind him. As senior agents, he and Tom had shared one of the glassed-in offices along the outer edge of the bullpen. He'd thought about inviting Walker to take the other desk but stopped himself every time, wondering if it was too soon, a disrespect to his former partner. Maybe he should be the one moving to the vacant desk in the cave instead. His mind rebelled against the notion, probably as Walker's would about the main floor location.

"How's it going with Jamie?" Mel asked, as if reading his thoughts.

"Good." Aidan closed the file and tilted back in his chair. "He was instrumental in making the bust on Byrne's case, and I've been running him through Academy basics."

"When I said assess him, I didn't mean test the things he's already cleared at Academy."

"I needed to see for myself."

She considered him for a moment. "And?"

"He kicked my ass at twenty-one." Aidan rubbed his left arm, remembering the soreness that had lingered after their pickup game. He had kept the score close but doubted Walker had felt like a ninety-year-old the next morning. "He's a natural behind the wheel. Not so much with a gun. Though given how fast he disarmed his target during Byrne's bust, he'll have the gun out of a shooter's hand before it ever gets that far."

"So you're comfortable taking him out in the field with you?" she asked, continuing to eye him. Nothing like being interrogated by your boss, who also knew all your secrets.

"I've already been out in the field with him. Like I said, top marks."

"That was Cameron's op." She crossed one leg over the other. "Are you ready to *lead* someone out in the field with you?"

"You cleared me." He kept his voice flat, giving away nothing.

They'd already had this conversation two weeks ago, and she had expressed her doubts then. He would have thought his performance on Byrne's case would have reassured her. Something else must have set off this particular interrogation.

"Gary called me," she revealed a moment later. "He said you reamed out his agents."

"There was critical information missing from the case file. I needed to determine if that was an oversight or intentional."

She tapped her trigger finger on her knee and measured her words. "Aidan, what I said that night at your place, it wasn't meant to imply there's a conspiracy around every corner."

Ah, so that was what she was driving at. He could allay this concern easily enough. "My reaming out Gary's agents had nothing to do with our conversation. Walker also noticed the missing information. We needed to be sure."

"All right, but you're not exactly winning friends and influencing people. Do you think those agents are going to want to work with you now?"

He shrugged. "Good cop, bad cop."

She raised a brow.

"Fine." Palms out, he propped his elbows on the desk. "I admit I was a little rough on them. I've got Whiskey for damage control. He'll go in there, flash his megawatt smile, and they'll be putty in his hands. Did you know he's best friends with Byrne?"

Her other perfectly plucked brow rose to match the first.

"No lie. I'm convinced he could charm a snake."

"Good. Should balance out the vinegar in you."

"Hey! Whose side are you on?"

She rose, a dash of mischief in her dark eyes. "Play nice in Texas."

He made the sign of the cross. "I'll be on my best behavior."

"Why doesn't that make me feel better?"

"You'll be at the house tomorrow, right?"

Sadness dimmed the spark of mischief. "Of course."

Saturday would be his first anniversary without his husband and Katie's first birthday without "Unka Gabe." Their goddaughter had been born six hours after they'd exchanged vows, Grace having gone into labor at their reception. While the past couple weeks had kept Aidan busy and distracted—Walker's findings had given him some measure of absolution—the ache in his chest grew stronger as the weekend approached.

"Thanks." He picked up a pen and spun it around his thumb. "It'll be good having people around that she knows and loves."

Mel snagged the pen and tossed it aside, keeping his hand in hers. "We'll all pitch in and do the best we can." She squeezed his fingers. "By Katie and by you."

He returned the tight grip, only dropping Mel's hand when a second visitor knocked on the door, making his presence known.

"Sorry to interrupt," Walker mumbled, studying his shoes. "I can come back later."

"It's fine, Jamie," Mel said. "I was just leaving."

"Everything okay?" Walker asked once she was gone.

"Fine." Aidan picked up the pen and set it spinning around his thumb again. "Party planning for a preschool princess."

"Pfft, that's easy. Ice cream, sprinkles, pink balloons, and a pony."

"A pony? You speak from experience?"

Walker beamed as he settled into the visitor chair Mel had vacated. "Twin nieces."

His smile was infectious, and Aidan couldn't help but return it, feeling improbably lighter about an event that had had him tied in knots. "Good to know."

"Anytime. You get the BSL-4 list?"

Aidan reopened the file, pulled out the inventory, and pushed it across the desk.

Blue eyes tracked down the page and Walker whistled low.

"Not a place we want breached," Aidan said.

"We're still working the bioweapon theory?"

"Why else hack GNL?"

Walker repeated Aidan's litany of motives from yesterday. "Fame, glory, sex. Or maybe our hacker's making a statement about lax security."

Aidan shook his head. "CDC's a better target for that kind of statement. No, I think GNL was targeted because it's on an academic campus instead of a closed government compound. More exposed. Any breaches overnight?"

"Nothing detected. Maybe it was an isolated incident. The knock didn't work, and our hacker gave up."

He folded his hands over his stomach. "Would you give up?"

Walker smirked. "Of course not."

Aidan drummed his fingers against his belly, intercepting the wave of heat racing south. That smirk was trouble. "Did you get the additional networks logs from GNL security?"

Walker tossed the folder he'd carried in onto the desk. "Nothing to indicate any breach of the internal firewall. Air gap did its job."

Aidan flipped through the expanded security log. "If the air gap held, is your monitoring working on the internal network?"

"Look who's catching on." Walker's prideful tone drew Aidan's gaze and his approving smile warmed Aidan through. Certain that heat showed on his pale face, Aidan bent over the logs again and pretended to be engrossed. "I can't set up monitoring inside the air gap until we're onsite," Walker continued. "GNL security knows to monitor around the clock until we arrive."

A knock on his door preceded Aidan's secretary pushing a rolling cart stacked with boxes into his office. "I have those files you requested."

Rising, Aidan gestured to his partner, who was already on his feet. "Leah, I'm sure you know Agent Walker."

She parked the cart beside his desk, then, in what was becoming less of a surprise, went up on her tiptoes and pecked Walker's cheek. "Jamie, dear, it's good to see you out of the cave."

"I might disappear in a puff of smoke at any second," Walker teased back, dramatically dodging a ray of sunlight before bending to return Leah's embrace.

"You better not," she said with a wink. "We're all enjoying the scenery too much. The both of you in here . . . mmm, mmm, mmm."

"Careful, Leah, or you'll scare the kid away again."

She tittered as Aidan lifted two boxes onto his desk and Walker unloaded the other two onto the floor. "Hope to see you out here more often, Jamie."

"Thanks."

She rolled out the cart and Walker lifted the lid off one of the boxes on the desk. "What are these?"

"Personnel files of everyone at UT Med with access to GNL's BSL-4 labs."

He ran a finger over the tops of the files. "We can't take all these on the plane with us."

Aidan removed the lid from the other box, yanked out a stack of files, and dropped them on his desk. "Maybe I should start calling you Sherlock."

"Would be better than *kid*." Barely a whisper, but Aidan caught it and the underlying bitterness.

"Walker—"

"Looks like we've got our work cut out for us." He knelt and peeked under the lids of the other two boxes on the floor.

"Grab a box and have a seat." Aidan motioned to the empty desk behind his.

Avoiding his gaze, Walker gave a sharp shake of his head and rose with two boxes in his arms, carrying them as if they weighed nothing. "I'll take these with me to the cave."

Aidan stepped out from behind his desk. "You don't have to do that."

"It's fine, Talley." He glanced over his shoulder with blank eyes. "Call me if you find anything."

"Likewise," Aidan said, but Walker was already gone, disappointment and regret trailing in his wake. Aidan didn't like the feeling now any more than he had when Walker shut down after the jock comment two weeks ago. All the progress they had made since, gone in a puff of smoke, right along with Walker. Determined to apologize, to fix this before it festered and undermined their fledgling partnership, Aidan lidded and stacked the remaining two boxes. He opened his desk drawer to grab his phone and wallet, intending to go work beside his partner in the cave, lack of windows be damned.

He had just picked up his phone when it vibrated. He slid his thumb across the screen and brought it to his ear. "Talley."

"It's Byrne. Federal prosecutor has a few follow-up questions for us on the child exploitation case. Can you spare a few minutes? I've got him on the other line."

Aidan stared at the boxes and his fleeting opportunity to set things right with Walker.

"Talley, you there?"

The mental image of a kidnapped Katie flashed in his mind, reminding him of the need to put these people away for good. "Conference me in."

"Katie asleep?" Aidan shrugged into his jacket as he juggled the phone.

"Aye," his mother replied, the snick of a door closing in the background. "Out like a light. You're off story duty tonight."

"I still want to swing by. I'm leaving the office now." He yanked the last quarter of the personnel files out of the second box and tucked them under his arm. He crossed the darkened bullpen on his way to the lobby elevators, admiring San Francisco's nighttime skyline through the surrounding office windows. "Giants game ended an hour ago, so traffic should be light. I'll be there in forty."

He pocketed his phone and punched the elevator call button, stepping back as he waited for the cab to climb thirteen floors. A light down the hallway caught his eye as Springsteen's "Born to Run" reached his ears. Realizing the likely source, he wandered down the hall, into the cave, and through the server racks. He was grateful the music drowned out his gasp when he emerged into the mini bullpen.

The sight before him was something to behold. His partner, asleep at his desk, face planted in a stack of open personnel files. Walker looked so young, so beautiful, in sleep. Long, burnished lashes fanned against darkening under-eye circles, cheeks pinked, lips parted as he lightly snored. Unable to resist, Aidan reached for the light brown waves that had fallen over his forehead, intent on brushing them back, but then Walker stirred, and Aidan snatched his hand away. He cleared his throat to alert him to his presence.

Walker came awake at once, blinking rapidly and scattering files with his flailing limbs. Once he recognized a familiar face, he relaxed back into his chair.

"I think you might need more coffee," Aidan said.

"Where's a twenty-four-hour Blue Bottle when you need it?" Walker ran his hands over his face and rubbed his eyes with the heels of his palms, just like a little kid.

Reminded of the apology he needed to make, Aidan leaned against the desk. "I'm sorry about earlier. You're not a kid, and I shouldn't refer to you as one." Walker smiled wider than Aidan expected, lifting a heavy weight from his chest. "From now on, I'll keep my nicknames to the adult variety."

"I can live with that and thank you." Walker held his gaze several long seconds before eyeing the files under his arm. "Please tell me those aren't more files for me to review."

"For me," Aidan said. "Cure for insomnia."

Compassion flooded Walker's countenance. "Since the accident?"

"Since the IRA put a bomb under the family car."

Walker's eyes widened.

"Sure you don't want my personnel file now?"

His reply was slower this time but still "No."

The faith Walker put in him felt somehow undeserved, and Aidan wanted to earn it. He would try to do that on this next case together, starting with something simple. Setting his files on the desk, Aidan grabbed a pen and Post-it and scribbled his address on it. "Give me a lift to the airport tomorrow?" Walker nodded and Aidan handed him the slip of paper. "Our flight is at eleven-thirty. We should leave the house by ten."

Lifting a hip, Walker pulled out his wallet and tucked the note inside. "Got it."

Aidan picked his files back up, along with half of Walker's stack. "I'll see you tomorrow, Whiskey."

"Irish," Walker called, and Aidan paused at the opening of the server racks. "Good luck with the party tomorrow. And remember, when all else fails, ponies."

He smiled. "Ponies, got it."

SIX

Aidan rocked in the swivel chair at one end of the patio table, watching a gaggle of kids play chase around the big ash tree in the middle of his backyard. Katie, dressed as a fairy princess, was in the lead, a tiara tangled in her headful of strawberry-blond curls. At least half the kids trailing her, his other niblings, were one shade or another of redheaded. All the kids—Katie, her cousins, a handful of preschool playmates—appeared to be having a good time, laughing and running, grabbing handfuls of chips and cookies and a juice box whenever they needed a break.

They would have had more room at his parents' place in Woodside or at Grace and Chuck's house in Sunnyvale, but Katie had insisted on having her birthday party at Aidan's. With Chuck deployed, Grace pregnant, and his mother already keeping Katie several nights a week when Grace worked late, Aidan had agreed to host. He'd give Katie anything she wanted. He shouldn't play favorites, but given the circumstances of her birth and the promises he had made at her christening, Katie was the closest thing he had to a daughter of his own. Hosting her party today made his heart light, just as carrying out those promises alone, instead of with his husband, made it heavy.

He pulled out his phone and flipped through her christening photos—he and Gabe, smiling, happy, wedding bands on their left hands and a tiny cherub-faced baby with red fuzz in their arms. They had hoped to adopt one day, but now this moment, captured on his phone, would be the closest they would ever come.

Two mojitos appeared on the table in front of him, and the chair beside him squeaked as his middle sister, Chloe, fell into it with a huff. "How you doing, Ai?"

He pocketed the phone and took a sip of the refreshing, minty-lime beverage, more than welcome in the late summer heat. "Katie seems to be having a good time, though I'm not sure my yard will survive the stampede."

She shifted her chair closer, out of the sun and under the shade of the umbrella. "You should tear up the grass and go native." She waggled her brows, and Aidan groaned, rubbing his hands over his face, not wanting to get into it with the family environmentalist today. He liked his green lawn, thank you very much. Chloe let him off the hook—only to spear him with a bigger one. "And I didn't ask about your yard or Katie. I asked about you."

"Go easy, Clo." Grace hobbled into the chair on his other side and patted her huge belly. "We agreed. Interrogation-free day."

"Where is Siobhan?" Aidan asked, reminded of the practicing lawyer among them. The oldest of his three younger sisters was a no-show, even though her three kids were among the tornado tearing up the yard.

"Board meeting in Chicago," Chloe answered. "She and Danny flew out this morning."

"That explains why Dad's been on a call since he got here." Aidan twisted in his chair and waved at his father, who was on the phone in the sunroom Aidan had converted into his home office. His father was still CEO of the family company, but Siobhan was general counsel, and his youngest sibling, Daniel, was COO, responsible for running operations and for presenting to the Board of Directors, a task his father had happily relinquished.

Grace tapped his shoulder. "Mel said you're flying to Texas tonight?"

"Houston, then driving down to Galveston. Just for a few days, and I'll check in regularly." He diverted his gaze and picked at the mint leaf garnish he'd pulled from his glass. "I don't want Katie to think—"

Grace gripped his arm, squeezing tight. "She knows you're still here, and we'll make sure she understands you're coming back. You've got to do your job. You need that."

"Speaking of work," Chloe said in her devious, meddling-sister voice. "Tell me about this new partner. Whiskey Walker, did I hear that right?"

"You heard right." He picked up his glass, swirled its contents, and took another swallow.

"Ooh." Grace lowered her voice, picking up on their sister's conspiratorial vibe. "I've seen him on TV. He's a looker. What's he like?"

"What happened to interrogation-free day?"

"I make exceptions for super-hot athletes."

He chuckled. "Former athlete, and you're both happily married."

She eyed him shrewdly. "I wasn't asking for me."

Time to shut down his meddling sisters, for all the reasons he had shut himself down and put Walker in the friend zone. A *good* friend and partner, he was learning, but that was all there would be. "One, he's straight. Two, he's young, just turned thirty. Three, we work together. Big no-no. And four . . ." The sudden lump in his throat caught him by surprise, but he forced the words out. "It's not even been a year."

"Ai, you need to get back out there," Chloe said, earnest and stern all at the same time, the perfect high school guidance counselor. "Gabe wouldn't want you—"

He cut her off before the lump in his throat blocked words and air completely. "Please, Clo, not today."

Before either sister could press further, their mom appeared outside with her arms full of presents, Mel a step behind with a tray of fresh drinks for the grown-ups. She couldn't cook to save her life, a tragedy given her upbringing, but she could bartend with the best of them.

Spotting the gifts, Katie let out a shrill, preschooler battle cry of "Presents!" and everyone under the age of ten charged the table. His mom spread out brightly wrapped boxes while his sister-in-law exchanged old glasses for new. Not *former*. Mel's title was sealed, no matter that Gabe was no longer with them. Her presence today was proof of that.

Shooting Mel a grateful look, he took a sip of the fresh drink, then, owing to Grace's belly, hefted his goddaughter onto his lap. Holding her steady as she tore through wrapping paper, Aidan let her excitement distract him from thoughts of those missing around the table. But as Katie's enthusiasm began to wane, her unwrapping not so frantic, her delight at revealing what was inside each box not so ecstatic, he began to worry if she was overtired or also feeling the loss of her Unka Gabe.

He hoped he had the perfect gift to cheer her up.

"Over, Munchkin." He boosted her up to hand her over the armrest to Chloe.

She wriggled around to face him and threw her arms around his neck. "No leave."

As if he didn't already feel guilty enough. Taking her wrists in his hands, he pulled Katie's arms away from his neck and sat her back on his knees, keeping hold of one hand and straightening her crooked tiara with the other. "I'm not going anywhere, Munchkin, except to get your present."

Like night and day, the little girl's face went from abject misery to pure joy, a bright smile dimpling her cheeks and lighting her green eyes.

"You'd like that?"

She nodded enthusiastically, jarring the tiara sideways again.

Laughing, Aidan straightened the crown once more and lifted her over the armrest, sitting her in his sister's lap. "Be good for Aunt Clo, and I'll be right back."

"What's this one?" Chloe brought another brightly wrapped gift toward them, distracting Katie as he rose from his chair and went inside.

Aidan skirted through the kitchen and living area and down the hallway to his room. He pulled the gift bag from his dresser drawer, extracted the jewelry box from the tissue paper, and lifted the lid. Until yesterday, he still hadn't known what to get Katie. Gabe was always the one who'd picked out their goddaughter's gifts. Last night, though, Walker had given him an idea and the jeweler was happy to oblige, even on a rush basis. Aidan made sure the pony charm on the silver bracelet was positioned just right, closed the lid, and dropped the box back in the gift bag. After taking a moment to run his hand over his and Gabe's wedding picture on his dresser, he checked the spare room for stray gifts, or kids, and headed back through the house.

In the sunroom, his father was finally hanging up the phone.

"Everything okay, Dad?"

John Talley nodded, his thick silver hair bouncing. "Boarding meeting is done. Your brother and sister handled it well. Less than a month back for you. Sure I can't convince you to make a career change?"

His father had been trying to convince him to make a career change the past fifteen years.

"Sorry, it's a G-man's life for me."

"Well"—he pushed up from the chair—"can't blame an old man for trying. Each one of you kids at the company is one less meeting I have to attend."

Aidan laughed, looping an arm through his father's and tugging him toward the door. "Let's go, old man. There's a meeting with your granddaughter you can't miss."

He moved toward the door, but the body linked with his failed to budge. Turning back, Aidan was met by his father's intense black gaze.

"These past months have been hard on all of us. We lost Gabe, and we almost lost you. I don't know how any of us would have gone on after that, but you have. You've had the hardest road of all, and you've hung in there. I just wanted to say how proud I am of you."

The lump materialized again in Aidan's throat. His dad was such a big man—in stature, in personality, in success. A loving, doting, stern but attentive husband and father who Aidan idolized. Sure they had argued, a lot, but there was no one he looked up to more. His father's words now meant everything.

"Thanks, Dad," he choked out hoarsely.

"You're welcome, son."

Buoyed by his father's words, Aidan couldn't wait to get outside and give Katie her gift. Smiling, he pulled his father, arm in arm, outside. As soon as they rounded the corner of the house, Katie looked up from where she sat in her aunt's lap.

And burst into tears.

Aidan rushed to Chloe's side, dropped the gift bag on the table, and pulled Katie into his arms. "What's wrong, Munchkin?" Settling in the swivel chair, he held the little girl close, rocking, as Grace scooted closer and patted her daughter's back. The other adults were herding the rest of the kids inside with the promise of cake and ice cream.

He shifted Katie back a little and Grace pushed the strawberry-blond curls off her tear-streaked cheeks. "What's wrong, baby? Don't you want to see the gift Uncle Aidan got you?"

"Not what I want," she cried. Tears streamed from her green eyes and snot ran from her little pink nose.

Aidan was miserable, not sure what he should do. He pulled the gift bag closer and held it out to her, beseeching, "How do you know unless you open it?"

She gave the bag a passing glance and cried harder. "Not Unka Gabe," she wailed, before launching herself into her mother's lap, belly be damned.

Aidan's arms and heart were left empty.

SEVEN

Jamie parked his Jeep at the curb in front of Aidan's home and wondered if his partner had given him the correct address.

The black Vanquish in the driveway and the pink balloons and streamers wrapped around Craftsman-style porch pillars indicated he was in the right place, but it was difficult to reconcile the modest Silicon Valley cottage with everything he knew about Aidan and his late husband. Most of the houses in this Redwood City neighborhood were single-level, two-bedroom-one-bath starter homes on small, well-kept lots. Not where you would expect to find the heir to an Irish shipping fortune and his football player turned successful investment banker husband.

Jamie would've guessed Aidan and Gabe had settled in next-door Atherton or closer to Aidan's parents in nearby Woodside. They'd had the means to afford either. Then again, with their busy jobs, Aidan and Gabe probably hadn't been home much. A big house would have been a waste, and if they'd bought this property as an investment, it had paid off in spades. Real estate values on the Peninsula were skyrocketing.

The porch light flickered on, and an older woman stepped outside. She gave him a friendly wave, and Jamie climbed out of the SUV and rounded the hood of the car.

"You must be Whiskey," she said, accented voice raised.

"Yes, ma'am." He hustled up the short drive, then along the curved walkway in front of a bed of towering roses, before he stepped up onto the porch. In the soft light's glow, the woman's autumn eyes and auburn hair, streaked with silver and white, were unmistakable. "Jamie Walker," he said, hand extended. "You must be Mrs. Talley."

She held his hand in both of hers, her grasp as warm as her smile. "Please, call me Ellen."

"It's a pleasure to meet you, Ellen. Aidan asked me to give him a lift to the airport."

She released his hand, and the corners of her mouth dipped the other direction, the lilt in her voice following closely. "I'm afraid he's not here." She shuffled to one pillar, then the other, pulling down the streamers and balloons. Aidan's absence, taken together with Ellen's suddenly somber turn, told Jamie everything he needed to know.

"The party didn't go well," he surmised.

"It didn't. Little Katie . . ." Ellen piled the party decorations on the small square table between two wooden rockers. "She seemed okay for a bit but had a rough go of it in the end." She lowered herself into one of the rockers and gestured for Jamie to take the other.

"I'm sorry to hear that." He took the offered seat and scooted back in the chair, propping an ankle on his opposite knee. "With all your family's been through, I'm sure you know to expect more tough birthdays in her future."

"Oh, I know," Ellen said, her voice so full of loss it made Jamie's chest hurt. "You speak from experience too?" she asked.

"I lost my father when I was five."

"I'm sorry to hear that. Was it sudden?"

Jamie almost laughed. It wasn't often he found someone who didn't know his sob story. "It was a work accident," he said, not going into the details of the factory fire that had killed his dad.

"Does Aidan know?" Ellen asked.

Jamie diverted his gaze, distracting himself from the remembered loss by cataloguing the different color rose bushes. "It hasn't come up," he answered, though he had no doubt Aidan knew, between his personnel files and sports television.

"I'm sorry for your loss," Ellen said. "But if you have it in you to talk about it, maybe my son could better understand what Katie's going through, other than what her doctors tell us."

"The docs can only do so much." He recalled the woefully inept grief counselor his father's employer had been forced to hire. Katie probably had the best therapists money could buy, but for Jamie, it had been his classmates and teachers who had pulled him out of the dark place. "Is she back in preschool? That's what got me through."

Ellen nodded. "It was touch and go the first day. She's been glued to Aidan since the accident, but her teachers got her settled. She's a social butterfly, like everyone else in this family."

"But not today?"

"She thought—" Ellen paused, blinking rapidly and swallowing hard enough to hear in the otherwise quiet night. "She seemed fine most of the day, playing with her cousins and friends. We got to the presents, and Aidan saved his for last. It was a bracelet with a silvery pony charm on it." Jamie's breath caught, but he didn't say anything, and Ellen continued. "He'd called the jeweler on the way home last night and paid God only knows how much to get it delivered in time. He would do anything for that little girl. She didn't even unwrap it. Just burst into tears because Aidan hadn't gotten her Uncle Gabe for her birthday."

Jamie dropped his foot and leaned forward, propping his elbows on his knees and covering his gaping mouth with his fingertips. He knew all too well the crushing disappointment Katie had experienced. The first Christmas after his father died, he had been sure Santa would bring him home. He remembered the pain on his mother's face when he'd said as much on Christmas morning. Aidan had probably worn a similar look earlier that afternoon.

"I'm sure that was hard on Aidan," he said.

"The last thing he ever wanted to do was break his niece's heart even more."

"And now he has to leave."

"Can't be helped." Ellen wiped her eyes and slid to the edge of her chair, straightening her spine as she angled toward him. "My son's been an FBI agent for a while now. We—all the adults—know how this works. He promised to call every morning and night. Can you help make sure he keeps that promise?"

"Yes, ma'am." He stood, absently wiping his hands on his jeans. "Where can I find him? I'll have that talk with him and make sure he's okay too." Jamie didn't care if he was overstepping. Aidan was his partner, and he wanted to be

Aidan's friend too—which, after a day like today, Aidan needed, even if Aidan was determined to keep him at arm's length.

Ellen stood, her long-fingered hands, so much like her son's, tugging her light cardigan snugly around her. "He took a cab to Woodside Tavern. You know it?"

"Yes, I know it." He turned to go, in a hurry to get to Aidan, but remembered his manners and turned back, holding his hand out once more. "It was nice to meet you, Ellen."

"You too, Jamie." She took his hand in both of hers again, some of the warmth returning. "I'm glad Aidan has you. After losing both Gabe and Tom, he needs more people in his corner."

"Truth be told, I'm not sure your son wants me there. Doesn't mean I won't dig my heels in and stay."

"Good," she said with a chuckle. "Thank you for that." She patted his hand as her smile turned into a smirk that was likewise unmistakable. "I raised a smart boy. He'll come around."

EIGHT

Polishing off his second Kentucky Sidecar, Aidan flagged down the bartender for another. Roy raised a brow and aimed a pointed look past him into the dining room. Aidan spun on his barstool, taking in the restaurant.

Woodside Tavern had been his go-to place for as long as he could remember. From family occasions to first dates and first jobs, to his and Gabe's engagement and wedding reception, the outstanding food and elegant décor befitted life's milestones. At one end of the space, where Aidan sat, was the ornately carved bar with three tiers of liquor stacked against a mirrored backsplash. A private dining room was hidden behind sliding doors at the other end, and in between, the main dining area was filled with white linen-covered tables, plush burgundy chairs, and dark leather booths. But despite the Tavern's rich appearance and humming undercurrent of Silicon Valley power, it still felt like a neighborhood bar.

A mostly deserted bar, as Roy was not so subtly implying. Only one booth was still occupied, a couple finishing off their soufflé, as staff scurried about, readying tables for tomorrow while bouncing to the ambient jazz music that had been turned up.

"I'll make it easy." Aidan spun back around with a plaintive look. "Just the bourbon. Take pity on me, Roy. I'm on a red-eye to Texas in two hours."

"You sure that's all this is?" the bartender asked. "I haven't seen you like this the past few weeks. My bourbon well wasn't depleted for a change, until tonight."

"Rough day," was all he answered. Roy had only started working at the Tavern six months ago. He wouldn't know the significance of today's date, or the role the Tavern had played in it.

"You got a ride?" the bartender asked.

"Right here."

Aidan glanced over his shoulder toward the door and the owner of the familiar Southern drawl. He usually favored men in suits—Gabe's default—but Aidan preferred his new partner like this. Dusty Chucks, weathered Levi's, a chambray button-down, sleeves rolled to his elbows. *Fuck it,* the bourbon said, and Aidan gave Walker the lingering once-over he had denied himself until then. When he reached the other man's eyes, thin rings of cobalt circled blown-wide pupils. Aidan chalked it up to the chambray shirt and dim lighting. "I take it Mom sent you," he said, not waiting for a response as he twirled back around to Roy. "Make it two."

"One's fine." Walker sidled up on the stool beside him. "Just water for me."

Aidan glared. "I wasn't ordering for you."

"Suit yourself. But don't expect me to hold your hair back in the airplane bathroom."

"Ha-ha."

"Your mess, you clean it up. And no way we'd both fit."

As soon as Roy set the whiskeys in front of him, Aidan downed the first, praying it'd burn away the image of him and Walker in an airplane bathroom. His partner's shirt torn wide open, those battered jeans around his ankles, his big hands in Aidan's hair for an entirely different reason.

"Your mom told me what happened at the party."

Instant fantasy killer.

"I'm sorry. I know that was rough," Walker carried on as Aidan sipped from the second glass. "Kids, they don't always understand death right away. I didn't after my dad died."

Aidan knew all about the factory fire that killed Walker's father. It was mentioned in his personnel file, in his psych evals, and any time he had been featured on sports television. The incident had made national headlines, not because of the mile-high flames that had burned all night or the popular brand name food processed there, but because the factory owner had chained the exit doors shut, trapping his supposedly thieving workers inside. Out of that came the legend of Whiskey Walker. The scrawny kid whose daddy died in the chicken plant fire, whose uneducated single mother struggled to raise him and his sister, who grew up to be a two-time NCAA champion, tourney MVP, and NBA lottery pick.

"Hearing your mom tell it and seeing you now . . ." Walker's words trailed off, and Aidan could feel the other man's eyes on him. "I'm even sorrier I said something similar to my mom that first Christmas after Dad died."

Aidan glanced over. "It's never too late to apologize."

"Already ahead of you," he said with a small smile.

"Called her on my way here."

"It's, what, one in the morning in North Carolina? You couldn't wait until morning?"

"No, I really couldn't." Walker's hand covered his where it lay on the bar, and Aidan was captivated by its size and warmth, by the blanket of comfort it provided. When Walker withdrew it a moment later, Aidan instantly missed the contact, not realizing until then how desperately he had needed it after the awful day. But then Walker spun on his stool, propped an elbow on the bar behind him, and their shoulders brushed, renewing the connection. "This is such a cool place."

"Been here before?"

"Once, on a date."

Aidan laughed, and Walker twisted, angling toward him. "Something funny?"

"My first date was here," he confessed, staring into his bourbon glass. "If you consider a quinceañera after-party with my family and hers a real date."

"So you've dated men and women?"

Aidan's head jerked up, meeting Walker's curious eyes. Not the question he'd anticipated. It wasn't a stretch to say they had become friends, but he didn't fancy a gossip about his love life with Walker any more than he had with his sisters. Not today, on his wedding anniversary that wasn't.

"When I was younger." He intended to leave it at that, then the bourbon got the better of him again. "And you?"

Gaze steady, Walker answered, "Only men."

And Aidan's world tilted, thrown off balance yet again by Jameson Walker. He would have fallen off his stool too if Walker hadn't shot out a hand and grasped him by the arm, keeping him upright. "You okay, Irish?"

"You're not straight?"

"Nope." He dropped his hand and looked away. "Never have been, never will be."

Aidan cast his mind back over the past couple weeks. To how those same eyes darkened tonight as Aidan blatantly checked him out. To Walker's abrupt movements and deflections whenever Aidan flashed him a grin, to his sharp, inhaled breaths if they passed too close, to the blush that colored his cheeks when Aidan favored him with a compliment, and the wounded look when he called him *kid*. To the way Walker had dropped his voice and described his eyes that first day together in the cave.

He had been flirting. Walker was gay. And interested in him.

And down goes Frazier, he heard Chloe cheer in his head.

Shit. And *fuck* and *damn* while he was at it.

Maybe he didn't belong back in the field after all. Was he this off his game, or had he just been willfully oblivious to the truth staring him in the face? A truth that would complicate their partnership. A truth Aidan was in no state to handle, especially not tonight.

"I've never seen you with—" He cut himself off, trying to recall if he had ever seen Walker with a companion of any gender. "Anyone," he answered his own question.

Walker's eyes, when they met his again, were hard and years older than thirty. "I'm not closeted, if that's what you mean. Just careful. When it comes to the press, I learned my lesson."

"Really? Because the reporters seem to love you."

"It's not fair to expose someone else to that."

Interesting. So he'd been burned, or almost burned. Was that why he had suddenly dropped out of the NBA and moved across the country? It fit with everything he had learned so far about Walker. He was cocky, sure, but his interactions with Leah, with Byrne, with him about Katie and Gabe, and the late-night call to his mother, hinted at a deep consideration for others. The well-mannered Southern boy who didn't want to make waves but couldn't seem not to.

"Tell me about this quinceañera date from hell," Walker invited.

Recognizing the deflection but still too stunned to do anything about it, Aidan answered, "Lots of dancing, ill-fitted tuxes, big hair, and big dresses. It was a wild night."

Walker chuckled. "Who was the lucky lady?"

"Isabella Crane."

"Tom's wife?"

"Isabella Cortez then, but yes, the very same." His voice grew quiet as sorrow crept in. "I set them up after Academy." He took the last sip of whiskey and pushed his glass across the bar to a passing Roy.

There was a scraping sound and when next Walker spoke, he was closer, his hot breath coasting across Aidan's neck. "Why don't you show me some of these dance moves?"

Aidan whipped his head around, bringing them nose to nose. "Don't be ridiculous."

"I'm serious." Walker grinned, the temptation and levity in his bright blue eyes chasing away the sorrow of the day, of the past eight months. "Impress me," he said, using Aidan's own words against him.

"Whiskey," he warned, low and tight, fighting his instincts.

"Come on, it's just us here."

Glancing over his shoulder, Aidan confirmed the other couple was gone, Roy was nowhere to be seen, and the only two servers left sat folding napkins in the private room.

Walker, standing between their stools, inched closer and laid his hand over Aidan's again. "Dance with me, Talley."

Hooked, the offered comfort reeled Aidan in. Tugging his hand, Walker pulled him off the stool and into his arms. As they swayed gently to the music, it wasn't dancing with Isabella Aidan remembered but dancing with Gabe after their wedding. Held in Walker's arms, knowing what he did now about his partner's sexuality, Aidan allowed himself to notice the physical similarities between Walker and his husband. Both accomplished athletes, they were bigger and stronger than him, larger in height and mass. He liked being surrounded in a bigger man's warmth. He also liked dominating that when he had a mind to. And Walker was one hell of a specimen.

Relaxing into the embrace, Aidan coasted the hand not in Walker's up his cut biceps, over his broad shoulder, and around to his back where rock-hard delts stood out beneath the rough chambray. Closing the inches between them, he pressed his chest to Walker's and bit back a moan at finding the front of him as warm and firm as the back.

Walker dipped his chin, his stubbled jaw nuzzling Aidan's temple. "Something tells me this isn't how you danced with Isabella."

"No, it's not." He breathed deep and fought not to melt completely. Everything about the moment enticed him to bury his face in Walker's neck and let go—that deep molasses voice, the tempting cologne, a warm embrace after months of cold loneliness.

Just as Aidan closed his eyes, just as his legs and arms

began to lose their form, a shrill ring shattered the moment, and cold air rushed between them.

Swearing, Walker released his hand and dug his phone out of his pocket. He glared at the screen. "It's Cruz."

Aidan stepped the rest of the way out of his arms. "Take it. I'll settle the tab."

Walker headed for the other end of the bar and Aidan riffled through his wallet, pulled out several bills, and placed them in the leather folio Roy had left on the bar. He turned back around and took in the empty restaurant once more. Defenses down, memories crashed through his heart and mind.

Bringing Gabe here for their first date, New Year's Eve ten years ago.

Gabe paying a small fortune to buy out the private dining room the night gay marriage was legalized in California so he could get down on one knee and ask for his hand in marriage.

Their friends and families gathered here to celebrate their nuptials.

Guilt slammed into Aidan, causing him to stagger back into his barstool.

"Whoa, there." Walker rushed toward him, arm outstretched. "You okay, Irish?"

Aidan skirted out of reach, cursing himself for betraying his husband in a moment of weakness, for taking comfort in the arms of another man in the place that had been theirs. It hadn't been long enough. He wasn't ready to move on, no matter what his sisters or anyone else said. Gabe was the love of his life. There was no moving on from that.

He avoided Walker's question and his gaze. "What did Mel want?"

"You weren't answering your phone. She wanted to make sure you were okay and that we were on schedule to make our flight."

Aidan moved to the closet at the end of the bar where he had stored his coat and suitcase. "We need to get a move on."

He was stopped short by Walker's hand around his upper arm, demanding his attention. "Aidan," he started, those blue eyes darkened again by a stormy mix of emotions.

Confusion, disappointment, frustration, arousal.

Aidan met them defiantly, denying all the things he had put there. "We're going to be late."

Growling, Walker dropped his arm and ran a hand through his hair, the tousling making him infuriatingly more attractive. Aidan hurried for the door while he still could.

"Are you okay to go?" Walker asked, rushing to catch up. "If you need another day with Katie and your family, I'm sure Cruz would understand."

Aidan's chest constricted at the revival of Walker's disarming consideration. No care for the roller coaster he'd just put him through. Only concern. This kid—this partner—was too good for him. He needed to get his act together and be the friend, partner, and mentor Walker deserved too.

And that was as far as it would go.

Stopping in the middle of the parking lot, Aidan inhaled deep and turned to face the other man. "I'm fine, Whiskey." His voice was calm and even. "Thank you for asking." He waited for Walker's expression to gentle, for the tension in his broad shoulders to ease, then said, "Let's go. We have work to do."

NINE

Jamie leaned over the bathroom sink, soaked a plush washcloth in warm water, and brought it to his face, chasing away the last vestiges of jetlag. He hadn't slept a wink on the red-eye to Houston. Their last-minute booking had landed them in the back row of coach, and there was nothing his charm or Aidan's badge could do about a full first-class cabin. Despite the tight fit and upright seats, Aidan had slept most of the three-and-a-half-hour flight, so once they deplaned in Houston, Jamie had let his partner lead the way.

Past the rental car counters to a Mercedes E350 convertible in long-term parking.

Past the valet who had greeted Aidan by name when they'd pulled in front of a private oceanfront complex.

Past the opulent lobby, into the glass elevator, up four floors, and through the living area of an open-plan condo.

Jamie had only had eyes for the guest bedroom Aidan directed him to and the California king bed waiting there.

Four hours of dead-to-the-world sleep later, Jamie took

in his surroundings anew. The bathroom was floor-to-ceiling white marble, with a sunken jetted tub and glassed-in spa shower, the latter of which he quickly availed himself. Freshly showered, he spotted his luggage on a rack by the bedroom door. He tossed out clothes until he unearthed his athletic shorts and a gym shirt. Once dressed, he padded across the smooth bamboo floors to the far wall and found two wooden rods in the heavy blackout curtains. Pushing them apart, he gasped at the view revealed—rolling dunes, white sandy beaches, and the blue-green waters of the Gulf.

He opened the French doors set in the wall of windows and stepped out on the balcony. As hot, humid air surrounded him, he fondly remembered beach vacations as a kid. Money had been scarce growing up, but his mom always saved enough for a week at the coast. They had never stayed anywhere nice—motor lodges were all they could afford on a server's tips—but sand, sun, and water were entertainment enough for him and his sister, and his mom had been content reading a book on the beach beside them. Nothing had made Jamie happier than buying her an oceanfront house at Oak Island with his NBA signing bonus.

He wandered down the spacious balcony and reentered the condo at the next set of open French doors, unsurprised to find the living area as lavish as his room. A gourmet kitchen was equipped with top-of-the-line stainless steel appliances, expansive granite countertops, a large center island, and a raised breakfast bar, stools tucked neatly underneath. In the adjacent dining area, a long, rectangular piece of beveled glass sat atop two white stone pillars, surrounded by eight chairs, their blue gingham cushions matching those on the barstools. Beyond the kitchen and dining areas, in front of where Jamie stood, a pair of oversize couches and two swivel chairs faced a giant wall-mounted television, a media unit underneath with the requisite peripherals and multiple gaming systems.

Noticing the open door to his right, Jamie poked his head into the other bedroom. Nothing but Aidan's exploded luggage. Reversing, he searched the main area for a note or other clue as to his partner's whereabouts. As far as clues went, a lukewarm pot of coffee and a covered skillet weren't a lot to go on. He lifted the lid on the skillet and inhaled the enticing aromas of chorizo, peppers, eggs, and cheese, all arranged on a picture-worthy breakfast tostada. He poured himself a mug of coffee, slid the tostada on a plate, reheated both in the microwave, then carried his breakfast out to the balcony.

As near as Jamie could tell, glancing above and below the waist-high stucco balcony wall, the condo was on the top floor of a four-level structure, four units wide, except the first floor, which only had two units on either side of the lobby. The building was a narrow beach and row of dunes back from the ocean, which was calm today. A few kids played on the sand, two teens floated on body boards just past the breakers, and a little farther out, someone swam parallel to the coast. Jamie shoveled in the last bite of his tostada, set the empty plate aside, and picked up the binoculars on the table behind him. He adjusted the dials to focus on the swimmer.

A shock of blond hair and powerful broad shoulders breached the water's surface in smooth, practiced strokes. Jamie's face warmed, not from the late morning sun but from the memory of that amazing body in his arms last night, tight in apprehension then relaxing as they'd danced. He had gone to the Tavern with the single intention of making sure Aidan was okay. After learning from Aidan's mother about Katie's outburst and Aidan and Gabe's anniversary, he figured his partner needed a friend. But the intimate atmosphere of the place and their conversation had had Jamie thinking about more. *Wanting* more. Once Aidan had mentioned the quinceañera, the thought of dancing with him had become irresistible.

And that right there was problem one. Aidan was his *partner*, his *mentor*. Jamie admired him, had wanted him from afar for years, but fraternizing with a fellow agent was frowned upon by the Bureau. He loved his job and didn't want to do anything to jeopardize it, especially now that SAC Cruz was eyeing him for promotion. While he preferred to stay in the cave, out of the public eye he'd already had enough of, he wanted to do well and advance, which meant doing good, clean fieldwork and keeping his hands off Aidan.

Problem two, Aidan was very much taken. The flood of guilt had been painted clear as day on his face after Cruz called last night. Gabe still had a firm hold on his heart.

Problem three, Jamie recognized his own inclination to move too fast, to fall head over heels at warp speed and ignore the danger-ahead signs lining the path to destruction. The psychiatrist he'd seen during physical therapy after his injury, when he'd been at his lowest, had said his instant attachment tendencies came from the loss of his father at such a young age. She was right, to some degree. He didn't want to waste time when he knew how short life could be. Another part of it was the happiness hoarder in him that wanted to grab onto the good and keep it hidden close, out of the ruthless public eye that could destroy it with a single headline. While clips from his highlight reel still aired from time to time, the media had mostly left Whiskey Walker alone since he'd joined the FBI. Getting involved with his wealthy, older, widower coworker—a man—would be sure to thrust him back into the headlines. Their lives would be exposed and their jobs at risk. This time, Jamie had to pay attention to the warning signs. He had to curb his desire and steer clear of any romantic attachment to Aidan.

His partner, though, wasn't doing him any favors. Aidan sauntered up the wooden walkway from the beach, towel slung over one shoulder, his swim trunks molded to his lower body in a way that left nothing to the imagination. Groaning, Jamie turned his back on Aidan and the ocean and adjusted his shorts. By the time a key turned in the front lock and Aidan stepped inside, Jamie had his body and imagination mostly under control. At the sink washing dishes, he glanced over his shoulder, grateful to find Aidan had wrapped the towel around his hips, even if it did draw Jamie's gaze to the strip of auburn hair leading beneath the towel.

"Morning, partner," Aidan said.

Jamie snapped his eyes up, then meeting Aidan's knowing smile, promptly hid the warmth that hit his cheeks by turning back to his task at the sink. "Sorry I slept most of it away."

"Judging by your A-plus walking dead impression after the flight, I'd say you needed it. Can't sleep on planes?"

"Fifty-fifty shot if I'm in first class. Coach, never."

"Ditto, but with enough whiskey . . ."

Jamie turned and braced his hands behind him on the

counter. He felt like he needed to apologize, like he had somehow taken advantage. "Listen, about last night—"

"Thank you," Aidan said, as he fiddled with the coffeepot. "I had a rough day, and you were a good friend, so . . . thank you."

Jamie spun back to the sink before Aidan glimpsed the disappointment on his face. *Friend*. Not the zone he wanted to be in, but where they had to be. Hell, it was better than merely *partner*. He would take friend; he'd be happy with that. He didn't have a choice.

"You know, you don't have to do that." Aidan appeared beside him, two mugs in hand. "Daily housekeeping service."

His mood improved instantly. He shut off the water, wiped his hands on the dishtowel over his shoulder, and accepted the offered mug. "This ain't exactly the Holiday Inn."

"The building's owned by families with business in the area, mine included."

Jamie took a careful sip of the coffee, unsure how hot it would be, and was surprised to find it prepared how he liked it. Had to fight the grin that wanted to turn up the corners of his mouth. "What else is on the agenda today?"

"I called the field office before I went for a swim. It's Sunday, so skeleton crew, but Gary and his team will meet us at noon. Then we'll head over to GNL."

"How are we playing the field office? Friendly or foe?"

"I may have ruffled some feathers the other day."

"You think?"

"You'll need to flash that gorgeous smile and win us some friends."

So much for holding back that grin and blush. "Who do

you want to interview at GNL?" Jamie asked, feigning ignorance of both.

"Everyone who has access to the BSL-4 labs. I want to look them in the eye and see if we've got a coconspirator inside."

"And I have some follow-up questions for the network security team."

Aidan downed the rest of his coffee and handed Jamie his empty mug. "You're on point there. Technobabble and all that."

"Can you at least say jargon or lingo?"

Aidan used his forearms on the bar to lever forward, mouth twisted in a smug grin. "No promises."

"Asshole," Jamie grumbled, though it morphed into a laugh.

A laugh that died when Aidan gave him a wink, turned, and walked, sans towel, across the living area to his room, his firm backside on display beneath those damp swim trunks.

Partner, mentor, friend. Nothing more.

Good luck with that, came a voice in his head, one that sounded suspiciously like the cause of his torment.

Luck was not on Jamie's side.

Not when Aidan came out of his room dressed in worn cowboy boots, dark wash jeans, and a faded gray Western-style button-down, looking right at home in Texas.

Not when they crested the causeway bridge and his partner shot him a smile, his hair windswept, the midday sun reflecting off his silver-rimmed aviators.

And definitely not when a good-looking younger Latino man dressed in jeans and a V-neck tee entered the field office conference room and gave Jamie a slow once-over, eliciting a rumbling, sexy, hands-off growl from Aidan.

Before Jamie could ponder the stranger's interest or Aidan's reaction, an older white gentleman joined them.

"Agents Talley and Walker, I'm Gary Clark." Hand outstretched, Gary rounded the table to greet them. Despite his thinning gray hair, Gary's shoulders were broad, his figure trim, his skin wrinkled and tanned from a lifetime in the Texas sun. This was not a man you wanted to meet in a bar fight. "Pleasure to meet you in person," he drawled, his accented voice deep and commanding. "SAC Cruz speaks highly of you both."

"Aidan, please," his partner said, all trace of hostility gone. "Mel says the same of you."

"Glad to hear I'm on her good side. That woman scares the piss out of me."

Aidan laughed. "Try being her brother-in-law."

"Married to her sister?"

"Brother."

Gary's eyes widened slightly, but the Texas City SAC betrayed no other reaction. Jamie wondered how that reaction would differ if he'd made such a statement.

Aidan's introduction interrupted the thought. "My partner, Jameson Walker."

"Whiskey Walker." Gary shook his hand with enthusiasm. "It's a real pleasure, though I'm still holding that Final Four loss against you."

"I'd expect nothing less of a Longhorn alum." He had read up on their host during the flight from hell last night. "And your nephew made my Tar Heels pay for it in last year's College World Series. Hell of a pitcher. He's going to make some major league team very happy."

Gary's milky blue eyes lit with pride. "Rangers and Astros are already scouting him. So are a dozen other teams, but it sure would be nice to keep him close to home."

"May the draft gods be with you."

"From you, I'll take that."

Most people would. He'd been fortunate, or so it seemed. Drafted by the Charlotte Bobcats, back before they had become the Hornets again, he'd stayed close to home. That had ultimately been his downfall.

As if sensing his discomfort, Aidan spared him further draft talk by extending a hand to the younger agent. "Agent Talley," he said, a more formal greeting than he had offered Gary. "Agent Torres, I presume?"

"Yes, sir." The striking, dark-haired man—Jamie guessed near his own age—tucked the files he carried under his left arm and shook Aidan's pale hand in his light brown one. "You received those additional reports?"

"We did. Thank you very much."

He turned to Jamie, a blinding white smile splitting his tan face. "Oscar Torres."

"Jamie Walker."

"I'm a big fan too." Using their clasped hands, Oscar pulled him close and lowered his voice. "That demo you put on at the Black Hat convention in Vegas last year was something else." Oscar's hazel eyes gleamed with mischief and flirtation.

Jamie was surprised into silence by the fact Oscar knew of his not-so-legal recreational activities behind a computer screen. Before he could reply, a fourth voice joined the fray.

"Excuse me, coming through." A wiry thirty-something white hipster type entered with a box of files. He dropped it on the table and glanced between Aidan and Jamie. "I'm sorry I'm late. Agent Todd Barnes, at your service."

After another round of handshakes, Aidan jutted his chin toward the files. "What've you got there?"

Todd adjusted his too-tight black vest and pushed his thick-rimmed glasses up his sharply angled nose. "First responder reports from each breach. I thought you'd want to see these too."

Of course they would.

Frustration and anger flared in Aidan's eyes, and Jamie intervened before he exploded. "Thank you, Todd. Have you looked through them yet?"

"Briefly," he said with a cautious look toward Aidan. "We just received them from the local departments yesterday afternoon. I spent all night collating them."

Aidan shifted his irate glare to Oscar. "And what were you doing?"

"Sweeping network logs," he answered, then pointedly addressed Jamie. "I'd be happy to go through these with you." He nodded at the folders he'd laid on the table.

Sensing the tsunami of tension rolling off Aidan, Jamie shut the solicitous agent down. "We'll get to that later, Agent Torres." Using Oscar's own tactics against him, Jamie ignored him and spoke to Todd. "Tell us what you've found."

Todd's wariness vanished, Aidan relaxed, and Jamie breathed a sigh of relief. He pulled out chairs for him and Aidan. Oscar and Todd sat across the table, Gary at the head.

"In addition to the alerts to GNL network security, alerts

were also transmitted to UT campus security, GNL and UT biohazard units, and local fire and police departments." Todd pulled different colored files out of his box. "No tampering or interference detected with any transmissions. Response times varied from two to ten minutes, depending on the day and time."

Jamie rotated his chair toward Aidan and rapped his knuckles on the table. "Knock, knock."

One corner of his partner's mouth quirked up. "This game again?"

Smiling, Jamie knocked again.

Aidan rolled his eyes but played along. "Who's there?"

"I don't care. I just wanted to see how long it took you to answer the door."

Understanding dawned, the other side of Aidan's mouth lifting as his gaze sharpened. "Someone's gauging response times." He turned to Todd. "Was it a different shift for any of those response teams?"

"Yes. It varies by day and team. I'll have a correlated report to you by end of day."

Aidan was on his feet again, pacing the area between their chairs and the conference room windows, pen spinning around his thumb. Chair sideways, one eye on Aidan, the other on Todd and Oscar, Jamie asked the latter, "Any further breaches?"

"None, and the internal firewall behind the air gap remains untouched."

He rattled off a string of diagnostic and penetration tests, making sure Oscar had run them all, until his chair was spun around to face an exasperated Aidan. "English, Whiskey. Translate the technobabble."

Jamie shot out a hand, snatched the pen from Aidan's

grasp, and broke it in half. "Say *babble* one more time and I'll break something else."

By the challenge glittering in Aidan's eyes, Jamie knew a repeat of the obnoxious word was on the tip of his tongue. Gary interceded before war broke out. "I'd appreciate an explanation too, Agent Walker."

Smirking, Aidan raised both hands. "Last time, I promise." He moved to stand by Gary, and Jamie split his gaze between the two of them, explaining in plain English the pen-tests Oscar had conducted, including the one he'd missed.

"I should have caught that," Oscar said, his tone a harsh rebuke of himself. "I'll call GNL network security and have them run it right away."

"No, don't," Jamie said. "We're headed over there next. I'll do it myself."

"Planning to leave a little something behind?" Aidan asked.

"Maybe."

"Would you like us to join you?" Todd asked.

"We've got it," Aidan replied. "We'll take the GNL security and biohazard responder reports off your hands."

Todd dug the green and yellow file folders out of the box and pushed them across the table.

Jamie flipped through them as Aidan continued speaking. "That leaves you two with the fire and police responder reports, and Barnes, make sure you email us that correlated shift log. While you're at it, crosscheck all responders with anyone who has BSL-4 access at GNL."

"What're you thinking?" Gary asked.

"Someone inside GNL is trying to move something out."

Jamie followed his partner's train of thought. "If they

need to breach the internal air gap to do so, that inside person could be conspiring with someone directing response teams."

"Directing or monitoring."

Gary nodded. "Worth a look."

"We'll get right on it." Todd scribbled notes on a legal pad.

"Be sure to include all agencies who responded, including this one," Aidan said.

Todd's hand froze, the lead of his pencil cracking under pressure. His green eyes grew wide as saucers behind his black-frame glasses.

"You don't need to do that." Gary drew their attention away from the junior agent's blanched face. "I've personally questioned everyone here." The SAC's tone contained not a trace of defensiveness, only pure professionalism, and Jamie understood why Cruz regarded him so highly. For such a large man whose bearing might frighten some, his demeanor was calm and steady.

Aidan nodded. "Good, one more thing off our plate. Can we use this conference room for the rest of the week?"

"That shouldn't be a problem." Gary pushed up from his chair and addressed his agents. "Todd, make sure Nora reserves this room first thing tomorrow morning. Oscar, get IT to set up some workstations in here too."

"Yes, sir," they both answered.

Jamie gathered files as Aidan shook Gary's hand at the door. "We look forward to working with you."

Todd followed them out, having a much easier time with his lightened box.

Jamie held his and Aidan's share of the files to his chest with one arm and used his free hand to enter search parameters into his phone. Focused on his task, he nearly ran into Oscar, who was waiting in the doorway.

"Here's my card." Oscar dropped a business card in front of the files. "My personal number is on the back."

Jamie didn't miss Oscar's invitation. Neither did Aidan, judging by the pointed look he shot him once they stepped into the elevator. "Run that search on connections here to GNL."

"Already on it." Jamie flashed his phone at Aidan and almost dropped the files doing so. "Here, hold these." He shoved the files at Aidan and turned his attention back to his search algorithm, disregarding Oscar's card, which had floated to the floor.

"You can do that deep a search from your phone?" Aidan asked, snit forgotten.

Jamie waited until they were outside the building doors before letting his partner in on a little secret. "I can bring down an empire from this thing."

"Speaking of, I didn't know the FBI condoned its agents attending Black Hat conventions."

"Surprised you caught that," Jamie said without looking up from his phone. "Much less know what one is."

"I've seen every Michael Mann film ever made. And you didn't answer the question."

The smack of file folders hitting leather seats halted Jamie before he ran into the side of the car. Search variables entered, he pocketed the phone and leaned his hip against the side of the Benz. "Jameson Walker has never attended a Black Hat convention."

"I'm sure he hasn't."

He shrugged one shoulder. "Guy's gotta get his thrills somehow."

Aidan cut a glare in the direction of the brick office building. "I'm thinking Torres would like to give you some thrills."

"Not where I'm looking for thrills these days." The words were out of Jamie's mouth before he could catch them.

Heat flared in Aidan's eyes, but he shuttered it quickly and tossed Jamie the keys. "Your turn to drive. Top up, though, with those files in the back."

Jamie caught the keys one-handed, then ran his other hand through his hair, giving the longer strands a frustrated tug and mentally repeating his new mantra.

Partner, mentor, friend. Nothing more.

He slid in behind the wheel, waited for the convertible top to lift, and clicked the E350 into sport mode.

Aidan arched a brow. "Another source of thrills?"

"The good kind," Jamie answered.

An easy smile spread across Aidan's face, melting the tension between them. "Just remember, you break it, you bought it."

"Like you said, I'm good for it."

TEN

Sunday operated like any other day of the week at Galveston National Laboratory. People in white lab coats and biohazard suits moved behind sealed glass walls while countless others traveled the main hallways. Even with uniformed security guards outside the main entry to each BSL-4 lab, the sheer number of people circulating in and around GNL made Aidan's head hurt.

How were they supposed to narrow down their suspect list?

He reached up to wipe a bead of sweat from his brow, only to whack his gloved hand against the plastic mask covering his face. He had never experienced claustrophobia before. Sealed up tight in a biohazard suit, he imagined it felt a lot like this.

"As you can see, gentlemen, we've taken every precaution to secure these pathogens," a tinny voice said from the speaker inside Aidan's suit. Standing next to Walker, Henry Altman, GNL's director, had one gloved hand on the breast pocket of his suit, activating the lab-wide comm system, while the other rested on the keypad lock of a vial cabinet.

"Excuse me." Another suited scientist, this one a woman, brushed past Aidan to a different cabinet behind them, keyed in her code, and opened the door. She transferred a vial from the cabinet into a small box at the side of a large, enclosed hood, and air locks clicked in place. A robotic arm withdrew the vial from the box and moved it into the center of the hood, within reach of the black gloves she slid her hands into. Aidan suppressed a shiver as he wondered what deadly disease was uncapped inside the hood five feet away.

"These keypads are on the internal system behind the air gap?" Walker asked.

"That's right," Altman said. "And so are the doors from the changing rooms farther in. Each person with access has a unique badge and code assigned by GNL network security."

"Can those badges or codes be changed?"

"Only by network security, and it's not a frequent request. Most of us find it easier to memorize the first one they give us." Altman walked ahead of them. "That being said, everyone's badges were replaced, and codes were reset this past weekend."

"It's randomized. Less likely to be guessed or figured out." Walker's voice directly in his right ear caught Aidan by surprise, even though he had been the one to suggest concealed comm devices that would allow them to speak on a private, closed channel. "Looks like they took our advice to increase security."

"They've seen all the outbreak movies too. No one wants to be ground zero for an incident like that." Aidan tapped his front pocket for the open mic. "Dr. Altman, who's responsible for background checks on personnel with BSL-4 access?"

"Everyone goes through the same clearance process as CDC staff."

"And the hiring decisions?"

"Lab supervisors," Altman said. "Principal investigators, in a normal academic setting, which is one difference between CDC and GNL. Despite the shared terminology, we operate more like an academic institution, with students and academic researchers."

"Isn't that risky?"

The other suited scientist approached, the top of her head barely reaching Walker's shoulder. "I assure you, these are the best of the best," she said. "They'll save us all one day when an attack happens."

"Though not from our facility," Altman added.

"That's what we're here to ensure, Dr. Altman." Walker extended his gloved hand to the woman. "Jamie Walker, and this is my partner, Aidan Talley."

"They're with the FBI," Altman supplied. "They're investigating the security breaches."

"Dr. Naomi Griffin." The woman's sharp brown eyes assessed them through the plastic barrier. "Welcome to GNL. We study anthrax here in my lab."

Another chill raced up Aidan's spine, and by the quirk of Griffin's lips, he didn't think he hid that one so well.

"I also oversee the BSL-4 labs at GNL, including hiring decisions," she continued. "I have the utmost confidence in my people."

"It's a pleasure to meet you, ma'am." Walker flashed the smile that had everyone eating out of his palm. "I have to ask, though, is there anyone with access to the BSL-4 labs who you don't have final hiring say over?"

She glanced at Altman, who nodded. "Dr. Altman and his staff," she said.

"Okay, anyone else?"

She paused a moment. "Network security and building janitorial, though the janitors don't have access beyond the changing rooms."

"You do the interior cleaning yourselves?" Aidan asked.

"Yes, each lab has two lab managers responsible for upkeep, ordering and general lab maintenance. They keep this place running."

"Not an easy job."

"That's why there are two per lab." She finally cracked a smile, and Aidan thought he might like this woman. She reminded him of Mel. All business and protective of her people.

"Were they included in the personnel files you provided our colleagues?" Aidan asked.

She nodded. "They're professional lab managers, not students. They've had years of experience in other labs, and before starting here, they go through special training at the CDC."

"After you, I'm guessing they know more about what goes on here than anyone."

"You'd be correct."

"Let's make sure they're on the interview list," he said to Walker.

"Gentlemen," Altman interrupted. "I'm supposed to deliver you to network security in ten minutes, and we still have to go through decontamination. If you'll follow me, please."

"Thank you for your time, Dr. Griffin," Aidan said. "Are you available to meet later today for follow-up questions after Agent Walker and I finish our interviews?"

"I'll clear my schedule." Her smile changed, became suggestive. "And please, call me Naomi." He credited the woman's age, closer to his own, as the reason he, instead of Walker, had caught her eye.

Ignoring her interest, he followed Altman and Walker through the decontamination chamber and into the locker room. He had a much harder time ignoring his partner showering on the other side of a half wall from him, even though his back was to Walker and he hadn't once glanced in his direction.

After their dance last night, and the landslide of guilt that had followed, Aidan had resolved to keep things with Walker strictly professional. It had been only eight months since he'd lost Gabe. His husband deserved more, better, and Aidan had enough on his plate already. An ill-advised, destined to be ill-fated fling with his partner would unduly complicate matters. He would keep things friendly, all aboveboard.

Not an easy task.

For someone determined to live life under the radar, Walker's presence filled a room. It wasn't aggressive or dominant, traits Aidan knew he often projected. Rather, everything about Walker was nonthreatening and inviting. His appearance despite his size, his smile despite the model quality of it, and the easy flirtation that drew out of Aidan a sense of youth and playfulness he recalled from the early days of his relationship with Gabe. And a worrisome streak of jealousy, if his adverse reaction to Torres's interest was any indication. He chalked the former up to Walker's age, the latter to partner possessiveness, and the lying-to-himself part of it to self-preservation.

Several stalls down, Altman turned off his shower, and Aidan moved to do the same. Walker's hand shot across the barrier and grabbed him by the wrist. His heart tripped over itself—a cresting wave of heat, a pulling undertow of guilt—and his eyes shot to Walker's.

Wait, his partner mouthed. He jerked his hand back over the divider and stepped under the showerhead, right before Altman shouted, "I'm going to change and step into the hallway to make a quick call."

"We'll be right out," Walker returned.

The shower room door snicked closed, and now that he had been forced to turn toward Walker, Aidan couldn't tear his gaze away. Walker punched off his shower and ran his hands over his face and hair, sluicing off water and flexing muscles. Aidan's gaze was riveted on his exquisitely toned chest, on the sprinkling of hair, on the interlocking *N* and *C* tattooed on his left pectoral. He should look away, but his attention was transfixed on all the things he wanted to touch and taste, his body heating and hardening at the prospect.

That beautiful chest got closer, flexed bigger, as Walker braced his hands shoulder width apart on the dividing wall. He cleared his throat, and when Aidan's eyes met his, they were the same darker shade of blue they had been at the Tavern last night. "You can turn yours off now."

No, I can't would have been the honest answer. Instead, Aidan grappled for any defense, falling back on sarcasm. "I'm sorry. I was distracted by your *Baywatch* audition."

Walker rolled his eyes, reached across the wall, and shut

off Aidan's water. "I didn't want Altman to hear us. We need to talk before we meet with network security."

The case talk snapped Aidan out of his Whiskey haze. "What are you thinking?"

"That our inside man might not be a researcher in one of the labs, but a security tech."

"Thought crossed my mind."

"I don't remember seeing those personnel files in any I reviewed. Were they in yours?"

Aidan shook his head. "I'll text Barnes. Have him add it to our list of requests."

"Let's not." Walker handed him one of the plastic-wrapped towels from the ledge outside their stalls. "The files we received came from network security. We can't be sure they won't filter the files they send on themselves."

Aidan struggled with the plastic wrap around his towel. "So we ask Altman?"

Walker ripped his open with one tug and tossed the plastic on the ground. "Uncontaminated, so to speak."

"Very funny," he grumbled.

Laughing, Walker tossed the unwrapped towel at his face and snatched the other out of his hands, getting it open by the time Aidan detangled himself.

"Segregating information sources to check for tampering," he said, toweling off. "Good instincts. I'll speak to Altman on the way out. How do you want to handle the initial meeting with security?"

"We don't let on that we suspect them, obviously."

Aidan rested back against the far dividing wall. "Thank you, John Madden."

Walker resumed his flexed position on the half wall between them, and Aidan thanked all that was holy for the extra-large towel around his waist. "You'll need to distract them long enough for me to upload the monitoring program."

"How do you propose I do that?"

"Ask them to repeat everything in plain English. It's damn annoying."

"Tell me how you really feel."

Walker's gaze drifted down Aidan's body. "Don't think you want that either."

Aidan flipped through the binder of GNL network security's standard operating procedures while Walker peppered Dave Fuller, head of network security, with questions.

"I've reviewed the access logs, and Dr. Altman showed us the physical locking mechanisms. He said all the badges and access passwords were changed over the weekend."

Dave nodded. "As of midnight last night, all personnel with BSL-4 access were assigned new access cards for the external doors and new codes for all the internal keypads."

"Any issues?" Aidan asked.

Fuller rubbed his beady black eyes with the heels of his palms. A portly middle-aged white man with scraggly dark hair, he seemed a genial fellow, if a bit overworked. "Other than supposed geniuses forgetting their new passcodes and flooding the help desk with calls, no issues."

Aidan chuckled. "Absent-minded professors."

Fuller laughed with him. "You have no idea."

Walker asked about GNL's encryption system, and he and Fuller dived back into technobabble. No, *lingo*. Aidan tuned out, taking in his surroundings instead. They were in another fucking cave, only this one actually was in the basement. Located in the center of the building, it had no windows or immediate exits to the outside. A claustrophobic's worst nightmare. Were all cyber nerds predisposed to vampirism?

A booted heel collided with his shin and Aidan feared he'd said that last bit out loud, but then he remembered Walker saying that would be his signal to play dumb.

Not gonna be hard.

He looked up from the SOP binder and scratched his temple for effect. "Can we back up a second?"

Two sets of eyes turned to him.

"I'm sorry, but could you please explain those security specs to again, in plain English this time?"

Walker rolled his eyes, harder than usual, and Aidan considered kicking him back. Before he got the chance, Walker rose. "If you don't mind, Dave, I'm going to use the restroom while you enlighten my Luddite partner."

"No problem. Wife's a lawyer. I have to plain English the TV remote to her."

"That sounds about right for Talley here."

He couldn't reach his shin, but Aidan rammed his heel down hard on his partner's toes.

Walker shot him the bird behind the desk so Fuller wouldn't see, then asked for a visitor's pass to get in and out of the security hub.

"A visitor's pass won't get you in here." Fuller pulled his ID card off the lanyard around his neck. "Take mine."

Did Fuller give his access card to just anyone?

"I'm guessing use of another's access card is prohibited?" Walker said, on the same wavelength.

Fuller shrugged. "If you can't trust the FBI, who can you trust? Besides, I'll hold your Luddite partner hostage until you give it back."

Walker took the card and tucked it in his pocket. "Fair trade."

"Hey!" Aidan gasped in mock outrage, which drew laughs all around and a just-kidding shoulder bump from Walker before he left.

"So, Agent Talley," Fuller said, "You want to understand the encryption we use?"

"If you wouldn't mind."

Fifteen minutes and several diagrams later, Walker rejoined them. "You got it now?"

Aidan crossed one leg over the other and folded his hands in his lap. "Yeah, in fact, I do. Dave's a much better teacher than you."

Walker flashed him an indulgent grin as he flipped through diagrams. "These are good."

Fuller's face lit with pride. "I teach at the community college. Introduction to Cryptography. I find drawings always help the noobs."

Aidan ignored the slang he recognized from decades of gaming. "How many nights a week do you teach?"

"Three."

"And there's always someone on staff here when you're not?"

"At least two. Night shift used to be just one of us. We've upped that since the breaches."

"We'd like to meet with each member of your staff, starting with the teams who were on during the breaches."

"Bruce, who you met when you came in, was here with me during the two day-shift breaches. He went up to one of the BSL-2 labs on a service call. You can talk to him when he gets back. Emily and Jake will be in at six. They were on during the first early morning breach. Our other team, Mike and Colin, will be in tomorrow. They're the lucky ones; missed all the action."

And shot straight to the top of Aidan's suspect list.

"Do you have any theories about what might be going on?" Walker asked.

"Well, seeing as it was a hack on the exterior firewall, I'm thinking they either don't know about or don't have access to the interior one. Since they haven't tried again in almost a week, I'm hoping it was just some hacker punks."

"Is there a CompSci program here?" Aidan asked.

"Not at UT Med. Only at the community college."

"Could you provide a list of crypto students you think capable of this level hack?"

Fuller hesitated. "I'll have to check with the dean. And don't discount the med students here. Some of them are pretty tech savvy, and they've all got God complexes. What's a little hack on the building with the deadly viruses for someone with an ego that big?"

"Why not just walk out of the building with it?" Aidan said. "Why bother hacking in at all?"

Walker glanced over at him. "Like Dave said, ego, and to cover their tracks."

"Something we should look into."

No sooner had the words left Aidan's mouth did alarms begin to sound all around them. On the bank of computers behind Dave, on the phone and tablet lying on the desk, on the phone in Walker's pocket.

"What's happening?" Aidan asked.

Dave had already spun to face the bank of computers.

"Intrusion alert." Walker perched on the edge of his seat. "Another breach."

"Right now?"

Walker nodded and Aidan, recalling he'd tampered with the security system, mouthed, *Did you do this?*

His partner shook his head and stood, peering over Fuller's shoulder.

"Shit! They've breached the exterior firewall around two of the labs," Dave said. "Looks like they're going for three and four. Where the fuck is Bruce? He should be back by now."

Bruce got moved up Aidan's list as well.

"I can help." Walker circled the desk and pulled up a chair in front of the second bank of computers. "Log me in."

Dave reached across, and with a few quick keystrokes, the screens in front of Walker came to life. A Matrix-like maze of numbers and diagrams flashed across the computer screens and technobab—techno-speak flowed between Walker and Dave, faster than Aidan could keep up with. Even from this angle, he could see the rapt attention in his partner's frame, in his eyes reflected on the screens. Aidan got lost in his head for a moment, wondering what it would be like to have all that attention focused on him in a decidedly unprofessional context. But then Dave and Walker's voices escalated, snapping him out of it.

This breach was different than the others.

"They've breached the air gap," he heard among the directives slung back and forth.

Aidan flew out of his chair and crouched by Walker's side, one hand on the computer desk for balance and the other on the back of Walker's chair. "Can you shut them down?"

Not sparing a glance, Walker moved his fingers over the keyboard faster.

After what felt like an hour but was probably closer to two minutes, Walker pushed back from the keyboard and cracked his knuckles. "It's done. They're locked out."

Aidan released the breath he'd been holding and moved his hand from the chair to Walker's shoulder. "Good job, partner."

Walker graced him with a wide smile, and Aidan's heart did that lovely-awful tripping beat again, before Fuller's voice cut in.

"I've got a back trace running to the source."

Aidan stood, hands on his waist. "So we might have this solved by tonight?"

Walker looked less than hopeful. "If they're good enough to hack this far, they've probably got countermeasures in place."

"He's right." Grim-faced, Fuller rose and stretched his creaking joints. "I'm going to call in Emily and Jake. Mike's out of town until he's on shift tomorrow, but I'll get Colin down here now. All hands on deck."

He ducked into the hallway, phone to his ear, and Aidan skirted behind Walker to collapse in Fuller's chair. "He's awfully trusting of us, with his space and his access cards."

"I noticed that too. Sure made planting my bug easier."

"And you're certain that had nothing to do with what just happened?"

"Positive."

"Okay then, explain to me what just happened. What did they breach?"

"That's the odd part. They flipped the switch on one of

the doors from the decontamination chamber to a BSL-4 lab."

Aidan snatched a pen off Dave's desk, spinning it around his thumb. "How'd they skip the shower door? And why not flip the switch on one of the vial cabinets first? None of this is worth it if they can't access the toxins."

"If that's the target at all."

"This is like a fucking game of Mouse Trap."

"Welcome to Hacker 101."

Aidan glared. "I'm gonna need a lot more coffee for this."

ELEVEN

Jamie was interviewing Jake and Emily when a text came through from Aidan.

Topside, ASAP.

He had no idea what kind of trouble his partner had gotten into. After two hours coordinating with local authorities and first responders, then another three questioning the BSL-4 personnel who were at GNL today, Aidan had pitched a minitantrum about descending again into "that goddamn cave" to interview Dave's team. Having just sustained a breach, Dave was reticent to excuse any extra manpower from the security hub, so Jamie had descended the stairs alone, leaving Aidan to follow up with Dr. Griffin.

"You need to get that?" Jake Young asked, a little too eager for Jamie's liking.

The security engineer's shifty green eyes would meet Jamie's every few seconds before darting to Emily or focusing on a nick in the desk he worried with a nail. Sitting next to him, Emily Richards could have been his twin in appearance and anxiety, but Jake's nervousness seemed the cause of hers, not the interview itself.

"It can wait." Jamie pocketed the phone and flashed his most disarming smile, hoping to put them at ease. "Now, you were about to tell me where you were at the time of each breach. Dave mentioned you two were on shift during the first one."

"That's right." Emily brushed aside her long blond bangs. "The one early Sunday morning."

"And you were both here"—he circled a pen in the air, indicating the cave—"during that incident?"

Jake glanced at Emily, as if seeking guidance. When she offered none, he returned his attention to Jamie. "Yes, we were both here."

"What about the breaches on Monday and Tuesday?"

"I was surfing Monday afternoon. At the gym Tuesday morning."

"And someone saw you at both those places?"

Jake nodded.

"I'll need their names," Jamie said. "What about you, Emily?" She hesitated, and Jamie inched forward, bracing his forearms on the edge of the desk. "Where were you on Monday afternoon and Tuesday morning?"

"I visited my father at an assisted care facility in Houston on Monday."

"And Tuesday?"

"Home asleep. Alone." The way she added that last word, making a point of it even though it meant she had no alibi, was not flirtation. Jamie read it as a need to protect someone's identity more than herself. A bedmate? Jake, maybe? That would explain the weird tension between them. Or was there someone else she felt she had to keep secret? Jamie knew the signs better than most.

His phone vibrated again.

Sensing he was onto something, he ignored the phone and sat back. "Had either of you noticed any unusual network activity in the days leading up to the first breach?"

"What do you mean by unusual activity?" Emily said.

"Off-hour logins by your colleagues, repeated requests for new access cards or reset codes, fragments of programming code where they weren't supposed to be." Both sets of eyes on him widened. Dave must not have told them he was an expert. Good, less chance they would find the ghosts he'd left behind.

"I don't recall seeing anything," Emily said.

"Mike's the one responsible for fragment sweeps," Jake added.

The absent Mike was looking better and better as a suspect.

"Tell me about the process you go through to issue new access cards and codes." The breaches so far had not been tagged to any active logins. Whoever was accessing the system was creating one-off logins, cloning orphan cards or codes, or skirting the logins altogether and diving directly into the system.

"You mean if someone forgets theirs?" Jake asked.

Jamie nodded.

"For the external access badges, they have to come to us to get a new one reissued."

"Is the old one immediately deactivated?"

"Yes. No orphan cards should be out there. Same for the access keypads."

"For the keypads, it works like resetting the PIN on

your bank card," Emily said. "Call or email us with the request and we reset it, except the code is randomized. The user has no say."

"Is there email confirmation?"

"Only that it's been reset. The actual code is provided on paper."

"And who issues *your* access cards and codes?"

"Dave," Emily answered.

"What happens if you forget your card or code?"

Jake looked positively offended. "You think *we* would forget codes?"

Even Jamie had to laugh, holding up his hands. "Point taken. What about forgotten cards? Surely someone leaves one at home every now and then."

"In that case, a new card is supposed to be issued," Jake said.

"Supposed to be?"

Jake looked to Emily, who, after a deep breath, answered, "Dave keeps a few spares in his desk drawer."

Why hadn't Dave given him one of those spares earlier today instead of his own card? Because he didn't want the FBI knowing he had them? In his gut, Jamie didn't think Dave was involved, but the evidence placed him a solid number two behind Mike on the suspect list.

"Agent Walker." Colin, who he had already interviewed, poked his head around the server racks from his and Mike's workstations one row over. "Your partner called the main number. He requests your presence upstairs. Immediately." By the distressed look on Colin's face, the message had not been delivered quite so politely.

Jamie checked his phone, seeing another five texts from

his partner. The last one read, **WHAT PART OF ASAP IS FUCKING HARD TO UNDERSTAND?!**

"I need to get going." Rising, he pulled two business cards out of his wallet and handed one each to Emily and Jake. "Please call if you remember anything else or see any unusual activity in the system. As I mentioned to Colin and Bruce, the FBI would appreciate you staying in town until this matter is resolved. I'm sure Dave would appreciate the extra hands too, in case another breach occurs."

"We'll be here," Jake said.

Emily nodded.

"Thank you both."

After a quick goodbye to Bruce and Dave, who were at the main bank of computers, Jamie took the stairs two at a time to the main level. His partner was in the hallway outside Dr. Griffin's office, looking furious and desperate.

Aidan grabbed him by the arm. "What if I'd been in a shoot-out up here?"

"If you'd been in a shoot-out, you wouldn't have been texting me."

"If I tell you to be somewhere, as my partner, I expect you to be there."

"Then text SOS," Jamie snapped. "I understand ASAP just fine. It means *as soon as possible*. I was onto something with Emily and Jake, and I thought it pertinent to *our* investigation to finish interviewing them first."

Jamie had him there and Aidan knew it, judging by his frustrated glare.

"I don't have time to explain." Aidan tugged him toward Dr. Griffin's office. "Follow my lead."

He opened the office door, and it was like someone flipped a switch. Aidan's hand, which had been wrapped tight in anger around his biceps, smoothed down his arm to lightly grasp his elbow. Aidan ushered him from the bright hallway into the dim office, shut the door, then moved his hand to the small of his back. Jamie bit back a surprised gasp while hoping the low light in Dr. Griffin's office would hide the blood rushing to his face.

Wait . . . Low light.

Jamie almost laughed out loud when it hit him. He wasn't the cause of Aidan's fury and desperation. It was the woman behind the desk who had her office lights dimmed, a bottle of bourbon on her desk, and her eyes locked on Aidan's hand on his back.

Some emergency. A senior FBI agent caught in a cougar trap.

Jamie swallowed his amusement as Aidan directed them to the visitor chairs across from Dr. Griffin.

"Doctor, why don't you tell my partner"—Aidan laid an arm over the top of his chair—"what you told me about Director Altman's lab staff."

There was no mistaking the impression Aidan projected —that the two of them were more than work partners. Jamie knew he should protest, but to do so would mean losing the warmth of Aidan's arm across his back. He struggled to focus on Dr. Griffin's response instead.

"As I mentioned earlier, Director Altman hires his own staff. While most of his day is filled with administrative tasks, he does maintain a small operating lab. There's been a lot of turnover and accusations of nepotism."

"Is the turnover related to the alleged nepotism?" Jamie asked.

"There's nothing *alleged* about it, and no, the turnover's because he's a bad scientist and worse mentor."

"Yet he's the director," Aidan said.

"He's a politician in a lab coat. He knows how to play well with the higher-ups who continue to promote him. The turnover is because the little science he still does is suspect at best and no student can get his attention long enough to graduate in a timely fashion."

"And the nepotism?" Jamie said.

"His niece, who somehow did graduate with her PhD in five years, and his son, Terry, occasional lab manager, when he's between jobs."

"I thought you said all lab managers went through CDC training?"

"Except Terry. In fairness"—she shifted in her desk chair, crossing her legs more slowly than called for—"Director Altman's very small lab doesn't deal with anything above BSL-2 pathogens, and Terry is a PhD dropout, so he's had some training."

Aidan crossed his own legs toward Jamie and tilted over the armrest into his space. "Let's see what we can find on Altman the Younger."

Jamie nodded, all the while watching Dr. Griffin out of the corner of his eye. He didn't like her now doubly interested look. "I'll get on that." He rose and offered Aidan a hand up. "First, we have to get back to the field office for a debrief with Gary and his team."

There was no meeting. They just needed an escape route.

"Yes, we better get going or we'll be late." Aidan stood, hand lingering in his. "Dr. Griffin, thank you for your time."

"I'm happy to help." Hips swaying, she glided around her desk. "If there's anything I can do for you two, you'll let me know."

"Yes, ma'am." Jamie followed Aidan's swift retreat out the door.

He made it all the way to the Benz before laugher bubbled out of him.

Jamie used extra-long kitchen tongs to pull the last golden-brown piece of chicken out of the bubbling fry oil. He laid it atop the mountain of chicken on the platter by the stove, spooned scoops of string beans and stewed greens onto a separate plate, then turned off the burners. All set, he carried the serving dishes around the kitchen island and slid them onto the bar between the two place settings.

Aidan stared at the food, eyes wide and longing, practically drooling. "All for me?"

"I did not go through all this trouble"—Jamie twisted to grab the basket of steaming corn muffins off the island—"just for you."

"Well, that sucks." Aidan gave him a mock pout that morphed into a smile as he began dishing food onto their dinner plates. "Where'd you learn to cook like this?"

"Soon as I could get a job, I bused tables at the diner where my mom worked."

Jamie came out from behind the kitchen bar and climbed onto the stool beside Aidan. "It was run by this five-foot-nothing slip of a Black woman named Regina. She referred to herself, in the third person, as 'the Queen.'"

"Sounds scary."

"She was, but the Queen could cook, better than my own mama."

"Don't let your mama hear you say that."

"Nah, Mom would be the first to agree. No better fried chicken in the South."

They dug into their food, and it wasn't until after Aidan killed a drumstick and wing that he asked, "So, you hung around and learned all the Queen's secrets?"

"I was there in the mornings before school, when she made the muffin batters and fry coating, and each afternoon, after I got out of practice."

"And she let a scrawny white boy steal her recipes?"

"Same scrawny white boy who convinced her to open a second location in Chapel Hill that tripled her profits."

"Well played." Aidan raised his glass, and Jamie tapped his against it. "You liked it there in Chapel Hill? I always wondered what it would be like to go to school in a real college town."

"Palo Alto doesn't count?"

"Hardly." He grabbed another muffin from the basket. "You didn't answer my question."

"It's hard to describe. All that energy contained in a four-by-five block on top of a hill." Jamie stared ahead, not seeing the mess he had made in the kitchen but the big green lawns and towering trees of Carolina's main quad, the two-century mishmash of buildings around it, and the throngs of people filling its crisscrossing sidewalks. "Coming from a small town, I'd never been exposed to anything like it. The architecture, the diversity, the freedom."

"I'm sure that was quite liberating for a gay kid from the country."

"Yes and no." He spooned the last bite of beans into his mouth and washed it down with sweet tea. "Carolina's a huge state school, so an average person can fade into the crowd, enjoy all those things, and live their life without anyone noticing."

"You weren't the average student, though."

Jamie gave him a small, resigned smile. "No, I wasn't."

Aidan's eyes went soft with sympathy. "Jamie."

It was the first time Aidan had called him by his first name, and he liked the sound of it. Too much. Before his partner's raised hand reached his arm, Jamie slipped off his stool and rounded the bar. He opened the fridge and pulled out the pitcher of tea. "Stanford was different?"

"It didn't feel like a college campus at all. Grad students outnumber undergrads, and so many of the students are local or intend to stay local after graduation. It's preschool for Silicon Valley moguls."

Jamie reclaimed his stool and refilled his glass. Aidan was sipping his tea slowly; probably too much sugar. He often forgot not everyone was raised on the sweet kind. "Did you live on campus?"

"Yeah, but home was ten minutes away. Family dinner each week, at least until I told them I was wasting the business and law degrees they'd paid for on a career with the FBI."

"You were expected to go into the family business?"

Aidan nodded but didn't say more.

"Why didn't you?" Jamie asked between bites.

Aidan returned his earlier resigned smile. "Aced criminal law, almost failed tax."

Jamie chuckled. "There must be more to it than that."

Rather than answering, Aidan stretched over the bar and grabbed the unopened bottle of Maker's Mark. He cracked the red wax and poured a generous shot into his tea. He offered the bottle to Jamie, who waved it off. Aidan set the bottle back on the other side of the bar, swirled his drink, and took a long swallow despite his previous hesitation.

Jamie grew wary of the answer to his question. Before he could dismiss it, Aidan cleared his throat. "I could have gone into the family business, helped rebuild the empire here in the States, but I was nursing a two-decades-old grudge."

"Against the IRA?" Jamie recalled Aidan's comment last week about car bomb–induced nightmares.

"My family didn't discriminate. We were equal-opportunity employers and business partners. That didn't make us popular with militant IRA factions." His gaze drifted over Jamie's shoulder to the darkness outside. "When my older brother, Sean, was killed by the car bomb, we got out."

Food forgotten, chest aching, Jamie clasped his partner's shoulder. How much had this man lost in his life already?

Aidan didn't pull away, accepting the sympathetic touch Jamie had shirked earlier. His gaze remained unfocused, his mind far away. "My first big bust with the FBI was an Irish gang trafficking in illegal arms. Funding what's left of the cause, so to speak."

"I'm sure your family understands now."

Aidan's gaze swung back to his, and the sadness there robbed Jamie of words.

"They do." Shrugging off his hand, Aidan slid from his stool and moved into the kitchen. He grabbed a bowl out of the fridge, a small pot from a lower cabinet, and began cooking something on the stove. Curiosity getting the better of him, Jamie collected their empty plates, dumped them in the sink, and peered over Aidan's shoulder.

"What are you making?"

"Reheating. Arroz con leche. Mexican rice pudding."

Jamie ran soap and water over the dishes, pretending to wash them for several minutes, as the sweet mix of cinnamon and vanilla filled the air. "For an Irishman, your cooking repertoire is suspiciously Latin."

"Gabe's dream was to open a restaurant." The smile in Aidan's voice eased the lingering tension from their previous exchange. "His family owns several in Miami."

"Can SAC Cruz cook too?"

Aidan let out a strangled noise—half cry, half laugh—something clattered to the floor, and he cursed, his Irish accent bleeding through.

"I'll take that as a no."

Bent over, ass in the air, Aidan rescued a wooden spoon from the floor and tossed it to him at the sink. "Never let that woman near a stove. The Cruz food gene somehow skipped her."

"You two seem close."

"Academy classmates. We wrapped training a week before Carnival, and she took me home to celebrate. We've been tight ever since."

"What happens in Miami, stays in Miami?"

Aidan chuckled and clicked off the burner. "Something like that."

"Was that when you met Gabe?"

"Love at first sight," he said, voice wistful.

Jamie shut off the faucet, wiped his hands on a dishtowel, and boosted himself up on the island. "How long were you two together?"

"Ten years." Aidan opened the drawer next to Jamie's dangling legs, pulled out two spoons, handed him one, and set the other on the opposite counter.

Jamie tapped the utensil against his thigh as he did the math in his head. "You weren't together right away?"

"No." Aidan split the steaming pudding mixture between two bowls. "He was still playing football, and I was still playing the field."

"You weren't always a one-person man?"

"Far from it." He handed Jamie a bowl, then, with his own bowl in hand, grabbed the other spoon and hopped up on the opposite counter. "Mel wouldn't let me near him until I was celibate for at least a year."

"How'd that go?"

Aidan blushed, his pale cheeks flaming an attractive red. "Embarrassing. Mel and I were in the San Francisco office already. Gabe blew out his knee, retired, and moved out to get his MBA at Stanford. We were inseparable since."

The earlier tension rushed back in, and Jamie was too far away to offer more than shared sympathy. "I know it's not easy, getting over a broken heart."

Aidan's gaze shot to his, begging the question.

He hadn't intended to get into his own past, but Aidan had shared, and Jamie felt he owed him a tiny bit of his own story. "I can't imagine what that must have been like for you. My situation was different. I had control over how things ended."

"You were the one who walked away?"

Not exactly walked. Jamie recalled that bright summer day outside the rehab facility in Charlotte. His entire body had hurt from a grueling PT session, but no joint, no limb, no ligament, had hurt as badly as his heart when he'd limped away, on crutches, from the love of his life. "I do know what it feels like to lose your other half."

"The media got wind of the relationship?"

"They were closing in." He picked up his bowl and finished off the pudding. "Derrick, my boyfriend, was a new professor at a conservative college nearby, Mom had a steady job, and my little sister was head of the high school cheerleading squad. Everything was good, everyone was happy. A news story like that would have disrupted all our lives."

"So you sacrificed your career and your own happiness?"

"I loved Derrick, and I loved playing ball, but I wasn't happy. And I had no interest in being a poster boy for gay athletes in the NBA. I realize that's selfish, that I should have taken a stand, been out and proud, but I was so tired of being the center of attention. It's like the media latched on when I was a kid and never let go."

"That's why you like Cyber, why you stay in the cave?"

He nodded. "I like the anonymity behind the screen. I'd been in front of it for so long. And I aced Crypto, almost failed Political Science."

Aidan laughed at the flipped phrase and slid off the counter. He took the bowl out of Jamie's hands, his countenance serious once more. "You can't hide forever. That's no better than being back in the closet."

"I don't see you getting out there."

Aidan dumped the bowls in the sink. "You sound like my sisters."

Jamie let him get away with that deflection, seeing as he had done the same earlier. "Irish, Southern, we're from the same stock."

"I think you might fit in better with my family than me."

"They sound like a fun bunch." Jamie hopped off the island as Aidan headed for the dining table where their case materials were spread out in Jamie's typical disorganized fashion.

"Back to not fun." Aidan rounded the table and took a seat on the far side. "What do you make from the interviews this afternoon?"

Jamie seated himself across from Aidan. "Dr. Griffin is in the clear. Director Altman too, though I want to dig into his son."

"Agreed." Aidan pulled Griffin's and Altman's files out of the leaning stack of personnel files and tossed them on the floor.

"I think we can also exclude the lab manager with the ancient laptop. Between his antiquated hard drive and million cables, I'd say he's a member of the Luddite camp with you."

Aidan glared across the table but dug out the lab manager's file and tossed it on the floor with the others. "That leaves two dozen scientists and students, seven lab managers, Altman's son, and"—he slid another haphazard stack of files between them—"GNL network security."

"If you can do a prelim review on those"—Jamie nodded to the network security files—"I'd like to examine the back trace I ran after the hack today and dig deeper into persons we flagged already. With GNL, you should focus on Jake, Mike, Emily, and Dave."

"Dave?"

"I don't think he's involved, but that stash of extra key cards gives me pause."

"On it. What are you looking for?"

"Online aliases, hacker histories, the like."

"How's an FBI agent going to do that?"

"An FBI agent isn't. StickyHeel12, on the other hand . . ." He had created the alias in college, a play on his alma mater's mascot and his jersey number.

"Very clever. And I don't want to know any more. What do you need for this hackathon?"

"A full pot of coffee."

"I can do that." He moved to stand, and Jamie caught him by the wrist.

"It's not the same, you losing Gabe and me losing Derrick, but I think, *I hope,* for both our sakes, that it gets easier. The heart's a resilient beast."

"I hope so too." Aidan's eyes met his, the warm brown swirling with a little bit of sadness and something else Jamie couldn't identify.

Something that stoked the hope in him and made the beast in his own chest stir again.

TWELVE

The siren call of sizzling bacon and the rich aroma of fresh brewed coffee lured Aidan out of his room the next morning. Two steps into the living area a wrapper crinkled under his foot, and glancing up, he took in the devastation that had been wreaked on the living room. A pair of laptops sat open on the pickled-wood coffee table, a beige couch cushion on the floor in front of them, a Walker's-ass-size dent in the middle cradling giant headphones. Multiple coffee mugs and a minefield of snack food detritus littered the table and floor. And everywhere among the rubbish, stacks of colored files teetered, and pages of yellow legal pads covered with Walker's chicken scratch fluttered in the breeze from the overhead fan.

On the other side of the mess, a certain hacker hurricane bounced in front of the stove in the kitchen. Hair in disarray, wearing yesterday's wrinkled clothes, Walker hummed CCR's "Fortunate Son" and tapped out the melody with a spatula on the counter. Aidan was ninety-nine-point-nine percent certain his partner hadn't slept a wink.

Aidan skirted around the scattered files and paper and dropped his own stack on one of the barstools before sneaking into the kitchen from the far laundry room side. "Should I take your song choice as a personal indictment?"

Walker jumped a mile. "Dude!" He swung around to face him. "No sneaking up on me when I've got burners going."

Aidan raised both brows. "'Dude'?" he said as he got the coffeemaker going.

"What's wrong with *dude*?"

"You're too young to appreciate it."

"I own not one but two"—Walker held up two fingers—"copies of *The Big Lebowski*. That entitles me to use the word *dude*."

"If you say so."

"Pour me one of those?"

Aidan cast his gaze about the living and dining areas, counting six used mugs. "Haven't you had enough already?"

"Are you judging me?"

"Maybe a little."

Walker pointed the soup spatula at him, expression and voice mockingly stern. "No pancakes for you."

Aidan narrowed his eyes. "Do I know you?"

Walker laughed, easy and carefree, and Aidan, enjoying the lighter mood, filled another mug for his partner, against his better judgment. Walker split a pile of steaming silver dollar pancakes between two plates and crowned each with mouthwatering slices of crispy, thick-cut bacon. Aidan snagged the bottle of syrup with a pinky and followed Walker and the plates to the other side of the bar.

"I'm surprised you can eat anything after ingesting all

that junk food." Aidan placed the syrup and their coffees between their plates, then climbed onto the stool next to Walker. "Where did you get all the foodstuffs for this feast? I'm sure none of it was in the pantry."

"There's a twenty-four-hour Walmart on the island." Walker said it like he'd found the Holy Grail. "I borrowed the car. Hope you don't mind."

"I guess I should be glad this was all you came back with."

Walker snickered. "Don't look in the pantry."

Aidan watched in horror as Walker doused his entire plate in syrup. "Do you really need more sugar?"

"Sugar and caffeine are all I'm running on right now." He shoveled in a bite and washed it down with a giant gulp of coffee. "Gotta mainline it to get through the day. Oh, that reminds me . . ." He dropped his fork, jumped off the stool, and bounded over to the dining table.

Aidan stifled the Energizer Bunny comment on the tip of his tongue when Walker turned to him, wide-eyed and earnest. "I got us a lead."

After a few quick bites, Aidan extricated a slice of bacon from Walker's maple moat and walked over to the table, careful not to drip any syrup on the floor. "You need to eat."

Hands full of folders and legal pads, Walker bent and ate the bacon right out of his hand, lips brushing over his fingertips. Aidan gasped as his heart kicked, triple-beating over itself.

Walker didn't even notice, mind and words on hyperdrive. "Usual hacking channels didn't turn up much last night. An illegal file-share here, a gaming account there, which, by the way, I found your *Destiny* stats, and bravo." He made a circular clapping motion with his hands.

"Whiskey, focus."

Walker narrowed his bloodshot blue eyes. "You owe me a game."

"Fine, get to the point, Sonic." At some point, the image in his head had transformed from the Energizer Bunny to the supersonic hedgehog.

"I may be fast, but I ain't that fast." He held this thumb and forefinger an inch apart in front of Aidan's nose. "And I am a wee bit taller than a hedgehog."

Aidan swatted the hand away and his voice took on the annoyed edge he sometimes got with his niblings. "The lead, Walker."

"Oh, right." There was no hostility in the other man's voice, just his tired, overstimulated brain jumping from one topic to another. "Dave's in the clear. His alibis check out. And I talked to him this morning about those cards. They're dummies. He keeps them as a check on his staff."

"Smart, though I'm guessing that's not the lead you walked away from pancakes for."

"No, but I like Dave, and I wanted him to be clear."

"Walker."

"Sorry, lead, right." He flapped his hands around, as if somehow clearing his mind. "I remembered what Dave said about med students playing God."

"Go on."

"I focused my searches on students getting both their MD and PhD." He placed a hand on a small stack of manila and red file folders in the middle of the table. "Much smaller pool."

"I'd imagine so. Takes a certain kind of masochist."

"Like you getting your MBA and JD?"

"It's a very special hell."

"Which is where I went looking for our potential bioterrorist." Walker picked up the top two folders and handed him the standard manila one first. "May I introduce Kevin Currie. Grew up in Philly, undergrad at Penn, three years into his PhD at UT Med, and just finished his first year in the MD program."

Aidan flipped through the standard biographical data and background search he'd read last week. Nothing had warranted a flag.

Walker handed him the red file. "May I introduce KrnuL_PaniK_1013."

"KrnuL_PaniK?"

"When spelled correctly, an operating system's internal kill switch, in plain English. I assume 1013 is an *X-Files* reference."

"Dorks."

Walker punched his arm. "At least he has some creativity, FBIGuy74."

Aidan shrugged and returned his attention to the file. "The red folders are cyber aliases?"

"Walmart to the rescue!"

"More like you stole Agent Hipster's idea." He skimmed through the alias information Walker had gathered. "What has Mr. PaniK been up to?"

"Aside from attending every major Black Hat convention in the northeast when he was at Penn and in southeast Texas since moving here"—Walker reached over the top of the folder, flipped a few pages, and pointed at a list he had highlighted—"he's hit some impressive targets."

Aidan whistled. "How come they didn't catch this when running his background check?" He tossed the folders on the table and stepped back to the bar to grab their coffees.

"His alias is buried deep. Someone this good covers his tracks."

He handed Walker his mug and took a sip from his own. "He's first on our list today."

"Already called Dave. He's sending over Kevin's class schedule. Did you find anything in the network security files?"

Aidan set his mug on the table and retrieved his stack. He held the top green folder out to Walker. "Not as much sugar was consumed, but I still found the bad guy, or girl, rather."

Walker opened the file and his blue eyes widened. "I would have figured Jake, not Emily. He seemed more squirrelly when I interviewed them yesterday, though I did think she was keeping a secret." He tossed Emily's file onto the table with Currie's. "What'd you find?"

"Single, mother died, father requires full-time care for early-onset Alzheimer's. She's barely making ends meet. Plus, she's got no good alibis for two of the attacks."

"Neither one of them? She said she was alone for one of them, though I expect she wasn't, but she said yesterday she was at the care facility with her dad during the other."

He was rambling a mile a minute, drawl thickened, and Aidan needed to break down and better understand the various parts of what he'd just said. He leaned a hip against the table and took the mug out of Walker's hands. "Back up . . . What's this about her not being alone?"

"I got a vibe when I questioned her and Jake. I was almost certain she wasn't alone during the Tuesday morning breach. I thought she was protecting someone—Jake maybe, since he kept looking to her for guidance—or that she didn't want people to know who she was with. I would know something about that."

Yes, he would, but that wasn't what caught Aidan's attention in his partner's run-on sentences. "What do you mean Jake kept looking to her for guidance?"

"He didn't want to answer questions without her go-ahead. Though by the end, I thought that might have more to do with protecting their boss. I ruled Dave out, so there goes that theory."

Walker reached for his coffee and Aidan shifted in front of it, blocking him until he finished unpacking everything Walker had said. "Jake's alibis checked out. If you're right, and she wasn't alone during the Tuesday morning breach, it wasn't him. She's hiding something, and he's careful with his words around her. Either he knows who she was with that morning, or he knows something else they don't want us to know."

"Maybe something to do with the breach they did work together."

Aidan nodded. "Let's add Jake to the list of interviews today, and we'll question him without Emily this time." He reached back for Walker's mug and handed it to him.

His partner guzzled it down in one long swallow, then slammed the mug on the table. "I almost forgot . . ." He darted into the living area and returned with one of the laptops, setting it on the end of the bar. "I got us another lead."

"Someone besides Kevin and Emily?"

"Not that case." He woke the sleeping laptop, and after logging in through an encryption window, familiar bank account ledgers appeared on-screen. "I had some time last night while searches were running and this isn't the office, so we can talk about it here, right?"

Aidan moved directly in front of the computer. "What'd you find?"

"The accounts didn't trace back to the detectives." Walker reached around him, their arms brushing, as he minimized the account ledgers and revealed an internet browser window. "This"—he pointed at the homepage for KAG Holdings—"is who owns those accounts."

Aidan racked his brain and came up blank. "I've never heard of them."

"I doubt you would have." Walker shifted to stand beside him, one arm braced on a barstool. "It's a Bahamian holding company."

"What do they hold?"

"Well, that's the odd thing." He nodded at the computer. "Try the links."

He gave Walker a skeptical look then began clicking on the links. About, Holdings, Contact Us . . . They all led to an Under Construction page. "Nothing's here."

"Meaning the site's actually under construction, or . . ."

"It's a dummy corp."

"I'd venture a guess KAG's only assets are those bank accounts. But somebody was smart enough to set it up in the Bahamas."

"Favorable tax regime." Aidan recalled overhearing something of the sort at one of Gabe's office functions.

"Per Google, after tourism, financial services account for fifteen percent of the Bahamas's GDP."

"Thank you, interwebs." He closed the laptop and turned to face Walker. "Is it possible KAG is a holding company for the detectives' dirty money?"

"Or for anyone involved in orchestrating the crash. You said there were more files on the flash drive. Maybe there's something there."

"I left it in my safe at home." Walker got that hurt look on his face again, and Aidan didn't want him to think it was a matter of trust or doubt. "It wasn't on my mind when we left Saturday, and even if it had been, I wouldn't have wanted to risk traveling with it. I'll get it to you when we're back in California. For now, can you follow the website anywhere?"

His face brightened and he yanked his phone out of his pocket. "Already on it. You drive, I'll keep digging," he said, turning for the front door.

Aidan grabbed him by the back of his wrinkled T-shirt, the momentum yanking Walker backward into his chest. "A shower and clean clothes would be appreciated."

Walker turned his head, their noses inches apart. "By who?"

This close, Aidan's gaze wandered over his face, seeking comfort in the striking features. Blue eyes, electric in the early morning sun. Toffee waves falling over his forehead, begging to be brushed back. Matching stubble covering his jaw and neck, rough where the former appeared the texture of silk. Add the scent of coffee, lingering cologne, and pure man, and Aidan was tilting forward. He splayed the hand in Walker's shirt, feeling the firm muscles beneath it, and Walker leaned into the touch, a live wire crackling as heat ran in a feedback loop through that single point of contact. Walker's face dipped toward his, lips scant inches apart, and the circuit overloaded, sparked to fire, then died as icy guilt flooded Aidan's veins.

"Go, Jamie." He pushed the other man forward, and in a

repeat of last night, Walker grabbed his wrist. Aidan's heart stopped and ice melted where skin met skin.

Walker smiled wide. "Thank you for trusting me."

Aidan's heart beat again, a little softer for the warmth that seeped in around it. He made a joke to ward off thoughts of things he couldn't have. "I've never seen someone so happy about potential hours of beating their head against a wall."

"Not why I'm smiling." Thumb flicking over his pulse point, Walker dropped his wrist and strutted to his room, holding up his right hand, two fingers raised again. "That makes two."

Two what?

THIRTEEN

Jamie unbuttoned his charcoal suit jacket and propped a foot on the wall behind him, staying out of his partner's way. Pacing a ten-foot circuit up and down the hallway, Aidan couldn't seem to stand still, and it wasn't only his legs in motion. He fidgeted with his cuffs and tie, checked his holster repeatedly, and tilted his head side to side like a fighter prepping for the biggest match of his career. Given Aidan's recent experiences with hospitals, Jamie supposed that was about right.

"You're going to wear a hole in the linoleum," he said the next time Aidan passed.

"I don't like hospitals."

Technically, they were in the medical school, but the antiseptic smell and bland white walls were enough to fool anyone's senses. "You were fine in GNL yesterday."

"GNL is more like a government lab, and I was distracted by the anthrax, the cougar, and the suit of doom."

"We'll grab Kevin and take him outside for a chat."

"I'll be fine."

Jamie pushed off the wall, intercepted Aidan's circuit and laid a hand on his arm. "We'll take him outside."

Autumn eyes shot to his. Last night's heat flared to life again, breaking an endless moment later when the door behind them swung open and students flooded the hallway. Jolting apart, both of them flushed. Jamie ducked his head and pulled up Kevin Currie's picture on his phone.

Long, thin face, dark brown skin, shaved head, brown eyes.

A lanky Black man matching Kevin's picture exited the classroom between two other students.

Aidan stepped forward. "Kevin Currie?"

Kevin's file indicated he'd run track. Taken together with his hacktivist activities, it was no surprise that when the young man looked up and saw two suited G-men, he dropped his bag and sprinted the other direction. Aidan took off running, Jamie following once he grabbed Kevin's bag off the floor and slung the strap across his body.

"FBI, stop!" Aidan shouted.

Kevin crashed through a door at the end of the hallway and led them careening into a stairwell. Their suspect was halfway down the first flight of stairs, dodging students, when Aidan put both hands to the rail and vaulted over it, taking Kevin down on impact. The surprised crowd of students scattered, stalling Jamie's descent and providing enough chaos for Kevin to slip away again. By the time Jamie reached where they'd been, Aidan was up and running again, following Kevin out of the stairwell into another hallway. Jamie recognized it as the breezeway to GNL. On the run, Kevin yanked a key card out of his back pocket. Red, the cards reserved for BSL-4 access.

"If he gets through those doors," Aidan said, "we're locked out."

Dave was supposed to have key cards for them this morning, but they weren't getting BSL-4 access without an escort.

At least that was what Dave and the rest of GNL network security thought.

The doors opened, Kevin darted through, and they slid shut behind him, leaving Aidan cursing.

"Have a little faith, partner." Jamie pushed him out of the way and dug a key card out of his suit pocket. He flashed it in front of the access panel, and the doors swooshed open. He grinned over his shoulder at Aidan.

"I don't want to know." Aidan zipped past him. "Take left. I've got right."

Jamie sprinted left, catching a glimpse of Kevin as he dodged students and scientists in white lab coats. He was gaining on him. "Kevin, stop. We just want to talk."

The young man reached an intersecting hallway and looked back at him. With his attention diverted, he didn't see the Irishman bearing down on him from the opposite direction. Aidan hit him, arms wrapping around his body, and they fell to the ground on their sides.

Jamie skidded to a halt next to them and took over for Aidan. "Kevin, stop moving." He rolled their suspect onto his stomach, pulled out a pair of cuffs, and snapped them around the other man's wrists. "You're not getting out of this."

"I didn't do anything. You can't arrest me."

"You're not under arrest," Aidan said as he got to his feet.

"Then what's with the handcuffs?"

Jamie hauled Kevin up. "You like to run." He glanced over at Aidan, who was cradling his left arm. "You okay?"

"Fine." Yanking Kevin out of his grasp, Aidan pushed him into an empty conference room, and Jamie shut the door behind them. Aidan shoved the student into a chair. "Kevin Currie, that's you, right?"

"Yeah. Who wants to know?"

Aidan pulled out his badge and tossed it open on the table. "Special Agent Aidan Talley. This is my partner, Special Agent Jameson Walker."

Jamie felt a flicker of relief when Kevin didn't recognize his name or his face.

"I'm not telling you anything."

Aidan pocketed his badge and claimed a chair across from Kevin. "KrnuL_PaniK_1013, that's you too, correct?"

"I have no idea who that is," Kevin said with an insolent shrug.

Jamie pulled out his phone and brought up the screenshot of the back trace he had run last night. He set the phone on the table in front of their suspect.

Kevin gasped. "How'd you get this?"

"He's a better hacker than you," Aidan said as he crossed his arms and leaned back in his chair.

Jamie picked up his phone and resumed his position against the wall. Kevin slumped in his chair, pretending not to give a damn. "I don't believe it."

"I don't care what you believe," Aidan said. "What I want to know is where you were yesterday evening."

"I stayed in the lab until midnight."

"And what about Monday afternoon and Tuesday morning last week?"

"I have classes on Mondays and Wednesdays. I'm in lab Tuesdays, Thursdays, and Fridays."

Jamie caught the dodge. "Were you in class and lab during those times last week?"

"I was in lab on Tuesday."

"And class on Monday?"

The young man ran his hands over his shaved head and left them locked behind his neck. He didn't look guilty so much as bone tired. "I skipped. I'd taken the red-eye home Sunday morning from my sister's wedding in Seattle, and I was jet-lagged. I was home asleep."

"You got roommates?" Aidan asked.

"Yeah, but they weren't home."

Things were not looking good for Kevin. He had an alibi for two of the breaches, but there was nothing to say he couldn't have had a laptop open in lab or in class, running the hack with no one around him the wiser. Then there were the two intrusions he didn't have an alibi for—Monday afternoon and the day before, when he had been on a plane. If that plane had Wi-Fi, then he could have pulled off the breach from thirty thousand feet.

"Wait, does this have to do with the increased security around GNL?" Kevin leaned forward and braced his forearms on the table. "I didn't hack anything, I swear."

"You've been to every Black Hat convention near where you lived the past eight years."

"I wouldn't target GNL. That's not why I'm in this."

"In this?" Jamie said, the earnest shift in Kevin's voice catching his attention.

"Working at GNL. And hacking, for that matter."

"What *does* your hacking have to do with then?"

He clammed up again. "I'm not saying."

"We can get a warrant and find out," Aidan said.

Kevin wanted to say something, Jamie could tell, but he hesitated, wary eyes locked on Aidan. Jamie thought about his crypto classmates and the other hackers he knew. Few scientists and even fewer hackers engaged in illegal activities would respond to Aidan's dominance and authority. But hacker to hacker . . .

Jamie shoved his hands in his pockets, making himself appear as nonthreatening as possible. "Aidan, you should probably check in with Gary."

His partner shot him an inquisitive look. Jamie kept his posture and manner calm. Aidan considered him a moment, nodded, then pushed back from the table and left the room without another word. Jamie closed the door behind him and slid into his chair.

"I don't believe you're a hacker," Kevin said.

Jamie lowered his voice. "I'll keep your secret if you'll keep mine."

"O-okay."

"You asked how I found you." Jamie tapped at his phone, brought up the profile from which he'd conducted the back trace, and pushed the device across the table.

Kevin stared at the phone as if he were afraid to touch it. "N-no way," he stammered, shaking his head. "No way you're him."

He waited for Kevin to come to terms with the impossible, then shifted back in his chair, one leg crossed over the other. "I've shown you mine, now you show me yours. Not that I can't find it myself, but we're in a bit of a hurry."

"You won't arrest me?"

"Not my concern." He nodded to the phone sitting on

the table between them. "Mutual assured destruction. I arrest you, you report me. I don't want that either."

Kevin's eyes flickered to the door where Aidan had exited. "Your partner know?"

"He does."

Brown eyes swung back to his. "You must trust him."

"I do. Now, are *you* gonna trust me?"

Eyes downcast, Kevin threaded his fingers together and twiddled his thumbs. "My father's an investor and a crook. Problem is, they can't nail him on anything, so I've been skimming his accounts and making anonymous donations of his money."

Jamie straightened in his chair at the unexpected response. "Donations where?"

"Shelters," Kevin mumbled, barely loud enough to hear. "For battered women and kids."

Jamie gave the downturned face a closer look. A crooked nose, broken more than once. A round scar on his biceps that could be mistaken as a vaccine or acne scar. Faint raised lines on the inside of one wrist below black rubber bracelets. Kevin Currie had not had an easy childhood, but he'd pulled himself out and up.

Jamie grabbed Kevin's bag and pushed it across the table. "Your laptop in there?"

Kevin nodded.

"Mind if I take a look?"

"Mutual assured destruction, right?"

"Agreed."

Kevin pulled out the laptop and brought it to life. While he waited for Kevin to log in, Jamie stuck his head out the door. Aidan was jogging down the hallway toward him.

"Where'd you go?"

"Just took a walk," he replied. "He's not our guy?"

"Don't think so, but I'm going to check."

"Ready," Kevin called, and Jamie led Aidan back into the room. They took the seats across from Kevin, Jamie accepting the offered laptop as Aidan resumed asking questions, treating Kevin more like a witness than a suspect.

"Have you seen anything unusual around GNL the past week? Anyone new or the regulars off their normal shifts?"

"No, but you should ask Dr. Griffin. She's here around the clock. She's even got a cot in her office."

"What about network security? We know they issued new access cards and codes this past weekend. Have they made any other protocol changes?"

"None, though, you know . . ."

Jamie glanced up. "What?"

"The other day, when I was out there, covering my tracks"—Kevin nodded to the computer—"I noticed unusual activity on the firewall. I thought it was network security running pen tests."

Jamie turned the computer back to him. "Go there. You can navigate your history faster."

Kevin nodded and handed the laptop back in less than a minute. "There's your IP address. Want me to keep digging and see where it leads?"

"I'll do that." Jamie took over once more, digging further and catching his breath when he pulled up a familiar profile. "Got you."

"You know the source?" Aidan asked.

"Yep." He snapped a screenshot before deleting all of Kevin's history. When he was finished, he handed the laptop back to its owner.

"No way! It took me weeks to build those algorithms

and find the paths I needed, and you just erased it all." The young man looked angry and defeated.

"We should get going," Aidan said as he stood. "Thank you for your cooperation."

Kevin cursed under his breath as he pounded keys, trying to restore what had been permanently deleted. Jamie waited for Aidan to leave, then pulled a card and pen out of his pocket, scribbling his cell number on the back. He handed the card to Kevin. "Call me next week. I'll help you rebuild the relevant histories."

"Why?" Kevin asked, a little awestruck as he pocketed the card.

Jamie thought about the account ledgers on Aidan's flash drive. About what else might be on it. His specialty was cracking defense and security frameworks. This kid's specialty was hacking financial mainframes. "I think there's something you might be able to help me with."

"It's a deal." Kevin gave him a surprisingly strong parting handshake.

Leaving him to pack up, Jamie rejoined his partner in the hallway.

"Where's the trail lead back to?" Aidan asked.

"Right where you thought it would this morning. Emily Richards."

FOURTEEN

Aidan pulled to the curb in front of Emily Richards's home and parked behind a red F-150 and a Bureau-pool sedan. The ramshackle cottage looked like it hadn't been repaired since the last hurricane hit the area. The wire fence circling the property bent and bowed in a dozen places, rotting two-by-fours supported a nonexistent roof over the front porch, and on either side of the buckled front walkway, knee-high weeds swayed in the summer breeze.

A light snore rumbled from the slumbering giant in the passenger seat. They had just crested the causeway bridge, heading to Emily's in Texas City, when Walker pocketed his phone and said he was going to "rest his eyes." Before they reached the end of the bridge's span, he'd been out like a light. Zero sleep and too much sugar and caffeine had finally caught up with him. Not even the change in momentum or the silenced engine had woken him. He looked so peaceful in sleep Aidan hated to disturb him.

"Hey, Whiskey." He lightly shook the other man's shoulder. "Wakey, wakey."

Lashes fluttering, Walker cracked open his eyes, then immediately slammed them shut again. "Why's the sun so bright in Texas?" he groaned, forehead wrinkling.

"I suspect the sun's bright anywhere after not sleeping for twenty-four hours." Aidan pulled the aviators off his head. "Here, take these."

Walker blindly flailed his hand between them until Aidan caught it and curled his fingers around the sunglasses.

"There you go." Aidan withdrew, not lingering on the remembered comfort of Walker's big warm hand wrapped around his the other night.

Walker donned the glasses and laid his head back on the headrest. "Don't suppose you have a candy bar or something stashed in here?"

Aidan reached into his inner coat pocket and withdrew a king-size Kit Kat.

Walker lolled his head to the side, a wide grin stretching across his face. "Where'd you get that?"

"GNL vending machine when you were questioning Kevin. I knew the crash would hit eventually."

Unlike with the sunglasses, their hands did linger over the candy bar, Walker's thumb trailing over his before pulling away. "Thanks," he said, as quiet as Aidan had spoken earlier, creating a kind of intimacy between them usually reserved for dark, cozy places rather than convertibles open to the bright midday sun. "You're officially my favorite person on Earth." He unwrapped one end of the candy bar and took a huge bite.

"On all of Earth?"

Walker waved the candy bar around and glanced at him

over the top of the sunglasses. "Well, on this godforsaken sunny patch of it."

Aidan's laugh died before it fully formed, the sight of a shiny-suited Torres approaching, hazel gaze trained on Walker, shattering their cozy convertible world. "Pretty sure Torres wants to be your favorite."

Walker scarfed down the rest of the Kit Kat, then ran his hands through his hair, adjusted his coat and tie, and pushed the sunglasses up the bridge of his nose. "Best not keep him waiting."

Jealousy seared through Aidan, sharp and fierce, and on its heels, a plan he should have discussed with Walker first, but his partner was already out the door. Walker had followed his lead yesterday with Dr. Griffin. Could Aidan count on him to do the same today?

"Jamie," Torres said. "Agent Talley," he added as an afterthought.

"Agent Torres," Aidan said, then to Gary, who'd joined them with Barnes, "What've we got?"

"Knocked," Torres answered. "No one's home."

"Did you look around yet?" Aidan asked the assembled group.

"We were waiting on you." Gary led their group through the wire gate hanging by a single rusted hinge and up the cracked and pitted walkway.

"We'll check out back," Walker said, assuming he would follow.

"You'll stay here," Aidan countered. "Torres, you're with me on the left," he continued before Walker put words to the consternation on his face. "Gary, you and Barnes take right."

He didn't give anyone time to argue, breaking left and

expecting the others to fall in line. He wove through the knee-high weeds, sidestepping debris and rusted-out car parts, as he made his way to the front left window. He cupped his hands around his eyes and peered inside.

Living room, deserted. Matching leather couch and recliner, cracked and lined from regular use. Bare bookshelves, end tables devoid of lamps and coasters, a tube television at the far end of the room, all of it collecting dust.

Aidan stepped back from the window and headed for the path along the side of the house. He slowly neared the corner, hand hovering at his side in case he needed to draw his weapon.

"How long have you and Jamie been partners?" Torres asked behind him, giving away their presence to anyone hiding there.

Finding the side path empty but for more piles of junk and plywood, Aidan held in the simmering diatribe. He wasn't there to mentor Torres, and he didn't think the other agent would take the correction well. The job didn't seem to be his primary focus.

"How long, Agent Talley?" he asked again, proving Aidan's point.

"Three weeks tomorrow." Aidan glanced through the first side window. Just the other side of the living room. Moving on, he walked carefully along the crumbling cement, watching for snakes and other critters hiding under the scattered piles of junk.

"Only three weeks? Really?"

"Yes, really." Aidan bypassed the narrow, frosted bathroom window and focused on the last window ahead.

"I would have thought longer."

"Why's that?"

"You two seem . . ." He paused, in speech and in motion, and so did Aidan, waiting for him to finish. "Connected. I didn't want to step on anyone's toes."

"Working together?"

"Sleeping together."

Aidan's brows raced north. "Excuse me?"

"I want to sleep with Jamie, but I didn't know if you two were more than work partners."

He had suspected as much about Torres's intentions. He did not expect him to come right out and say it, though. He also didn't expect the near uncontrollable urge to strangle him. For everyone's benefit, Aidan crossed his arms and throttled the instinct to strike.

"How do you know Walker would be interested in sleeping with *you*? He could have a wife and kids at home."

Torres flashed a knowing smile. "Come on, Agent Talley. You've been working this job long enough to know appearances can be deceiving."

He held the other man's stare but didn't answer. How had Torres picked up, in two days, that Walker was gay when Aidan had been so oblivious?

"The path's clear, then?" Torres asked.

"I'm not going to comment on my partner's sexuality or his love life other than to say it's Bureau policy to discourage fraternization."

"Discourage, not prohibit."

Rather than arguing semantics, Aidan turned back to the last window.

Another deserted space, this one a bedroom. Queen bed neatly made, heavy wood furniture, another older television, likewise all collecting dust. Bending, Aidan adjusted his view and the sun streaming in over his shoulder glinted off something shiny in the far-right corner. A tall silver pole, a hook at the top, a stand with four wheels at the bottom—an IV hanger. This must have been Emily's father's room before he was moved into assisted living.

Straightening, Aidan backed away from the window and continued around the corner to the backyard.

Torres cleared the corner behind him. "Good thing I won't be with the Bureau much longer then."

Aidan rocked to a spinning stop. "How's that?"

Before the other agent could answer, a screen door screeched open and Aidan grasped the butt of his gun, almost pulling it on his partner.

"Fucking hell, Whiskey! A little warning next time." He made sure the sidearm was still secure as Walker descended the back stoop. "How'd you get in?"

"I knocked and the door opened. Guess it wasn't shut all the way."

Aidan's gaze shot to Torres. "I thought you said you knocked."

"I did," Torres replied as Gary and Barnes rounded the opposite corner.

"She left in a hurry." Gary removed his cowboy hat and wiped his sweat-drenched brow. "Drawers and closet doors in the bedroom on our side were flung open. Clothes and personal items were strewn everywhere."

"Our side was clean," Torres said. "Unused living room and guest room. Couldn't see in the frosted bathroom window."

Gary headed toward the back door. "Let's take a closer look."

As Torres passed, Aidan grabbed him by the arm, holding him back as Barnes and Walker followed the SAC inside. "What was that about leaving the FBI? Does Gary know?"

"He knows." Torres wrenched his arm free. "One of our former agents opened a private security firm last year. I'm done at the end of the month. Gary's scouting Jamie as my replacement. I sure wouldn't mind having him here." The last was said with a leer that made Aidan want to reach for his sidearm again.

What the fuck? Did Mel know about this? He had zero interest in mentoring an agent—one he had to spend an inordinate amount of time resisting—who would be gone in less than a month. One case did not a lesson make. Aidan scratched a call to Mel on his mental to-do list.

He marched up the steps, ignoring a wary glance from Walker.

"Dave confirmed she worked her entire twelve-hour shift yesterday," Walker said as they joined Gary and Torres in Emily's crowded bedroom. "She called in sick today."

"So she split this morning?" Torres said.

"Maybe she had a reason to head out of town." Barnes entered from the connected bathroom. "A scheduled trip? Toothbrush and toiletries are gone."

Aidan checked the drawers of the bedside table closest to him. Both were empty. He rounded the end of the bed, crossing in front of Walker, who asked, "What are you looking for?"

He opened the top drawer of the table on the other side of the bed and found it. He withdrew a roughed-up older-model tablet from the drawer and handed it to Walker. "Think you can find something on here?"

"I'm offended you have to ask."

"Just do it."

Walker flinched at the harsh tone and Aidan instantly regretted it. A few taps later, Walker passed the tablet back, calendar app opened. "No trips scheduled this weekend."

"I'll get an APB out right away," Gary said.

"As of right now, Emily Richards is our prime suspect." Aidan dug his keys out of his pocket and tossed them to Walker. "Go back to the condo and handcuff yourself to the computer. I want everything you can find on her." Next, he turned to Barnes and Torres. "You two, she's got a father in assisted living in Houston. Get up there, find out when was the last time she visited, and interview him and anyone else she regularly interacted with." Last, he addressed Gary. "After you call in that APB, let's canvass the area. See if anyone saw her come home this morning or if she left directly from GNL."

They all nodded, but no one moved.

"Let's go, people!" He clapped his hands together and everyone broke into action. He was following the local agents out when Walker blocked the doorway.

"Everything okay?"

"Fine," Aidan snapped.

Walker narrowed his eyes, not buying it one bit.

Had it really only been three weeks together? No matter how in sync they were, though, this partnership likely had a shelf life, according to Torres. Another reason not to get attached. Another reason to move ahead with his plan.

"You have a job to do, Agent Walker. Or do you need me to make that an order?"

"Unnecessary, Agent Talley."

Aidan hated the chill in Walker's voice, hated this plan of his. Pocketing the keys, Walker tucked Emily's tablet under his arm, turned on his heel, and exited with frightening rigidity, Torres's eyes on him the entire way.

Aidan might hate his plan, but it was working.

Darkness hung heavy over the coast when Aidan returned to the condo, entering to the sound of relaxed male voices and the enticing aroma of mole. At the far end of the dining table, heads together, Walker and Torres were laughing over something. Neither of them acknowledged his presence. He cut through the laundry room to the kitchen and surprised the other agents when he flipped the kitchen overheads on and tossed his suit coat across the bar onto a stool. "This doesn't look like 'handcuffed to the computer.' "

Exhaustion was written all over his partner, from the wrinkled dress shirt and suit pants to his sagging shoulders and bloodshot eyes.

"Oscar brought over dinner. Oaxacan mole." Walker's false enthusiasm was obvious to Aidan, but judging by Torres's wide smile and his knee brushing Walker's under the table, the other agent hadn't noticed.

"The real deal," Torres said. "From a hole-in-the-wall joint only locals know about."

"There's plenty left for you," Walker said before he turned back to Torres, lowering his head and voice so Aidan wouldn't hear their conversation.

Aidan bypassed the open containers of food on the kitchen island in favor of a beer. He popped the cap and took a long swallow of citrusy pale ale. "I'm going to change. When I get back, I want to hear what you've found, and it better be more than Agent Torres's favorite food joints."

Walker didn't bother to look up, just waved a dismissive hand in the air. They were a long way from this morning's supersonic hedgehog who'd eaten out of his hand. No better at weathering that depressing thought, Aidan set his beer on the end of the bar and headed to his room, leaving the door cracked behind him.

A chair scraped back from the table. "I'm going to go," Torres said. "Unless you want me to stay."

A second chair slid back. "No, I've got it. Thank you for everything."

Not wanting to contemplate *everything,* Aidan tuned out the rest of their goodbye. Undressing, he pitched his dirty clothes into the hamper hard enough to tip the wicker basket over. He was angry, irrationally so. He had no claim over Walker. He couldn't—wouldn't—pursue a relationship with him. And he had been the one to put this particular quarrel in motion without getting his partner's go-ahead. Walker didn't deserve to be the target of his anger. Aidan was sure he'd done the work requested, and by the look of things between Walker and Torres, he had also run with the plan Aidan hadn't explained. Walker wasn't the problem; Aidan was. The threads of his personal and professional life were winding themselves together faster than he could untangle them.

Aidan pulled on a T-shirt and jeans and slipped his feet into his flops. When he reemerged from his bedroom, Walker stood with a shoulder leaning against the open balcony doorjamb. "You want to tell me what that was all about?" he said.

Aidan grabbed his plate from the fridge and popped it in the microwave. "What do you *think* that was all about?"

"You suspect someone in the field office. You want them to think we're not getting along, so they'll try to divide and conquer and, in doing so, show their hand."

Walker was better than good, and not just with computers. His field instincts so far had been spot-on, and he had slid fluidly into a new partnership. Better than Aidan had. The tension in Aidan's back eased and he favored his partner with a tired smile. "You catch on fast."

"I also think it's about you acting like a jealous prick."

Spot-on instincts indeed.

Their gazes locked, sparked, only disconnecting when the microwave chimed. "I wasn't sure who was on the take. I'm thinking Torres." Aidan retrieved his food. "He knew that door was unlocked, he's a sloppy investigator, and he's leaving the Bureau at the end of the month."

"Where's he going?"

"Private security. Gary wants you to replace him."

Walker collapsed like an extra-long noodle in the chair at the head of the table. He stretched his long legs to the side, bare ankles crossed, and dangled his equally long arms over the armrests, fingers skirting the floor. "Did Cruz know about that?"

"I called her on the way here. She claims not to."

"You don't believe her."

"Until I look her in the eyes, I can't be sure." Aidan grabbed his beer bottle from the bar and took a seat at the opposite end of the table by Walker's disarrayed files and laptop. He beckoned with a tilt of his head. "Come show me what you've found on Emily."

Walker looked for a moment like he might object,

having just situated himself, but he wasn't in any more of a mood to fight than Aidan after a long afternoon of playing at it. He moved to the chair in front of his computer and handed Aidan a red folder.

Aidan set aside his fork and skimmed the first few pages of the file. "This is a dossier on a different Emily Richards. What's she got to do with our Emily?"

"That"—Walker pointed at the file in his hands—"is Jo Ann Richmond's alias."

"Who's Jo Ann Richmond?"

"Our Emily." He handed over Barnes's original green file on Emily. It was substantially thicker than it had been this morning, supplemented with financial history, credit card usage, and travel activity for two persons. Stapled on the inside left cover was a picture of two young women in green graduation gowns, so similar in appearance—green eyes, blond hair, freckled, sun-tanned skin—that anyone would mistake them as sisters, twins even. Aidan picked up the red file again and flipped pages until he found the inevitable.

A death certificate.

"She covered her tracks incredibly well," Walker said. "GNL security didn't find it. I didn't find it on the first pass either."

"What about Emily's father in the nursing home? I thought she was in debt up to her eyeballs caring for him."

"She is, but that man, Dale Richards, is the real Emily Richards's father."

"And he didn't recognize his own daughter? Or rather her imposter?"

"For all intents and purposes, Jo Ann is also his daughter. She was a foster kid who met Emily Richards in grade school. They were alphabet buddies, last names so close they were always seated next to each other. They became best friends, and she spent all her time with Emily's family. She must have made Emily a promise to care for him if something ever happened to her."

"In exchange for Emily's identity?"

"Maybe, maybe not. Maybe she was just doing her best friend a favor."

"That's an awfully big favor."

"Assuming Emily's identity certainly made taking responsibility for Mr. Richards easier. They relocated from New Orleans five years ago. When she couldn't care for him any longer, Jo Ann moved him into the assisted care facility. There are more details in the file." Walker closed his laptop, pushed it forward, and propped his elbows on the table. He hung his head in his hands and rubbed his temples.

Standing, Aidan gathered his plate and empty bottle in one hand and laid his other on Walker's shoulder. "Good work, Whiskey."

Walker smiled, tired but true. "Thanks, Irish." He moved to stand, and Aidan pressed down, keeping him seated.

"Two minutes," he said, and Walker nodded, closing his eyes.

In the kitchen, Aidan dumped his plate in the sink and grabbed several items from the pantry and fridge. "I met with Jake again this afternoon." He mixed chocolate, cinnamon, and milk in a ceramic mug.

"Twitchy fella, isn't he?"

Aidan chuckled. "Good to know it wasn't just me." He put the mug in the microwave and zapped it for a minute.

"Did you find out what was going on between him and Jo Ann?"

"She was on duty, but she wasn't there when the breach occurred."

"Where was she?"

"He thought she was taking an emergency call about her father. He didn't tell us earlier because he didn't want to get her in trouble."

"Did he know who she might be sleeping with?"

"He'd hoped it would be him. He liked her. I suspect the 'Alone' you mentioned was for his benefit, especially if she needed him to cover for her." He pulled the mug out of the microwave and stirred its contents.

Walker shook his head. "I didn't get that from her. I think there's someone else."

By now, Aidan knew not to doubt Walker's instincts. "We'll look into it." He pushed the steaming mug under the younger man's nose. "Drink that."

"What is it?"

"Mexican hot chocolate."

He took a careful sip and made a sound in the back of his throat that sent Aidan to the kitchen for a double shot of Maker's.

Walker smiled over his shoulder. "It's good."

"It's even better with coffee, but you're cut off for the night." He slid into the chair next to him and enjoyed the peaceful sounds of the ocean as he sipped his bourbon. After a while, the mug in Walker's hand teetered, his eyelids closed, and his head bobbed in semisleep. Aidan eased the mug from Walker's hand, causing him to jerk awake.

"Sorry. Must have dozed off a minute." He stood and began stacking the files. "I'll keep digging."

Aidan grabbed Walker's wrist, halting his actions. "You'll go to sleep is what you'll do. You're dead on your feet."

"But we're back to square one."

"No, we're not." He tapped Jo Ann's file. "This woman's involved somehow. She's our in. You're running more searches?"

"Always running searches."

"We'll follow those leads in the morning." Aidan squeezed, then released his wrist. "*After* you sleep."

Walker chuckled. "Okay, boss."

"You did good today. Getting Kevin to cooperate, catching on to Operation Divide and Conquer"—that got him another laugh—"and uncovering what no one else did about Emily Richards."

"I learned a lot too. Good teacher." He shuffled across the bamboo floors to his room, faltering over the threshold when Aidan called out, "Whiskey."

Aidan waited for him to glance over his shoulder before offering the apology he deserved. Before offering the truth. "I'm sorry for being a jealous prick."

"Operation Divide and Conquer. You were acting." Walker closed the door behind him.

Aidan tossed back the rest of his bourbon and whispered his truth to the night. "I said *being*, Jamie."

FIFTEEN

Aidan twirled a pen around his thumb as he reviewed the papers scattered on the conference room table, searching for answers in the data Walker's overnight searches had produced.

Emily Richards died five years ago, the summer after she and Jo Ann Richmond graduated from Tulane. Why had Jo Ann assumed her best friend's identity? Who or what was she running from? Was her past connected to the present security breaches at GNL? Who was she with Tuesday morning?

Familiar voices in the hallway grew louder as they approached. Aidan's gut clenched. Laughing, Walker and Torres entered, their heads close like they had been last night. Aidan had set this farce in motion, and he liked it less and less by the minute. "Sampling more of the local cuisine?"

Walker withdrew the arm he'd started to extend, curling the cardboard cup he held toward himself instead. "I picked up this Mexican coffee for you, but I think I'll keep it for myself now." He took a sip and sat across from Aidan.

Torres claimed the chair next to him. "Any luck, Agent Talley?"

"Striking out." Aidan stared down the other man. "Like you."

Ignoring them both, Walker opened his laptop. "Let's see if Magnum's had better luck."

Disregarding the ridiculous, adorable fact that Walker had named his computer after a fictional detective—albeit a very hot one, in his prime—Aidan kept his attention on Torres. "No one at the nursing home had any idea Jo Ann wasn't Dale Richards's real daughter?"

"As far as anyone there knew, Jo Ann Richmond was Emily Richards. She'd arranged Dale's admittance and visited twice a week. Staff said she sometimes looked a little frazzled, but no more than the kid of any other patient with early-onset Alzheimer's."

"And he played along with it?"

"By the time she admitted him, he couldn't remember his own name. If he slipped up and called her Jo Ann from time to time, no one thought anything of it."

"I may have something," Barnes interrupted from the doorway.

Aidan gestured to the seat beside him. "Let's hear it."

Agent Hipster eagerly took the offered seat and placed a thin orange file folder on the table. "We received Jo Ann's foster records this morning. I've been going through them to see if she crossed paths with anyone local."

"Any hits?"

From the file, he pulled out a grainy black-and-white copy of a Louisiana driver's license. "Eric Hamilton. He was Jo Ann's foster brother in her last home before she moved on campus. Eighteen months ago, Hamilton was discharged from the navy. Six months ago, he got a job at the Port of Galveston."

Aidan riffled through the meager contents of the background search. In addition to the driver's license were copies of Hamilton's Port employment application, his union card, and a list of known addresses. There were no military discharge papers. "What was he discharged for?"

"His file is sealed."

Aidan slammed the folder shut. "We're the fucking FBI."

Barnes rolled his chair back a bit. "It's classified. Gary's working on it."

Across the table, Walker cleared his throat and gave Aidan a calm-the-fuck-down look. Aidan reined in his temper and channeled his frustration into the pen he tapped against the table. "Was Hamilton on shift yesterday?"

"Yes, swing shift," Barnes answered. "He's on again at three this afternoon."

Aidan glanced at the clock on the digital display of the conference room phone. "That gives us three hours. You two"—he pointed the pen at Barnes and Torres—"call the Port foreman back. Get us a list of all Port personnel on shift during each breach. Let's see if we've got any more connections."

"Or," Torres said, "you could help Todd with that, and I could help Jamie. Two hackers are better than one."

Aidan looked to Walker, who met his steely gaze head-on. "He's right."

"Fine." He threw the pen down and headed for the

door. "Barnes, I also want you to walk me through that first responders list."

"Yes, sir."

Aidan stopped in the hallway, and Barnes, who was on his heels, let out a gruff, "Sorry, sir," when they almost collided.

"I need to make a call," Aidan said. "Grab your laptop and the first responders list and bring them back to the conference room."

"Maybe we should work someplace else." Barnes's gaze drifted to the side and Aidan's followed.

Torres was booting up his laptop next to Walker's and the too-smooth agent had slung an arm over the top of Walker's chair. Aidan watched as Walker leaned back into the other man's arm, crossing his legs in Torres's direction. Blood boiling, Aidan struggled not to growl. As it was, his voice was rough, the Irish brogue irrepressible, when he ordered Barnes to meet him back there in five. Reading the warning signs, Barnes scurried away, and Aidan stomped down the hallway in search of another empty conference room. Three doors later, he found a small room with a round table for four. He had just sat down and pulled out his phone when Walker snuck in behind him.

"Who are we calling?" Walker closed the door and slid into the chair next to him.

Aidan scrolled to the contact he needed and dialed, turning the speaker on. "Laying it on awfully thick with Torres, aren't you?"

"This was your ridiculous idea."

"Aidan's got a ridiculous idea. Must be Tuesday." The dig from the other end of the line was shouted over a racket of background noise, and Aidan couldn't help but laugh.

"Love you too, baby bro."

"Sorry, Ai, had to be said. And sorry for the noise. I'm standing on a cargo ship in Oakland trying to figure out why we're short containers."

"You're the COO. Isn't that someone else's job?"

"You want something done right . . ."

"Do it yourself, yeah, yeah, yeah. Dad taught us all the same. Need a favor, Danny."

"Of course you do. Give me a second to find someplace quiet." There was a half-scraping, half-groaning sound, followed by a thunderous boom, then complete and utter silence until Danny spoke again. "You're gonna have to deal with the echo."

"Is he in a shipping container?" Walker asked.

"I am. Is that the new partner?"

"Daniel Talley, Jameson Walker. Whiskey, my brother, Danny."

"Nice to meet you, Danny," Walker said. "And please, call me Jamie. And please also tell your mom I said 'hi' next time you see her."

Aidan shoved Walker's shoulder. "No ganging up on me."

"Mom says he's cute. You're hosed, bro," Danny mortifyingly supplied. Walker's answering smile was nothing short of smug, but before either of them could say more, Danny asked, "What's this favor you need?"

"You still tight with that admin at the Port of Galveston?"

Danny's voice lowered. "If by tight you mean I know how tight certain—"

"Great first impression you're making."

His brother laughed, the sound full and boisterous. "Says the original Casanova himself."

"Danny," Aidan chided half-heartedly. His brother's good humor never failed to brighten his mood.

"What's the ask, Ai? I've got a company to run, remember?"

"If I send you a few time windows from the past two weeks, can you see if your admin friend remembers anything off about the shifts during those times?"

"What are we looking for?" Even though he was ten years Aidan's junior, Danny had always been a willing coconspirator.

"*We* aren't looking for anything." Aidan didn't want Danny anywhere near a potential bioterrorist attack.

Undeterred, his brother tried cajoling his partner. "Jamie, what are we looking for?"

Walker snickered as Aidan threw Danny's words back at him. "Don't you have a company to run?"

"Please, I can run the company in my sleep. This sounds way more interesting."

No sooner had he brushed off his day job than someone banged on the container door, shouting, "Mr. Talley!"

"Sounds like someone disagrees," Aidan said.

"Unfortunately."

"You'll call your Port contact?"

"As soon as I free up."

"Thanks, Danny."

More banging. "Duty calls." The earsplitting sound of the container door opening drowned out everything for a few seconds, then Danny was shouting over background Port noises again. "Nice to meet you, Jamie. Hope we can do it in person soon."

"Likewise."

"Ai, love you. Be safe."

"Love you too, baby bro." Said in jest before, Aidan spoke the words sincerely now, forced out over the lump in his throat. He was close with all his siblings. They had never been bashful about expressing their feelings for one another, even in front of others. After the accident, those expressions of love took on new significance. His siblings had rallied around him like never before, letting him know he was loved and wasn't alone.

"He sounds like a character," Walker said once the line went dead.

"He's the youngest of six. He had to be. Danny came out wailing. Never heard lungs on a kid like that before or since."

"And he's running the company now?"

Aidan nodded. "Our father's still CEO, but Danny's COO, and my oldest sister, Siobhan, is general counsel. They run the day-to-day operations."

"You think he can find out more than we can?"

"Danny can be very charming."

Walker leaned over the arm of his chair, deep into Aidan's personal space, that damn attractive smile bordering on a seductive leer. "And I can't be?"

Oh, he was charming all right. Between him and Danny, Aidan had been charmed out of his bad mood and into a comfortable new place. A place that, if he were honest with himself, included Walker fitting in with his family, maybe better than Gabe ever had. At the moment, the promise of that comfort, and the other comforts Walker could provide, felt hot enough to melt the blanket of icy guilt and fear he had wrapped himself in since Gabe's death. It also had the potential to burn him alive. The lure of the fire, though . . .

A knock on the door sent them reeling apart. Torres didn't wait before barging in. "Everything okay, agents?"

"We're fine." Aidan stood. "Just checking in with SAC Cruz."

"Todd's waiting in the conference room with the files you requested."

"We'll be right there, Oscar," Walker said.

Torres hesitated then relented, leaving them alone again.

Aidan glared at the open door he left behind him until Walker clasped his shoulder and lowered his voice. "Rein it in before you go in there and scare Todd off. He's good. We need him on the team."

"I can't help that Agent Hipster's jumpy. Do you think he's a suspect?"

Walker shook his head.

"Then why do I scare him?"

A soft smile played across Walker's face. "Because he admires you." His hand trailed down Aidan's arm, all the way to his wrist, tweaking the gold and emerald cuff link there. "You're more of a force than you realize."

"I don't scare you," Aidan said once he found his voice again.

Cobalt eyes clashed with his brown ones. "You scare me, Irish. More than you know."

Suffocating in one of the Port's mobile offices—a glorified trailer—Aidan stood by the narrow open window and let the foul-smelling harbor breeze waft in over him. The mix of stagnant water, diesel fuel and machine exhaust would turn most people's stomachs, but growing up in a shipping family, he had become immune to the nauseating blend. And right then, the need for air circulation was paramount, especially with the Walker-Marge showdown heating up behind him.

"I understand it's a big place, ma'am," Walker drawled, attempting to cajole the stern-faced receptionist. "But if you could please try locating Mr. Hamilton again, we'd appreciate it."

Marge was not Danny's playmate. With gray hair and weathered skin, the surly-tempered woman had likely been at this post most of her life, a seasoned shieldmaiden who provided the last line of defense against outsiders.

And outsiders he and Walker were, having already been treated, over the past several hours, to the tight-knit, tight-lipped, closed communities that were ports. They might have gotten further faster if they'd used his name—Talley Enterprises still did a fair bit of business there—but Aidan didn't want to disrupt his family's interests or Danny's information gathering. They had agreed Walker would do the talking while he flew under the radar and observed.

Marge, however, seemed as immune to Walker's charm as Aidan was to dock stench.

"As I told you twice already, Agent Walker, you should have called ahead and made an appointment to meet with Eric."

"We did call ahead, three hours ago, and again when we arrived at the main office."

"That's not enough time. I need it the day before so I can put it on his time card. That way he'll know to be here."

"I'll take it from here, Marge," came a deep, commanding voice behind them.

Turning, Aidan knew at once the tall, muscled white man standing in the doorway was Eric Hamilton. The crew cut hair and rigid posture screamed military, as did the lightning bolt and bomb tattoo on his right arm. Explosive Ordnance Disposal Unit. The navy's own bomb squad.

"Eric, I told these men they needed an appointment to speak with you."

"It's fine, Marge." He stepped into the office. "Paul needs you in Trailer Two."

Marge shot them one last hassled look on her way out and slammed the door behind her.

Hamilton's clear blue eyes flickered to Walker then back to Aidan. "I understand you're looking for me."

"Eric Hamilton." Walker took the lead, striding forward. "I'm Special Agent Jameson Walker, and this is my partner—"

"Aidan Talley." Hamilton didn't take his eyes off him. "I know who you are."

"How's that?" Aidan propped himself against the wall, the trailer suddenly seeming half its size. "I haven't introduced myself yet."

"Main building called ahead. Gave me your names."

Something in Hamilton's icy stare convinced Aidan his explanation was a lie, but before he could follow the hunch, Walker inserted himself between them. "We need to ask you some questions about Jo Ann Richmond."

Hamilton's gaze held Aidan's a moment longer, then slid to Walker. The two big men stared each other down, and Aidan watched, fascinated. His partner was impressive, didn't give an inch, even in the face of a highly trained combat vet.

"Ask away," Hamilton finally conceded after several long seconds.

Walker gestured to the single visitor chair. Hamilton disregarded his suggestion and claimed Marge's seat behind the desk. Not letting it rile him, Walker smartly took the rejected visitor chair and sat casually back in it, unbuttoning his coat and resting an ankle on his knee. "How'd you know Jo Ann Richmond?" he asked.

"She was one of my foster sisters in New Orleans." Hamilton leaned forward, placing his forearms on the desk. "Now, let's skip to the questions you don't already know the answers to."

"When's the last time you saw her?" Walker asked, unfazed.

"The day I shipped out with the navy."

"Have you seen her here in Galveston?"

Hamilton didn't flinch, didn't blink, just replied flatly, "Jo Ann's in Galveston?" He knew she was in Galveston all right, but he wasn't going to admit it. Maybe they could get him to admit something else. The timing lined up . . .

Aidan pushed off the wall and came to stand behind Walker. "Did you know Emily Richards?"

"Jo Ann's best friend."

"Not anymore."

"They had a falling out?"

Was he playing them? Aidan went for shock and awe, seeing if he could get a telling reaction out of the other man. "Emily died the summer after they graduated from Tulane."

Zilch. Another blank stare. No reaction.

"We're looking for Ms. Richmond," Walker said. "She didn't report to work today, and we need to ask her some questions. You have any idea where she might go?"

He shrugged. "Like I said, I haven't seen her in almost ten years."

"You didn't visit New Orleans between tours? Didn't want to check on your siblings?"

"The home with Jo Ann was my tenth. I didn't make it a habit to get attached."

"Tattoos can symbolize attachments." Aidan braced his hands on the back of Walker's chair, leaning forward. "You were EOD?" He nodded to Hamilton's tattoo. "Based where?"

"Usual hot zones."

"EODs are in high demand."

"That's right."

"So why did they discharge you?"

Hamilton shifted back in his chair. Finally, a reaction. "You'll have to ask the navy. That's classified." Aidan made a mental note to have Cruz expedite those discharge papers.

"Why become a longshoreman?" Walker asked.

"Needed a job. Was used to the water."

"And you landed here in Galveston?"

"What can I say, I like the Gulf."

Aidan came around to the side of desk. "In the same place where your foster sister just happened to be?"

"Coincidence, Agent Talley."

"I'm believing in those less and less these days."

Hamilton smirked, a knowing glint in his eye. "Remember that."

Before Aidan could reply, a very round, very bald older

man came blustering through the door with a poorly suited younger man on his heels. "I'm Eric's union rep, and this is our attorney. You can't question him without us present. You should know better."

Aidan backed off, hands in the air. "We're just looking for someone Mr. Hamilton knows. That's all." He deliberately used *know,* not *used to know,* and by the smirk still on Hamilton's face, the other man knew it and didn't care. What was he playing at?

That smug grin stayed in place as he rose and crossed his arms, puffing himself up. "Sorry I couldn't be more help."

"Oh, you've been more than helpful," Walker said as he stood, and Hamilton's gaze shot to him, the icy arrogance faltering. Score one for the kid, though Aidan also wasn't sure what his partner was up to. Walker withdrew a card from his pocket and held it out to Hamilton. "If you hear from Ms. Richmond, please let us know."

Hamilton snatched the card out of his hand and pocketed it. "Of course."

"If that's all, agents," the union rep said, holding the door open for them. "Do you need an escort out?"

Aidan handed the union rep his card and watched as his eyes bugged out. "I think I know my way around."

"Mr. Talley, I didn't realize."

"Make sure your papers are in order." Striding out past him, Aidan knew he wasn't exactly flying under the radar, but the blustering rep's interruption and condescension had pissed him off. He felt not a small amount of satisfaction at his abuse of power.

"Show-off," Walker said, catching up to him.

He favored his partner with a grin. "I could say the same about you. What was that dig there at the end about?"

Walker stopped and held out a card to him. "Knock, knock."

Aidan snatched it out of his hand, his good mood evaporating in the face of yet another fucking knock-knock joke. "Enough with those already!"

"How many cards are in your hand?" Walker nodded at the pieces of paper.

Wait, pieces?

He had handed him two cards, not one. Looking closer, Aidan pried them apart to reveal a thin layer of adhesive and in between, a small metallic strip. "What is this?"

"Little something I picked up at a convention." He held up his phone, a moving red dot displayed on-screen. "Thankfully, I picked up a few."

Realization dawned. "It's a tracker. You pissed him off and got him to pocket the cards without noticing."

"Not just a tracker." Walker tapped at the screen again and when he turned it back to Aidan, it showed a download in progress. "Also a cloning device. He put it in his pocket with his phone."

"Whiskey, you big, beautiful genius." He smiled wide and swatted Walker's chest, thrilled and relieved to have finally caught a break. "We got him."

SIXTEEN

Jamie fell into the passenger seat of the Benz just as the sun set over the Gulf, the tall Port cranes casting long shadows in the orange glow. Sweaty and tired of being in a suit all day, he tossed his coat in the back, rolled up his dress sleeves, then checked his phone. "Hamilton's still on-site," he said. "Download's fifty percent complete."

Aidan was already dialing. "I'm going to check in with Gary."

"Agent Talley," the SAC answered after four rings. "What've you got?

He brought the phone to his ear. "Hamilton was less than helpful, and the rest of the Port stayed mum, but we've got a tracker on him. Expedite the warrant for a search on his place, and if the judge won't grant it, at least go look around. Does he have roommates? Does it look lived in, or is it deserted like Jo Ann's? And keep a car on both."

Aidan cranked the engine, the phone connected to the

car's system, and Gary's booming voice filled the inside of the car. "We're on it. You two headed back here?"

"We're going to keep an eye on things at the Port." Aidan drove out of the main parking area and steered toward the deserted bank parking lot Jamie had pointed out earlier. One waterway over and several blocks down, it had a good line of sight, and with the encroaching darkness the drive-through shelter would keep them relatively concealed.

"I can send Todd and Oscar to relieve you in a few hours," Gary offered.

At the next stoplight, Aidan glanced over. "You got your laptop?"

Jamie nodded.

"Okay on sleep?"

He nodded again.

"We'll be fine," Aidan replied to Gary. "But do get more teams out here in different positions. We can't cover it all."

They exchanged logistical details as Aidan wove through alleyways, hanging up just as he pulled the car into the rear entrance of the bank lot.

"Something's going on there." Aidan put the car in park and killed the engine. "I'm used to how ports work. Tight-knit, Union-run. No one wants to rat on their friends, but Hamilton's the new guy. No way they would close ranks around him this fast."

"You think someone else there is getting paid too?"

"Multiple someone elses. That or they've been spooked, and not by us. Now that they know we're sniffing around, I want to see if Hamilton bolts and if they get any visitors."

"Well, if we're going to be here awhile . . ." Jamie

unbuckled his seat belt and reached into the backseat for his bag and laptop.

"What are you doing?" Aidan asked.

"I'm going to start going through the material we're downloading." He pulled out his laptop and began booting it up. "I also want to add extra alerts in the GNL security system. If someone knows we're onto them, they may try to move something out tonight. You're watching the Port. I'm watching the network." He toed off his shoes, yanked off his tie, and unbuttoned the top few buttons of his shirt.

"Good thinking, but don't get too comfortable yet."

Confused, Jamie glanced at his grinning partner. "I thought we were on a stakeout."

"We are, just not in this car. Not enough leg room for an all-nighter." Aidan bumped his knees against the steering wheel to demonstrate. "And the Benz is too noticeable in this area."

Jamie had spent time in cars with far less legroom, but his partner had a point about the Benz sticking out if anyone bothered to look for them.

Aidan punched the start button on the dash, reactivating the car's electronics without starting the engine. He tapped at his phone and the dial tone rang through the speakers.

"Mr. Talley," a woman answered. Jamie recognized the voice as one of the condo's concierge staff. "What can I do for you?"

Half an hour later, someone from the building staff showed up with an LR4, the backseat full of the other supplies Aidan had requested, including all of Jamie's snacks from the hackathon the other night. It was a smart move on Aidan's part. As the hours ticked by, they had space to spread out in the SUV, and in the sticky Texas heat, the extra breathing room and upholstered seats were much appreciated.

"I hope it wasn't too much trouble for them to bring all this out here." Jamie finished off his third can of Dr. Pepper with the last bite of a BLT.

Aidan, by now also sans jacket, tie, and vest, sipped from a thermos of coffee and filched another Oreo from the package on the console between them. "Unlike some of the other residents, our family doesn't abuse the concierge services, so they're happy to help when we do ask for a favor every now and then."

"Is your family ever all here together?"

"Once or twice a year, hence the big dining table. The nieces and nephews like the beach."

"Your family's tight?"

"We are."

"Is that because of what happened in Ireland?"

"Yes and no." Aidan took a long swallow of coffee and stole another Oreo. "Having lost a son and other friends and relatives, my parents place a high value on family time. So, yeah, we're tight, but Siobhan and I are the only ones who remember Ireland and the Troubles. The rest of our siblings were still very young when we left."

"That explains why I didn't hear any accent in Danny's voice."

Aidan nodded. "You'll hear it in certain words or phrases he's picked up from Mom and Dad, but otherwise, you're right. No accent. Siobhan and I were the only ones who had to work to hide it."

"Why did you? When I met your mother, she didn't hide hers, so it's not a safety issue."

Aidan shifted in his seat, angling toward him. "Were you always tall?"

Jamie startled at the abrupt non sequitur, but after his repeated knock-knock jokes, he played along, sensing this was going somewhere. "Always the back row of choir."

"I knew I heard a voice under there when you were cooking the other day."

Aidan reached for another Oreo, and Jamie snatched the package away.

"That'll be the last time you ever hear it, if you want another cookie."

"Please don't take the fake chocolate away." Aidan thrust out his bottom lip in an exaggerated pout, and Jamie laughed as he tossed the package across the console into his lap. The laughter, the joking was welcome after the tense show they'd put on for the local agents the past two days. He didn't like pretending to be at odds with Aidan. The strange thing about it, though, was Jamie sometimes couldn't tell when Aidan was acting and when he wasn't. Jamie had let him off the hook last night, but today in the office, it didn't feel like Aidan playing hot and cold for show. He was a raging bull in the conference room with Oscar and Todd and then his usual self when they were on the phone with Danny.

"Back to my point, though," Aidan said, bringing Jamie out of his thoughts. "You were always tall, right? Always stuck out?"

Ah, now he got it.

Aidan would have been a preteen when his family

immigrated, the worst time to stick out in a new crowd. From his own experience, Jamie knew that while accents fascinated adults, kids were not so easily amused. Adolescents, in particular, were prone to cruelty and ostracizing those they perceived as different. In a place like California where there was no accent or local dialect, Aidan's Irish brogue, probably also cracking at that age, must have put one hell of a target on his back. Add the . . .

"Was that also when you started dyeing your hair?" Jamie asked.

Aidan leaned against the driver's-side door and cast his gaze out over the water. "Siobhan went more mom's color, dark auburn. I, on the other hand, experimented with peroxide. Neither of us wanted to be the redheaded, freckled kids with the funny accents. On top of that, I liked guys as much as I liked girls. I knew that about myself even back then, just as I knew there was no changing it, so the hair and accent had to go instead."

"You could always let it grow back red."

Aidan chuckled. "I'm afraid of how much gray there'd be in it."

"A little gray hair is to be expected."

"You saying I'm old?"

"No, that's not . . . I didn't mean . . . Gray hair looks distinguished."

"Oh, so I'm the distinguished older mentor now?"

Jamie open and shut his mouth several times, trying to figure out how to dig himself out of his hole. Thankfully, Aidan gave him a hand up, albeit a sorrow-tinged one. "I thought about dying it back after Academy, but Gabe liked it blond. Now I have his stylist's number on speed dial." He ran a hand through his hair, wavier than usual in the Texas humidity. "After so long, this is me now."

"It's not a disguise anymore?"

Aidan speared him with dark, serious eyes. "Is playing FBI agent a disguise for you?"

"I'm not playing anything."

Aidan held up his hands. "Foot in mouth disease is apparently catching. All I meant—"

Jamie reached through the seats to grab another can of soda. "I know what you meant."

"Well?"

Jamie felt the pressure of another one of those times when Aidan had shared and so should he. After the past couple days, it felt almost necessary, like they needed to shore up the fledgling connection that had been beaten and picked at by Oscar and everything else around them. In the dark of night, in the intimate space they had created in the Rover, it seemed like as safe a time and place as any to let Aidan in a little more.

"I never planned to play basketball forever, and I was always good with computers."

"I know. I saw your transcripts. Aced your computer science classes at Carolina, graduated top of your crypto doctorate program at MIT. Why the FBI and not the private sector?"

"Either way, I wanted to move to the West Coast. I didn't need the money, and it's a lot easier to answer reporters' questions with 'I can't talk about my work.'"

"A lot easier to be *out* in California too."

"Yes, it's very different from home."

"You miss North Carolina?"

"All the time, but the career questions would always be there in a basketball-obsessed state. In the Bay Area, no one cares about March Madness."

Aidan's voice was a touch woeful, a touch introspective, when he said, "You can't hide forever, Whiskey."

Without thinking, caught up in that wave of somber reflection and the intimate atmosphere, Jamie reached out and brushed his fingertips through the darker roots beginning to show at Aidan's temple. "Neither can you, Irish."

Dark eyes shot to his and held his gaze, only breaking away when the shrill ringtone of Aidan's phone pierced the silence. His partner fumbled the phone once, twice, before finally answering and hitting speaker.

"Um, yeah, Danny, hey."

"You okay, Ai?" Danny said. "You sound a little rattled."

"Fine," he clipped, as Jamie asked, "What've you got for us?"

"I heard you and my brother caused a stir today at the Port."

"Our brand of charm didn't get us far, especially with Marge," Aidan said.

"And your brother couldn't help throwing his name around a little," Jamie added.

"So I heard," Danny replied. "A very nervous union rep called me."

"You handle him?" Aidan asked.

"Yeah, he won't say anything to anyone else."

"Good. Did your contact come through?"

"She did. At the times you gave me, there were several extra guys around. Ones that aren't normally on shift then."

"You got a list?"

"Just emailed it to you."

Jamie grabbed his laptop from the floorboard and logged into Aidan's email account, opening the new message from Daniel Talley.

Aidan gasped. "How did you get into my email?"

"Not the point right now." Jamie waved him off as his eyes tracked down the list, freezing halfway. He handed the computer across the console to Aidan, who'd set the phone on the dash. "Anyone's name look familiar?"

"There's our guy, Hamilton, second one down."

"Keep reading."

He knew when Aidan saw what he had, his partner's eyes widening and jaw dropping.

Terry Altman. PhD dropout and part-time lab tech for his father, the director of Galveston National Laboratory.

"Text Torres and Barnes. See where they are on pulling that background search."

Jamie was already typing a message when a lilting "Yoo-hoo" came from the phone sitting on the dash, reminding them Danny was still on the line.

"Sorry, bro," Aidan said. "Saw something on that list we weren't expecting. Think your contact could get us manifests of the ships in dock at those same times?"

"Sure thing, but Galveston does a lot of cruise ship business nowadays. Half the manifests I get for you will be passenger lists."

"Focus on the commercial shipping vessels first."

"That'll help narrow things down. I hate I'm missing all the fun."

Aidan huffed. "If you call fun sitting in a car for five plus hours with the Cookie Monster—"

Jamie swatted his arm. "Says the man who ate half the package of Oreos."

Danny laughed, big and loud. "Think I'll stay out of this domestic dispute."

"Good idea," Jamie said. "Hey, Danny, thanks for the list, and keep us posted."

"Same," Danny replied, before hanging up.

Jamie's phone beeped with a text from Oscar. "Local office is pulling everything they can on the Altmans," he told Aidan, then set the phone aside. "What are you looking for in the manifests?"

"Parts."

"Parts for what?"

"A distribution device."

Jamie put the pieces together. "For a bioweapon. Something could be coming in, not necessarily going out."

"Given Hamilton's EOD experience, we have to consider both possibilities."

"Why not have Danny also get the passenger manifests? Someone could be bringing it in on their person."

"Too huge a pool to consider at this point. All those passengers have already been checked at the point of origin and every port since. Checking the commercial vessels first will narrow the initial scope."

Aidan handed the laptop back, email closed, password likely also changed, if that was what he'd been typing when he was talking to Danny.

Jamie sank back in his seat. "I'd feel better with extra customs agents checking bags."

"I don't want to spook anyone yet by sending in a bunch of extra law enforcement. They know we're sniffing around, and if there's a leak in the field office, they'll know even faster. Let's keep an eye on things tonight and see what happens."

A prickle crawled across Jamie's skin. "I don't have a good feeling about this. There's something we're missing."

"Good field instincts. We still don't know if Hamilton's the head of all this or if he's a mercenary for hire and someone else is calling the shots. Or why they're doing it. Or even what they're doing."

"That's a lot we don't know."

Aidan tapped his thumbs against the steering wheel. "But I think we're getting closer."

Sprawled across the front seats, ass in the driver's seat, legs thrown over the console, Jamie was decrypting Hamilton's phone data and digging through background searches on Dr. Altman's son when Aidan's "getting closer" speculation proved true.

The little red dot on his tracking app died and two seconds later alerts rang from every electronic device in the car—the computer open in his lap, his phone propped on the steering wheel, the tablet lying on the dashboard, the phone somewhere on his sleeping partner in the backseat.

Aidan shot up, eyes squinting against the rising sun. "What the hell is that?"

"There's a breach occurring." Jamie swung his legs around and Aidan clambered over the console into the front passenger seat. "And Hamilton killed the tracker."

Jamie shot off a quick text to the GNL security team letting them know he would be working beside them, then opened the portal he had built into the network security mainframe and started activating countermeasures.

Beside him, Aidan had Todd on speakerphone. "You guys seeing this on your end?"

"We're on it," Todd replied. "Oscar's in the system, tag-teaming with Agent Walker."

Jamie nodded. Oscar had flagged him two seconds ago.

"The tracker's dead?" Aidan asked him.

Like he had done at the shooting range, Jamie split his attention, continuing to work while answering Aidan's questions. "Two seconds before the alerts."

"Were you able to get all the data off his phone?"

"Yes, but it's still decrypting."

"What did you find on Terry Altman?"

"Definitely didn't live up to his father's expectations. Squeaked by in community college. Dad used his influence to get him into the UT grad program. Dropped out after a year. His paychecks from UT Med line up with his dad's publications, which syncs with what Griffin said. He's got a steadier gig at the Port. Driver's license says he lives at home still."

"Negative," Todd chimed in. "Terry moved in with one of his dock buddies four months ago. Three guesses who."

"Hamilton," Jamie and Aidan answered together.

"Yes, sirs. We checked out their place an hour ago. Warrant didn't come through until this morning. It's in a similar state as Jo Ann's. Looks like they left in a hurry."

"Until thirty seconds ago, Hamilton was still on-site," Aidan said. "We didn't see him leave, Barnes. Check in with the other teams."

Sirens wailed outside the car, and Jamie glanced up. Police cars and fire trucks streamed by them, racing away from the Port toward GNL.

His computer dinged again, regaining his full attention.

"Shit! They're through the internal firewall. It has to be someone with system access. Jo Ann, wherever she is."

"Negative," Todd repeated. "I'm staring right at her."

Aidan leaned forward and clutched the dash. "What do you mean?"

"Sorry, sir. I should have started by telling you the marshals brought her in an hour ago. They picked her up after she used one of Emily's credit cards."

"So then who the hell did I just boot from the system?" Jamie said.

Aidan's head swiveled. "You shut it down?"

"Yeah." He straightened out of his hunch over the keyboard and cracked his knuckles. "But not before they accessed all the inner lab doors and the locking mechanisms on two cabinets."

"Barnes," Aidan said. "Make sure GNL is locked down. No one and nothing goes in or out."

"Yes, sir. First responders are en route."

An incoming call from Danny flashed on Aidan's phone. "Hold a minute, Barnes." Aidan switched to the other call.

Danny didn't bother with pleasantries. "One of those names on the list is at the Port right now, off schedule."

"Altman?" Aidan said.

"That's the one."

"Barnes said they were gone." Jamie shut his laptop and handed it to Aidan.

"Altman's meeting Hamilton here, and they don't want us to follow." Aidan uncurled from where he had bent to tuck the laptop into the bag on the floorboard. "You drive."

Not that Jamie planned to waste time switching. He was the faster driver anyways. Cranking the car, he familiarized himself with the controls, found the sport mode in two clicks, and launched them out of the bank parking lot.

"What else can I do?" Danny said.

"Nothing, that's it, Daniel." Aidan's voice brooked no argument. "I'm not sure what we're walking into, but you stay the hell out of it."

"Ai, Jamie, be safe."

"Love you, bro." Aidan ended the one call and switched back to Todd. "We've got Hamilton and Altman at the Port. Walker and I are headed in. Tell the other teams to converge."

"Yes, sir," Barnes replied, and Aidan hung up. "Faster, Whiskey."

Jamie gunned the Rover through the sparse early morning traffic, passing another fire truck and two more police cars headed the opposite direction.

"You noticing a trend?" Aidan said.

"All the emergency response vehicles are leaving the area."

"Perfect time for something illegal to go down at the Port."

"You think the hacks are a distraction?"

"In some part, yes. It's all connected somehow."

"Let's hope Hamilton and—"

Jamie's words were cut off by a jolt to their rear fender. An oversize dark blue SUV had burst out of an alley and rammed into the Rover's back end.

"What the fuck?" Aidan shouted.

Jamie wrenched the steering wheel and fought the skid, stopping them from spinning out and aiming them down the next alley instead. "We've got company." He kept one eye on the road ahead and one on the rearview mirror. The

SUV on their tail accelerated, gaining faster in the path Jamie cleared for them. Impact was inevitable. "Shit, hold on!"

The other car rammed them again, hurtling the Rover forward, he and Aidan straining their seat belts. He switched the LR4 into manual and tapped the shifter paddles, gaining some separation from their pursuer.

He cleared the alley, finding they had been diverted away from the Port.

"What the fuck is going on?" Aidan was white-knuckling the oh-shit handle above his door, torso twisted to look behind them, his face paler than Jamie had ever seen it.

"Someone doesn't want us at the Port." Turning hard right, Jamie aimed them down another street leading right back there.

And into the path of a second oncoming SUV.

A horrified "Oh God, no" escaped from his partner just as Jamie saw an under-construction on-ramp ahead on the left, orange-and-white-striped barrels blocking the entrance. He pressed the gas pedal to the floor and headed straight for the oncoming truck.

"Whiskey!" Aidan cried, head whipping forward and back. "What the fuck are you doing?"

Their pursuers were closing in on either side as bypassed alleys flew by left and right.

"You're headed straight for them. Turn, goddammit!"

But turning down one of those alleys would leave them cornered. There was only one path to escape.

Jamie grabbed the back of Aidan's head and pushed it toward his knees, screaming, "Hold on!"

At the last possible second, he veered left, out of the path of the oncoming SUVs and into the barrels. The SUVs in front and behind plowed into each other, exploding in their wake, the blast momentum propelling the Rover farther than Jamie had intended.

Through the barrels and past the unfinished on-ramp.

Through the guardrail.

And down the cliff on the other side.

SEVENTEEN

Aidan came to slowly. The acrid smell of smoke stung his nostrils, something wet dripped down the side of his face, and his head throbbed like someone had taken a hammer to it. Shattered glass tinkled all around as he lifted a hand to his temple, massaging the point of pain. His fingers came away sticky and wet.

Eyes closed, his aching brain was slow to catch on, but one by one, the pieces came together, and the terrible familiarity of his situation knotted his gut and tore at his chest.

Blood.

Broken glass.

Engine smoke and airbag fumes.

Not one but two SUVs barreling toward them.

Car accident.

Again.

Present events collided with past memories of a similar, horrible night eight months ago.

Tom clutching the dashboard with one hand and the handle above the Jag's passenger door with the other, bracing for impact, his face aghast in the oncoming high beams of the vehicle speeding toward them.

Gabe's frightened black eyes meeting his own in the rearview mirror, a second before his body was thrown sideways in the backseat, the crash of his skull against the window louder in Aidan's mind than the grinding metal and splintering glass.

Aidan's insides tossing and turning with each flip of the car, free fall at its most terrifying. The scrape of asphalt against his arm, metal piercing skin, twisting and turning, as death pinned him in its grip.

A weak gurgling cough yanked Aidan back to the present.

Whiskey.

Eyes popping open, he squinted against the bright morning sun and gasped at the pain piercing his head and radiating down his right side. Blackness encroached on the edges of his vision. Not long now. Fighting it, Aidan turned his head left and searched for his partner.

His partner who'd driven the Rover with stunt-worthy precision out of the way of two oncoming SUVs, through a barrier, and down a cliff into a ravine.

The hard landing had knocked Aidan out, but he'd woken upright and in one piece, relatively. Walker, just coming to, was held back against the driver's seat by the taut seat belt. He had his left hand up by his hairline, and when it fell limply into his lap, his fingertips were covered in blood. The strained belt snapped, and he began to crumple forward.

"Whiskey!" Aidan swatted the deflated airbags out of the way and pressed Walker back into the seat, holding him upright. "Stay with me."

Groaning, Walker rotated his head, his lashes dark against colorless cheeks. Bright red blood seeped from a gash at his hairline.

Ignoring the pain in his side and the anvil in his head, Aidan unbuckled his seat belt and stretched across the console to hold Walker's face in his hand. "Come on, Jamie." He gave his unshaven cheek a firm but careful pat. "Open those beautiful blue eyes for me."

Walker's forehead wrinkled and his eyelids fluttered open, the gaze beneath them hazy and unfocused. "Irish?"

Pure relief and blinding need propelled Aidan farther across the console. Fingers digging into Walker's neck, he slammed their mouths together and tasted the precious life flowing from his partner's lips. Aidan had wanted this the past three weeks but had denied the attraction between them. Because they were partners. Because he was still grieving. But in the aftermath of this latest accident, too much like the one that had stolen the last man he'd loved, Aidan needed to know the man beside him, the man he could but couldn't love, was alive.

Walker gave a surprised jerk, then caught on, angling his head and parting his lips, his warm breath rushing into Aidan's mouth. Granted entrance, Walker's slow kiss was no match for Aidan's desperation.

For the fear that laced each swipe of his tongue.

For the longing that shook his fingers and caused him to groan.

For the darkness that grew closer with each stolen breath.

"You'll be okay, Whiskey," he whispered against his lips.

Relief for Walker's safety, for his life, made Aidan's slide into darkness smooth, not the tossing and turning of his nightmarish memories.

"Irish, hold on," was the last thing he heard before falling forward into Walker's big body and letting oblivion take him.

EIGHTEEN

In the waiting area down the hall from Aidan's hospital room, Jamie answered the local police detective's questions, most of which he had already answered for two officers before him.

"You sure you didn't recognize either driver, Agent Walker?"

Elbows on his knees, head hanging in his hands, he absently picked at the bandage on his left temple. "I'm sure, Detective. I was too busy trying to save our lives."

"Anything else you can remember?"

"As I told your officers, both drivers were white men, early- to midthirties. One had a beard, dark; the other was clean-shaven. Both wore sunglasses, Ray-Bans the one, Oakleys the other. Ray-Ban had a ball cap on, Oakley a hoodie. The SUVs were the same make and model—Ford Expeditions, navy blue, early 2000s. Other than the front windshield, the windows were tinted. I'd guess beyond the legal limit. No other individuals in the cars that I saw."

"That's a lot of details, and yet you didn't recognize either driver?"

Jamie was done with this. His head hurt, his body ached, and all he wanted to do was get back to Aidan's bedside and talk his partner into waking the fuck up. "I remember the details because it's my job. I didn't recognize either driver because I don't know them."

"And they weren't this"—the detective looked down at the small notepad in his hand—"Eric Hamilton or Terry Altman that you and Agent Talley suspect are involved in your investigation?"

"No, they weren't Hamilton or Altman. They're in the wind."

Gary entered the waiting area, Oscar on his heels, carrying a small file box, and two other agents behind them. "Helms," Gary said, addressing the detective. "Agent Walker's been through enough today. He's already given you more than your average witness."

"This isn't an average accident, Gary."

"Understood, and you have our full cooperation. My agents here"—Gary gestured to the agents behind him and Oscar—"will accompany you, and you'll have the Bureau's full resources at your disposal in identifying the dead bodies pulled from the wreckage. Of which there were only two, correct?"

Jamie appreciated Gary's smooth backhanded verbal slap.

"I'll want to question Agent Talley as soon as he wakes."

"Assuming he wakes tonight, you can question him at the field office first thing tomorrow."

The bulldog-faced detective was not pleased, but confronted by a wall of federal agents, he conceded. He handed Jamie his business card. "Please call me if you remember anything else." Helms left with his new FBI escort, probably not what he had intended, and Jamie couldn't help but laugh, which in turn caused him to wince.

Oscar knelt beside him and laid a hand on his shoulder. "Brought you a get-well present of sorts." He handed him the file box and Jamie removed the lid. Inside were his laptop, tablet, and both his and Aidan's phones. "I couldn't bring them back to life, but maybe you can."

"Thank you," he said with a weak smile. By the look of the beat-up devices, he didn't hold much hope for rescuing the data on them, including the clone of Hamilton's phone. He had spare devices at the condo, but the past twelve hours would be lost.

The other agent put a too-familiar hand on his knee. "Is there else anything I can get you?"

Presented with the opening, Jamie took it. He needed to bring Gary up to speed, and his doubts about Oscar had solidified over the past twenty-four hours. "I'd love a soda and some chips. And another few pain pills if the doc says it's okay."

Oscar squeezed his knee and stood. "Let me see what I can do."

"What's going on there?" Gary asked once Oscar cleared the door.

"You mean your agent relentlessly hitting on me?"

The older man chuckled and took the seat next to him. "Oscar hits on every attractive person who crosses his path. He's a player, as my nephew would say. What I meant was why did you send him away just now?"

Jamie had to approach this delicately. He needed to think like Cruz and Aidan would on how to handle the politics of the situation. He had to choose his words carefully. "I know you've already questioned and cleared your agents, but—"

Gary held up a hand. "The door was not properly cleared at Jo Ann's house yesterday, and Oscar's a better-than-average hacker. With Jo Ann in custody during the last hack, he's your next best suspect."

"You've already considered this?"

"I didn't get to be an SAC by being the *worst* agent in Texas."

Jamie laughed and winced again. "Shit." He leaned back in his chair with a hand over his side. "Bruised ribs. Forgot how not fun this is."

Gary favored him with a sympathetic smile. "Oscar will be back soon with those pain meds, and I'll keep an eye on him until you two are up and running again."

"There's something else we put together during the breach this morning."

"What's that?"

"When the breach occurred, all the EMS vehicles left the Port area."

Gary nodded. "Headed to GNL, that's right."

"We think GNL could be a distraction, in whole or in part. We need to be sure adequate response teams remain at the Port. I was going to mention it to Detective Helms, but we didn't exactly hit it off. I think the order would be better received from you."

"I'll make sure he gets it," Gary assured him just as Oscar returned.

"Ask and you shall receive." He handed Jamie soda and chips, but no pain pills. "Doc said you have to wait another hour for more meds."

"Worth a shot." Jamie opened the soda and dug into the snack. He was halfway through the bag when Barnes came around the corner with doctors Altman and Griffin.

"Agent Walker." Dr. Griffin moved ahead of the other two and took his free hand in hers. "We came as soon as Agent Barnes told us what happened. Is Aidan okay?" Despite having been raised in the South with a mother who hugged everyone, Jamie was getting damn tired of all the contact from virtual strangers here. The only person he wanted to have any sort of contact with right now was lying unconscious in a bed down the hall.

"Talley got his head rattled," Gary answered for him. "We're waiting for him to wake up."

"I'm sorry about this," Altman murmured from where he stood, separated from the rest. "I never expected Terry to be involved in something like this."

Dr. Griffin's head snapped to the side. "Really, Henry? How many times did I tell you he shouldn't be working here?"

"Terry wasn't living up to his potential. I thought working in the lab would motivate him to reenroll and finish his PhD."

"That backfired," the woman spat.

From their interview with her on Sunday, Jamie knew Dr. Griffin wasn't a fan of Altman, but her claws were out and extra sharp today. He wasn't sure where the added animosity came from. He doubted it was mere concern for his partner. Angling for his job, maybe? Hiding something herself?

Altman spread his hands. "I made a mistake. Is there anything I can do to help fix it?"

Jamie withdrew his hand from Dr. Griffin and straightened in his chair, fighting not to cringe in pain. "Did you show him a picture of Jo Ann?" he asked Todd.

"Not yet. Dr. Griffin insisted we rush right here."

"Pull it up on your phone," he told Todd, since his device was dead in the box.

"Here you go," Todd said as he handed Altman the phone.

Recognition dawned on the doctor's face.

"You recognize her?" Jamie said.

"I thought her name was Emily. She and Terry dated off and on. Nice girl. They met at GNL during one of the times Terry helped me with a project. She's involved in this too?"

"We think she's responsible for the security breaches."

Altman gasped. "They were working together? Did she bring him into this?"

"More likely the other way around," Oscar said. "They were working with another man, Eric Hamilton. Do you recognize that name?"

"He's the fellow from the docks Terry moved in with. Only met him once. Intense guy."

"And you let your son move in with him?" Dr. Griffin said.

"Terry's a grown man, Naomi."

"And you're still trying to run his life, like you do everyone around you."

"I'm sorry." Jamie had had enough of the byplay he didn't understand. He glanced back and forth between the two scientists. "Is there something more going on here we should know about?"

"They were married," Todd said, and Jamie understood Aidan's frequent instinct to strangle Agent Hipster for hiding the ball.

"Is Terry your son, Dr. Griffin?" he asked.

"No," Altman answered. "I had Terry with my second wife."

"Four months after our divorce was finalized," Dr. Griffin snipped.

That explained the hostility, though the tangled web made Jamie's headache reappear. He rubbed a temple and glanced again at Dr. Altman. "Hamilton and your son are missing. Do you have any idea where they might have gone?"

"I'm sorry, no. We've only spoken a couple times since he moved out."

"Talk to Jo Ann," Jamie said to Todd. "See if she has any ideas."

"There's a string of no-tell motels out on I-45 on the way to Houston," Oscar added. "I'll make some calls and see if anyone fitting their description has checked in."

Jamie nodded and sank back in his chair, eyes closed against the intensifying headache. The pain must have shown on his face. He heard Gary's heavy footfalls and lowered voice ushering the doctors out, Dr. Griffin insisting the entire way she be kept updated on Aidan's status.

"You doing okay?" Oscar asked as he lowered into the seat next to him.

"Yeah. Head's just hurting from the feuding lab coats."

Oscar laid a hand on his back, rubbing his shoulders, and Jamie jerked away. He was deciding between an apology and an argument when chaos erupted down the hallway.

"What am I doing here? Where's my husband? Where's my partner?" Aidan's sleep and brogue-roughened voice rang out, followed by the clatter of metal. "They were in the car with me. Take me to them. Take me to them now!"

Standing faster than he should, Jamie swayed on his feet and was forced to accept a steadying hand from Oscar. Once the world stopped spinning, he hurried down the hallway and entered Aidan's room behind two nurses and a security guard. Hands out, they tried to calm his snarling partner, who was backed into a corner, holding his IV pole like a weapon.

Jamie moved in front of the nurses and guard. "Irish, calm down," he said, voice far steadier than he felt.

"Who the hell are you?" Aidan's autumn eyes were wide with bewildered terror, the whites bloodshot and the rims red from smoke and tears.

"I'm your partner," Jamie said.

"The hell you are. Tom Crane is my partner."

"Aidan, you're at UT Med in Galveston." He approached slowly, step by careful step. "I'm Jameson Walker. I work in Cyber. We're newly partnered."

"Where's Gabe? Where's Tom?"

He closed the last few steps between them and clasped Aidan's shoulder with one hand, his face with the other, bracing for impact. "They're gone. Killed in a car crash eight months ago."

"I don't understand."

"You and I were in a similar accident this morning." He ran a thumb across the matching bandage on Aidan's right temple. "Things may have gotten a little rattled in there. You're confusing our accident today with the other one, the one that killed Gabe and Tom."

Aidan blinked twice, slowly, and moisture pooled in his

eyes as the confusion cleared. "They're gone," he whispered. "They're gone, Whiskey."

Jamie breathed a sigh of relief at the same time his heart broke, glad to have pulled Aidan out of the past but hating to force him into the painful present. He glided his hand from the side of Aidan's head to the back of his neck. "I'm sorry, Irish. It's just you and me now."

This time when Aidan fell forward, Jamie caught him, wrapping him in his arms and holding tight.

NINETEEN

Aidan stared out at the ocean, inky black waves rising, falling, and crashing into the dunes as the tide rolled in under the full moon's light. Into the phone at his ear, he recited Katie's favorite bedtime story. He had memorized most of it sometime around the fiftieth read. By now, closing in on one hundred repetitions, he knew the words by heart, so most of his attention was on Walker making noise in the kitchen behind him—rustling around in the pantry, running water, clattering mugs, the whirring noise and beep of the microwave. After the day they'd had, after the horrible, black emptiness that had descended on him in the hospital, as dark and violent as the waves below, he needed the constant connection to the man moving about his condo. Since coming back to himself and the present, in Walker's arms, he hadn't let his partner out of his senses' reach.

And those senses, once restored, couldn't let go of the day's trauma. One second, he would recall the screech of tires and the smell of burned rubber as Walker swung the

Rover out of the path of the oncoming SUVs, and his head would pound with the remembered impact. The next, the ghost of Walker's lips would whisper across his own and his stomach would flip, reacting to the phantom kiss. A kiss he had forgotten those first few minutes of wakefulness in the hospital. The next, he would recall the measured sound of his partner's voice and the concerned look in his tired blue eyes as Walker coaxed him out of the corner of that hospital room, when he had been calling out for his late husband and former partner. The last, the boulder in his chest and gut as he had collapsed in Walker's arms, realizing his loved ones were gone. It was as if the past eight months had been honed into a single moment of grief and despair, drowning him under the tsunami.

The same defeat colored his voice now, despite his effort to remain upbeat for Katie. He leaned heavily against the balcony rail. The doctors had wanted to keep him in the hospital overnight, but he had insisted on sleeping in his own bed. He was still feeling it, though. He held the phone to his ear with one hand and curled the other around his neck, massaging the lingering pain just above the collar of his T-shirt.

Shuffling feet alerted him to his partner's approach and Aidan dropped his hand. Walker had removed the bandage at his temple, a bruise forming there around the gash held together by butterfly strips. His perfect façade marred just a little, but otherwise he was whole and here with him.

Walker set a mug on the wide stucco railing and laid two pills next to it, then made to retreat. Aidan shot out a hand and circled his wrist. Half on, half off the balcony, Walker looked to him for direction. Aidan wanted him closer, wanted to feel that big warm body sheltering his again, wanted that phantom kiss, the taste of life, to be real. Aidan gave a slight tug. Walker came closer at once, allowing Aidan to shift his weight from the railing to him. Aidan paused briefly in his bedtime story to Katie to take the pills and chase them with coff—*tea*—which he tried not to taste as he swallowed down the meds. He pitched the rest of the revolting liquid over the railing and Walker chuckled, the soft rumbling noise from inside his broad chest drawing Aidan closer.

Walker continued to drink from the other mug and grew warmer with each sip, the heat radiating through his tee and into Aidan's side. On the edge of his periphery, Walker's free hand flailed, but once Aidan relaxed further into him, he skimmed it up his arm and over his shoulder, around to the back of his neck where Aidan had been rubbing earlier. Digging his fingers into the knot there, Walker massaged gently enough not to do harm yet firm enough to cause the muscle to kick and release. Aidan became putty in his hands, sinking fully into him and wrapping his dangling arm around his waist. They hadn't been this close since the Tavern, and it felt just as right now as it had then.

And just as wrong, but Aidan was rapidly losing the will to fight, especially once Walker abandoned his mug on the balcony and circled him with both arms, holding him loosely until he finished the bedtime story with a whispered, "The End."

"Katie?" Aidan called for a response and hearing none, added, "Night, sweetie."

He lapsed into Gaelic as he spoke to his mother next, letting her know he was okay and that they would likely be delayed getting back. "Oíche mhaith, máthair," he finished, then ended the call and set his phone facedown on the balcony railing.

When Aidan didn't immediately move away, Walker gave him a nudge and Aidan turned fully into him, wrapping his arms around his waist and burrowing against his chest. His breath hitched, his shoulders shook, and he fought not to choke on the strangle of memories and a too reminiscent present. He shouldn't be here in another man's arms, his partner's, but he'd almost lost him—his mind, his body, his heart, before Aidan had really gotten a chance to know any. Nearly snuffed out the same way he had lost the last man he—Aidan cut off the thought before it ran further, admitting instead that if he had lost Jameson Walker today, it would've been a tragedy, any way he cut it.

Any way he lied to himself.

Walker cinched his arm around Aidan's waist and threaded his other hand through his hair, soothing him. "It's okay. I've got you."

"Today was too close. If you'd turned like I said, if you hadn't played it the way you did . . ." Aidan's words trailed off as his hold tightened, pressing his face into Walker's neck. The lingering aftershave and day-old scruff fired all his senses.

"Just doing my job."

"You did a good job, better than I did."

Walker palmed the side of his face. "We've been over this. There's nothing you could have done. Don't go back there. Leave the past where it belongs."

Easier said than done. Aidan shook his head, his gaze drifting past Walker's shoulder and out over the dark ocean. "The past was right there when I woke up in the hospital. I thought . . ."

"You were confused. It was understandable given the circumstances."

So willing to let him off the hook, but Aidan couldn't let himself off so easily. He swung his gaze back and met a strange mix of doubt and anticipation in Walker's baby blues. "Was it understandable that I kissed you?"

"Who were you kissing?"

A spear lodged in Aidan's chest. That was the last thing he expected Walker to say, the last impression he wanted to give him. When he had first come to in the car, when he had realized where and when he was, there had been only one person's life on his mind, only one person's life he had wanted so desperately to taste.

He laid his hands flat on Walker's chest. "*You*, Whiskey. I was kissing *you*." Walker's heart pounded beneath his palms, and Aidan curled his fingers into the cotton of his tee, wishing he could reach inside and feel the beating pulse of that organ, the very evidence Walker was alive and whole.

"Tell me why then," Walker said, "And I'll tell you if it's understandable."

Aidan laid the side of his face between his still-clenched hands, just above Walker's heart, listening to the steady, reassuring rhythm. "*Understandable*," he said after a moment. "Not the word I thought we'd use to describe our first kiss."

Walker's words rumbled beneath his ear. "You'd thought about it?"

Aidan chuckled without mirth. "Too damn much."

"Why then, Aidan? Why today finally?"

Fingers uncurling, he flattened his palms over Walker's now racing heart and leaned back, meeting his eyes, needing to dispel those doubts still swirling in his worried blue gaze. "Because you saved us. Because we were alive. Because I needed to remember what that felt like." He had been dead inside for months. Actually being near death had brought that fact into startling focus.

Walker pulled him back into his arms, cheek to cheek. "Understandable."

"I need . . ." The corner of his mouth brushed Walker's jaw.

"What do you need?" Walker angled his face in, more than a mere brush, noses nudging each other, mouths inches apart.

Life—big, beautiful life—and an end to the emptiness was right there for the taking.

Aidan coasted his hands up Walker's chest, coming to rest at the base of his neck, thumbs stroking his hammering pulse. "I need to feel alive again."

Walker's heartbeat kicked at the words, at the gentle caress. "Then kiss me, Talley," he whispered, and Aidan wasted no time crushing their open mouths together, his tongue diving in. He angled his head as he licked, nipped, and sucked, exploring every possible fit until he found the one that fused them together best. He hauled Walker close and wove his fingers into his silky hair, scraping his nails across Walker's scalp and eliciting a shudder.

Aidan's body reciprocated, trilling for more than just a kiss.

Reading correctly, Walker shuffled them back, pressing him against the balcony door, not hiding his body's interest. Moaning, Aidan drove a hand down his backside, grabbing his ass, and Walker answered with a powerful thrust of his hips. Heat spiraled through Aidan, aimed straight for where their cocks were grinding together, his own unleashed desire equally apparent.

Walker snaked a hand under his shirt, ran it up his abs and chest, hot and greedy, and Aidan threw his head back with a gasp. His hand on Walker's side clenched at the welcome attentions on his touch-deprived skin, but then, just as suddenly, he was left cold and bereft, the branding touch and solid weight gone.

"Are you okay?" Walker asked, voice concerned as his hands skimmed just over Aidan's clothes in a clinical manner. He must have misread the earlier reaction for pain, but the meds had dulled any aches Aidan should have been feeling while amplifying the rippling pleasure.

Aidan righted his gaze. Hoped Walker saw in it the desire riding him hard. "Don't stop, Whiskey."

A smirk hitched up one side of Walker's mouth and Aidan grabbed his shirt again, yanking him back against his body with a groan. Walker ran his tongue along Aidan's ear and nipped at the lobe. "What do you need, Irish? What do you want?"

There was only one possible answer to that complicated question. Aidan skirted a hand between them and cupped him through denim. "You, Jamie," he answered, with a slow stroke down the impressive length. "All of you."

Rocking back and grabbing him by the shoulder, Walker pulled him off the doorjamb and aimed them inside. Arms wrapped around him from behind, and Walker yanked his shirt off over his head. Aidan was usually the one calling the shots during sex, but with one of Walker's big hands grabbing greedily at his chest while the other worked his fly, he was too overcome with sensation to do anything but let his partner lead.

They kissed over his shoulder, hot, openmouthed, desperate, as they stumbled through the condo toward Walker's bedroom. They made it as far as the dining room table when one of Walker's roving hands dived inside Aidan's jeans and boxers, wrapped around his aching cock, and pulled it mercifully free. Skin caught against skin, but with one swipe across the tip, Walker had enough moisture to lessen the friction and glide smoothly, firmly, up and down. If Aidan had thought Walker's hands on his upper body had been searing, stroking his cock was enough to make him lose his mind. Lost in sensation, he lolled his head on Walker's shoulder as he rocked his hips, shoving his erection into Walker's fist while grinding his ass against his groin.

Knees going weak, he threw out a hand and clutched at one of the dining chairs for support. Walker shifted, brought his free hand down on top of his, and their entwined hands skirted off the chair to the table, slipping on papers and files until they found purchase on glass. Curling over his back, Walker kissed a path down his spine as his other hand continued to work his cock. Entranced by Walker's lips and tongue, by the steady, tortuous rhythm of his strokes, Aidan considered letting Walker jerk him off right there, but there was another emptiness growing inside him, one that demanded to be filled. He straightened and looked at Walker over his shoulder, confessing his need on a groan. "I want you inside."

Walker's eyes flashed, and for a second, Aidan thought Walker was going to take them to the floor right there. But then the haze cleared, and he licked a path up the side of Aidan's neck. "Stuff's in my room."

Pants and boxers falling, Aidan stepped out of them,

turned in Walker's arms, and claimed his mouth again, taking his turn at control and moving them where they needed to go. Walker gave way, stumbling backward as Aidan tore off his shirt and pushed him toward the bedroom. The door caught their fall, and Aidan used the opportunity to explore. He coasted his hands over that beautiful big chest he had admired in the showers the other day, his lips and teeth following in their wake, taking extra time on the interlocking *N* and *C* inked on his left pectoral.

Tattoos meant something. The Tar Heel logo was a symbol of Walker's past, inked into the skin over his heart. Whatever he'd loved and lost back then made the man here today, and Aidan gave the ink the adoration it deserved before continuing to kiss and lick down Walker's torso. He unbuttoned his pants and got a single hand in, one long stroke down his length, before Walker pushed them off the door, grabbed his kit off the dresser, and tossed it and Aidan on the bed. So much for directing this endeavor, but watching Walker kick out of his jeans and boxer briefs, seeing him stand at the side of the bed—strong, lean, fully erect, so very alive—and smiling, Aidan shivered with wicked anticipation and arched his body. "Something funny?"

Walker put a knee to the bed, spread his legs and trailed fingers up the insides of his thighs. "I have a plan for those freckles, but it'll have to wait." Before Aidan could contemplate what that meant, Walker bent at the waist and put his mouth on his cock.

All rational thought fled. "Oh God," Aidan moaned, eyes fluttering closed as his thighs tensed.

Walker held them apart as he licked up and down Aidan's length, stopping at the end each time to circle the sensitive tip with this tongue. Aidan wanted more but didn't have the words or mental capacity to string together the request. Walker, though, as they had been for weeks, was operating on the same wavelength. He checked his teeth, breathed out a hot gust that caused Aidan to shiver, then took him fully into his mouth, sealing his lips tight around his cock and sucking it deep, squeezing the tip in the back of his throat. Aidan bucked and shouted, begging for more. Always obliging, Walker slid up and down, breathing deep, tonguing the underside of the head on each pass, and adding his hand as the pace of Aidan's thrusting hips increased. So lost in the trance of pleasure, Aidan was almost past the point of no return when the other emptiness reasserted itself, demanding to be quelled.

"Stop," he gasped, repeated, and, when Walker didn't let up, reached down and raked his nails across his skull. Aidan's cock slipped from his lips with a pop.

Walker settled back on his haunches, his gaze wandering, and Aidan's body flushed under the heated stare, his cock standing at painful attention.

"What do you want, Irish?" Walker ran his hands over Aidan's hips and under his ass, lifting him into his lap and nestling his erection along Aidan's crack.

Walker knew exactly what he wanted, and *fuck,* the anticipation, the wanting, the end of the emptiness right there where Aidan needed it most was killing him.

He pressed his hips down on Walker's straining length, gliding back and forth, and Walker's head fell back on a moan. His cock swelled in Aidan's crack, and it was barely a breath before he shifted Aidan's hips off his cock and grabbed supplies out of his kit. He rolled on a condom, poured a dollop of lube in his palm, and slicked up his fingers and erection.

Aidan watched, groaning as Walker stroked himself, until he was silenced by Walker kissing him deep and his slick fingers sliding into his crease. Aidan tightened his arms around his neck. He wanted this too.

"This what you need, baby?" Walker's fingers teased Aidan's clenched hole. Aidan shoved his ass back in answer, and Walker smiled against his lips. He pressed in with a finger, and pain chased away Aidan's pleasure. "Relax," Walker whispered, petting and teasing, then trying to push back in.

Another flare of pain and Aidan tensed further. "It's been a while," he mumbled into Walker's neck.

Walker drew back and forced a meeting of eyes. "How long?"

"Eight months, twenty-seven days, three hours, give or take a few." Since his husband's death. But he didn't want to think of Gabe right now, of what he'd lost. He only wanted to think about the man in his arms, the life that had been saved, the emptiness he promised to fill.

"Why don't you top?" Walker suggested, and Aidan shook his head on the pillow.

"No. I'm so tired of feeling empty. Please, Jamie, I need you inside. I need—"

"Hush, Irish." He pressed his lips to Aidan's. "I understand. I'll give you what you need."

Walker shifted them to their sides, pulling off the condom and gathering him into his arms again. They kissed, long, slow, and the comfort pouring out of Walker was palpable. His hands roamed slower, building the burn and coaxing. When he took Aidan in his hand again, his strokes mirrored the long, slow swipes of his tongue through Aidan's mouth, devouring not in a frenzy but savoring every taste. Aidan's hands clawed and wandered too, into his hair, down his torso, and over his ass before he threw a thigh over Walker's hip to hold him close.

As they rutted together in a steady, sensual rhythm, Walker grabbed the lube again, slicked up his fingers, and made another pass at his hole. This time, after the buildup and added lubrication, there was only a moment of discomfort before Aidan's muscles gave way. Walker pressed a finger inside, caressing and searching, and pleasure took hold.

"More," Aidan begged. He arched his back and clasped their dicks in his hand, jerking them off together.

Walker added a second finger and stroked and stretched until Aidan was writhing on the edge of release. Only then did Walker pull back, and Aidan watched with panting breaths and heavy-lidded eyes as he ripped open a condom, rolled it on, and slicked his length. Pulling up his legs, Aidan spread himself, and Walker ran his hands under his ass again, lifting and positioning. Then slowly, oh so slowly, he pushed past the weakened resistance and inside Aidan, inch by tortuous inch.

At the halfway point, Aidan gasped at the impending, welcome fullness and Walker looked up from where he had buried his face in his neck. "You okay?"

"Yeah." Aidan's voice shook with the effort of staving off his orgasm, but the last thing he wanted Walker to do was stop. He curled up and claimed his mouth. "Keep going," he breathed against Walker's lips, arching his hips and leaving no option.

"Hold tight," Walker said with a grin before he thrust

deep, causing them both to shout. Seated firm, he ran one hand up Aidan's side to his shoulder, holding them steady as they picked up speed. With his other hand, he held Aidan's cock against his abs, their thrusts grinding it against the hair there and his ribbed abdomen, giving Aidan all the friction he needed.

"Oh God." Head thrown back, Aidan writhed and arched, holding on to Walker by the ass and biceps. "Harder, Whiskey." Aidan's cock swelled as Walker picked up the speed and force of his thrust. "Now, Jamie, now," he cried out.

Walker pounded inside him, nailing his prostate, and Aidan's world exploded, come spilling onto his abs and through Walker's fingers, his ass clenching around Walker's dick enough to send him careening over the edge too.

Once they caught their breaths and came back to Earth, Walker carefully slid out of him and flopped onto his back. Aidan reached for a tissue from the box on the nightstand and handed it to Walker. He rolled off the condom, wrapped it and the previous one inside, and pitched the wad of trash into the waste basket across the room.

"Nice shot," Aidan said.

"I did win two national championships." He snatched another tissue to clean up the mess on his stomach.

Aidan rolled onto his side and brushed Walker's hand and the tissue away. Ignoring the mess, he grabbed him by the hip, aligned them front to front, and threw his leg back over Walker's hip. The warmth between their bodies, the scent of their combined release, was intoxicating and he didn't want to let it go just yet.

"You're already going to hurt." Walker wrapped his

arms around him, a smile in his voice. "You fall asleep like this, and it's going to make it worse."

"I don't care," he mumbled. "I need this too."

"All right, then. You know, that's five times you've called me Jamie."

Aidan chuffed. "Of course you're counting. And it's six. You missed one." He kissed the tattoo once more and snuggled down. He had no idea where they went from here. But for tonight, he wasn't empty. He was holding life in his arms. Walker dropped a kiss in his hair and Aidan took a deep, contented breath of ocean and sex, of them, memorized it, and tucked it away so no matter what happened he would always have tonight.

TWENTY

Contrasting textures and temperatures nudged Aidan toward consciousness. Something cold and smooth rested on his hip, something warm and soft blanketed his back. He nuzzled into the heat and shifted away from the chill, chasing the blissful cocoon of sleep, until a hand covered his mouth and rocketed him awake.

Before he could strike, a big, heavy arm looped over his torso and pressed the butt of a gun into his chest. The pistol registered as familiar, as did the muscled arm and Southern drawl in his ear. "Someone's at the door."

Stilling, Aidan heard it—*scrape, scrape, scrape*—against the front lock. He rotated his head, eyeing Walker over his shoulder as he tapped two fingers against the gun. "Spare?"

"In the closet safe. Take this one." Walker handed over his weapon and rolled off the rumpled bed in the opposite direction.

Aidan dove off his side, spotted a pair of jeans on the floor, and yanked them on. He stopped to listen again.

Muffled voices, two at least, outside the front door.

He flattened himself against the wall and edged closer to the bedroom door, gun held at the ready. Walker, in nothing but gray boxer briefs, appeared out of the closet, backup weapon in hand, and assumed a similar position against the opposite wall.

The voices outside quieted and Aidan chanced a peek. A tall man stood on the other side of the glass door, an ominous figure in the early morning darkness. The stranger knelt and the lock scraping resumed. Aidan motioned for Walker to follow. Crouched low, they scurried past the dining table and hid, weapons drawn, between the barstools under the dining bar.

The lock on the front door gave with a loud click.

Familiar with their surroundings, he and Walker had the advantage in the darkness. Aidan motioned for a take-down. When the intruders pushed through the door and came around the front of the bar, they sprang from their hiding place, Aidan in the lead.

It took less than five seconds for him to wind up face-down on the floor, divested of his gun, with a knee to his back and his arms pinned behind him. The overhead lights flipped on, and Aidan lifted his head. On the floor at the far end of the bar, scattered papers and files lay next to an open briefcase. Above the mess, Walker pressed a dark-haired, suited man against the wall, his weapon trained on the back of the intruder's head.

An intruder Aidan recognized all too well, even from his awkward angle.

Face turning toward him, Danny widened his coal-black eyes, and his booming laugh filled the room. "Bro, you got taken down hard."

"Says the man pressed against a wall with a gun to his head."

"Yeah, but Jamie's a lot bigger than her."

"Her" was the sole focus of Walker's anxious gaze. He lowered his gun and backed away from Danny. The bruises on his sternum and temple and the bite mark on his tattoo were vivid on his blanched skin. "Ma'am."

Aidan didn't need to look over his shoulder to know who the "Ma'am" was pinning him to the floor. Only one woman could take him down that fast and that hard, as Danny so aptly put it. "You want to get your knee out of my back, Mel? I've got enough bruises as it is."

Snickering, she removed her knee and hauled him up, hands still clutched behind his back. His left arm ached, and the rest of his body protested yesterday's activities. All of them.

"You gonna perp walk me to my room?" he asked.

"I might need to. In case you get tangled up in Walker's jeans."

He knew what she saw. Too-long denim bunched beneath his feet, the frayed ends tickling his toes.

Danny whistled low. "Busted."

Walker's instablush tanked any chance of denial. "I'm gonna go get dressed." He avoided eye contact with everyone and cut through the kitchen and into his room.

Once the door shut, Mel spun Aidan to face her. She was impeccably dressed, as always. Not a wrinkle in her designer pantsuit, not a curl out of place, despite a late-night flight and textbook takedown. She grasped his chin and tilted his face side to side, inspecting yesterday's damage. "You want to explain?"

The injuries or the fact that he was wearing Walker's clothes. Neither was a question he intended to answer before coffee and pain pills. He needn't have bothered though, answering or holding his tongue. Mel released his chin, stepped aside, and swept the room with her assessing gaze. The answers were apparent everywhere. Melted ice packs in the sink, two bottles of pain pills on the bar, balcony doors open, abandoned mugs of tea and phone on the railing, a trail of clothes littering the path to Walker's room.

Her dark eyes, identical to Gabe's, swung back to him, and the guilt he had put out of his mind the past six hours rushed back in, closing off his throat, strangling his words, and heating his face. Her stern expression softened. "I didn't see anything."

What didn't she see, or rather, chose not to see? His betrayal of her brother, his husband? Or his and Walker's blatant disregard for Bureau expectations?

She click-clacked on mile-high heels into the kitchen, making a beeline for the coffeemaker. "Go get changed. I want a full debrief."

Grateful for the reprieve, Aidan shuffled to his room, picking up scattered clothes on his way. He had almost made a clean getaway when Danny snuck into the room behind him. "Not so fast." He closed the door and leaned back against it. "Mel might have let you off the hook, but I'm not."

"Why the hell were you picking the lock to your own condo?" Aidan deflected. He grabbed a clean pair of boxers and jeans from his suitcase and headed for the bathroom. "And why the hell are you even here?"

"I forgot my key."

"You didn't think to knock? Or ask the concierge to let

you in?" Aidan grabbed a washcloth, ran warm water over it, and wiped down his stomach, wincing as hairs came unstuck from his skin.

"Where's the fun in that? And I didn't know you were here. We thought you were still at the hospital. I suggested we get you and Jamie a change of clothes before heading over. Should've known you'd check yourself out against medical advice."

"The hospital called you?" Aidan inspected the rest of yesterday's damage, gently prodding the bruises on his head, chest, and side.

"No, Mom called me after you talked to her and Katie last night. I already had the jet ready. I was planning to personally deliver those cargo manifests."

Aidan brushed his teeth and spat, then, after rinsing the washcloth out, wiped it over his mouth and face. "I told you to stay out of this."

"When did that ever work?"

Never. Aidan didn't know why he expected it would this time. He had been the one to train Danny as the perfect accomplice. By age ten, his little brother's lock picking skills far exceeded his own.

Aidan was pulling on his jeans when the dark-haired devil appeared behind him in the mirror, blocking the bathroom exit. "Spill it."

He turned and rested against the sink, clutching the vanity's edge. "It's not going to happen again."

No matter how much he wanted it to. And after last night, he did. He wanted to run his hands through Walker's silky hair, drag them down his body, and grasp that most intimate part of him again. He wanted to drown in his lust-darkened blue eyes, his rich taste, his firm yet gentle touches. He wanted to feel that big, hard body on top of him again, and he wanted to know if the inside of Walker was as warm as the outside.

But he couldn't.

"You're allowed to move on," Danny said softly. "And there is no right or wrong time. Everyone's grief is different."

Aidan scrubbed his hands over his face. "It's only been eight months."

"Closer to nine now." Danny's hand landed on his shoulder. "See how fast time flies when you're having fun?"

Aidan smiled weakly, melancholy tempering his usual fondness for Danny's good-time antics. His reticence to start something with Walker was about more than honoring Gabe. Last night had been good. So good he had forgotten not only his husband but also the pain that came from losing something that good. Yesterday reminded him of that. So did seeing Mel. He had to shut down this thing with Walker before he wound up with another hole in his chest.

"Ai," Danny started, but then they both froze as the smell of something cooking wafted under the door. "Please, God, tell me Mel's not cooking."

Shaking off his brother's hold, Aidan shoved his feet into his flops and jerked on a T-shirt, wincing. If Mel was about to burn down the condo, he had to get out there and stop her, aches be damned. He bolted past Danny, then came to a halt in the living area. Mel sat on a stool, legs crossed, foot bouncing to some tune in her head, while Walker, dressed in jeans and a tee, stood in front of the stove.

"He cooks too, huh?" Danny jostled past and climbed

onto the stool next to Mel. "Smells good, Jamie. What're you making?"

"Sausage biscuits and gravy." Walker smiled over his shoulder, eyes snagging on Aidan before diverting to Danny. "Well, technically, biscuits and sausage gravy, but I grew up saying it out of order. Everyone says it out of order where I'm from. It'll be ready in a few."

Walker was rambling, uncharacteristically nervous. For someone who didn't like attention, he had garnered all the wrong kind this morning, from his boss no less. Aidan wanted to make it better, but he was confused enough as to his own feelings. Under the watchful eyes of Mel and Danny, he settled for fixing their coffees instead.

"So, boys," Mel said, "you want to tell me exactly what trouble you've been getting up to?" Her gaze bounced around to each of them.

Danny raised his hands in mock surrender. "I'm just the hapless accomplice."

"Hapless my ass."

He stretched an arm over the back of Mel's chair and tilted toward her. "And a mighty fine ass it is, Ms. Cruz."

She leaned into his space, forcing him to lever back. "That's Agent Cruz to you, gringo, and if you don't watch it, I'll take you to the floor too."

"Is that a promise, chica?"

Mel rolled her eyes and Aidan and Walker laughed, Danny's ribbing breaking the heavy tension. Aidan finished fixing coffees, popped open their pill bottles, and tapped out two for himself and three for Walker. He placed a mug and pills on the counter next to the stove and got a thankful smile for his efforts. He downed his own, then set mugs in front of Danny and Mel.

Once everyone was caffeinated, Aidan launched into his debrief, filling Mel in on the case and events leading to yesterday morning's accident, Walker adding technical details as needed. Midway through, Walker set a basket of biscuits, a big pot of sausage gravy, and four plates on the clean end of the table. Without having to be told, the rest of them moved to the table, following the enticing aromas. Aidan and Walker finished bringing their boss up to speed, pausing frequently to eat the first good meal either of them had had since Monday night.

"And what does the civilian have to do with this?" Mel asked, side-eyeing Danny.

"My brother has a contact at the Port who provided certain information. Speaking of"—he turned to Danny—"you mentioned manifests."

"Ah, yes, the hapless civilian being useful." Smirking at Mel, Danny retrieved three bulging pocket files from the mess still on the floor at the far end of the bar. He dropped the first one in front of Walker. "The list of ships docked at the Port during each breach." He pushed the second across the table to Aidan. "Manifests for the commercial ships on Walker's list." He handed the last file to Mel. "High-value targets currently at or coming into the Port this week. Pulled that one together myself."

"Look at you being the self-starter." Aidan riffled through the manifests in his folder. He stopped when he reached a commercial vessel whose point of origin was Morocco. "It's all here." He placed the alarming manifest in the center of the table. "All the parts for a biological dirty bomb, minus the toxin."

Danny pointed at the departure date on the manifest. "That ship's gone."

"So the bomb parts were moved off."

"But not out of the Port," Walker said. "The hacks on GNL are twofold—to remove a biological agent and to draw first responders away from the Port."

"The Port's the target." Mel slapped down another piece of paper, her red nails pointing at two entries. "Luxury liners scheduled to dock this afternoon. Two thousand plus passengers each. Combined with the Port workers, the number of casualties would be huge."

"Maximum loss of life, no responders," Walker said. "It'd be the biggest terrorist attack on American soil since 9/11."

"We don't have the time or manpower to search all the containers and ships at the Port, and no one there is going to help us," Aidan said. "They closed up tight when we went in last time and all our evidence was ruined in the crash."

"Not to mention they tried to kill you in that crash," Mel said.

Aidan saw the shudder Walker failed to suppress.

"We need to keep you two out of sight as long as possible," Mel added.

"Use the civilian," Danny chimed in.

Aidan furiously shook his head. "No fucking way."

"They're used to seeing me around."

"You don't think they can connect one Talley to another, especially that union rep?"

"I'll avoid him and Marge. As for the rest, you were accompanied by a very attractive, very distracting former basketball star, and name aside, we look nothing alike."

Mel tossed aside her file. "He's got you there. On both counts."

Aidan stewed in silent concession. There was no denying the distracting power of Jameson Walker, having fallen victim to it himself, nor that Danny, with his black eyes, black hair, and freckle-free skin, looked nothing like Aidan.

"I'll go with him," Mel said. "They don't know me."

"As my assistant," Danny suggested way too cheerfully.

"If by *assistant* you mean the brains of the operation that keeps your ass in line," she shot back. "We need to take this to Gary."

"Don't." They were finally getting to the topic Aidan had dreaded. Gary was Mel's friend, but someone on his team was conspiring with terrorists. "There's a mole in his shop, and I won't put either of you in jeopardy. This stays between the four of us for now."

"Fine," Mel said after a long, atypically indecisive moment. "But if you get even a whiff of an attack in progress, you converge on the Port with all the manpower you can muster. Can you narrow down the who or the what we're looking for?"

"We know the who already. Eric Hamilton and Terry Altman. We'll get you the rest."

Aidan ducked into the observation room on the other side of the two-way mirror from where Walker and Torres were questioning Jo Ann Richmond.

"Anything yet?" he asked Gary, who stood in front of the glass.

Gary removed his cowboy hat, tossed it on one of the chairs behind them, and wiped his brow. Nine in the morning and the AC was already struggling against the blazing late summer heat outside. "Just getting started. You get everything settled with Detective Helms?"

"I told him what I remembered, which I gathered from his scowl was less than Walker."

"Sorry I couldn't spare you that. He was waiting for us to unlock the doors this morning."

"He's just doing his job."

"You didn't recognize the drivers or the SUVs at all?"

"Like Walker said, the drivers were disguised, and the vehicles were generic. Helms said the plates turned up stolen. They're checking dental records against the bodies."

Gary made a stumped "Hmm" sound, and Aidan returned his attention to the other room. Torres was still going over introductory questions with Jo Ann, who had forestalled questioning yesterday by requesting an attorney. She didn't look any more comforted today by the public defender sitting by her side.

Walker sat relaxed at the short end of the table, his suit jacket open, shiny black shoe resting on his knee. Other than the bandaged cut at his hairline and the lines that appeared around his eyes and mouth if he moved too quickly, he showed no signs of yesterday's roller coaster.

None of it.

But out of sight didn't translate to out of Aidan's mind. While Walker's light blue dress shirt covered most of his bruises, including the one Aidan left in the center of his tattoo, Aidan could still taste the lingering salt of his skin, could still feel the remembered heat of him and the phantom touch of those powerful hands.

Stop it.

Even if thinking of Walker that way didn't feel like a

betrayal of Gabe's memory, there was no getting over the insurmountable fear of loss keeping Aidan from making any romantic attachments. He refused to go through that again. If being afraid kept him safe, so be it.

"You're afraid of Eric?" Walker's question, his use of the very word in the forefront of Aidan's mind, brought him back to the present. Walker leaned forward, voice calm and soothing. "We can help you, Jo Ann. You don't need to be afraid anymore." He expertly coaxed their suspect, and Aidan felt like he was being coaxed too.

The slight, haggard-looking blond cowered on the other side of the table, her green eyes locked on Walker like he was her last hope. "If I confess to hacking GNL . . ."

"You don't have to confess to anything, Ms. Richmond," the attorney said.

Walker ignored the interruption. "There will be consequences, but if you help us find Eric and Terry, we can recommend those consequences be minimized."

She bit her bottom lip, wavering, and Walker nodded encouragingly. She looked to the attorney. "Is he telling the truth? Will my sentence be reduced?"

"Most likely, yes, we'll be able to work out a deal."

She looked back at Walker and took a deep breath. "What do you want to know?"

"You and Eric were foster siblings, is that right?"

"Yes, in New Orleans."

"So he knew who you really were? Who Emily was?"

She nodded. "Emily and Eric dated in high school before he left for the military."

"When did you first see Eric here in Galveston?"

"I've been dating Terry off and on for a while. About three months ago, we went back to his place after a date. He wanted to show me his new apartment and introduce me to his roommate."

"Eric Hamilton," Torres supplied.

Of course.

Hamilton wasn't just a dockworker and former EOD specialist. He was a trained mercenary. He did his research, knew Terry had ties to GNL and dated Jo Ann. He could leverage them both. They were his way in.

"Eric said if I didn't help him, GNL and the authorities would find out what I'd done, that I'd stolen Emily's identity."

There had to be more. She could hack her way out of those offenses, if necessary. What else was she holding back?

"Was that all Eric threatened?" Walker asked, following the same train of thought.

Jo Ann swiped at the tears leaking from her eyes. "He said he'd tell our foster family where to find me."

By the twisted look on her face, half anger, half shame, Aidan didn't need to hear more.

Torres asked anyways. "What happened with your last foster family?"

"He . . ." She paused and took another deep breath. "My last foster father took liberties. With all of us. Even after I moved on campus, he would show up at my dorm and at school. He used to call at all hours of the night. He wouldn't leave me alone."

"So Emily died in a boating accident after your senior year at Tulane, and you assumed her identity in order to disappear?"

"And to take care of Dad. I mean Emily's dad, Dale. He's the only real parent I've ever had. He didn't have anyone left and neither did I. We were all we had left," she said, crying in earnest now.

Torres snagged a box of tissues from the credenza behind them. They waited for Jo Ann to pull herself together before Walker asked, "Did Eric or Terry tell you what the purpose of the hacks were? What you were after?"

"All they told me was which locks to hit and when to hit them. They wanted me to time how long I was in the system before I got booted out."

"Response times," Aidan said to Gary.

"Seems so," the other agent replied.

"There was a hack yesterday morning, Jo Ann," Torres said. "Did you set that one to run in advance?"

"The last one I ran was Sunday afternoon, before I came on shift."

"How were you getting into the system without being flagged?"

"I piggybacked in on someone else's login. Once inside, I used a randomly generated IP address."

"But you had to have already laid a groundwork of openings. Did you do that with your own login?" Walker asked, and Aidan recalled the unusual network activity Kevin had spotted.

Jo Ann nodded.

Walker leaned forward. "Did Eric or Terry ever give you any indication that they intended to remove a biological agent or toxin from GNL?"

"That was the odd thing. Terry would rattle off toxins from time to time, but Eric was always more concerned with timing and how long I was in the system."

A terrible theory formed in Aidan's mind. One he and Walker, with Mel and Danny, had touched on that morning.

Now, with Jo Ann's responses, the idea became frighteningly concrete. He tapped twice on the glass and waited for Walker and Torres to excuse themselves and join him and Gary in the observation room.

"The bomb's already there," he said, the instant the door closed behind them.

"But they only accessed the materials cabinet yesterday," Gary said. "Dr. Altman reported nothing missing. They don't have everything for a bioweapon."

Aidan shook his head. "Diversion." He still didn't know who on Gary's team was the mole, but the time for withholding information had passed. He had to follow Mel's orders. "This morning, we received cargo manifests for the ships in dock during each hack. We were looking for parts for a biological dirty bomb, and they were all there."

"Except the toxin," Gary reiterated.

"They don't need it," Walker said, catching on. "Put those existing bomb materials together with explosives already on-site at the Port, and you've still got a deadly explosive."

"Exactly," Aidan said.

Barnes burst into the crowded room. "We finally got Hamilton's discharge papers." He handed each of them a file folder, and Aidan skimmed through the papers as Agent Hipster continued to speak. "Hamilton was suspected of selling arms to local warlords and other known arms dealers. Never proven, so they didn't charge him, but it was enough to get him discharged. One of the parties he's suspected of dealing with is Pierre Renaud, a French émigré residing in Morocco, who Interpol believes is linked to terrorist attacks in Europe and North Africa."

Aidan flipped back to the photo he had passed several

pages ago. A color shot of a white male with green eyes and white-blond hair, standing in what looked like a North African or Middle Eastern bazaar. Taller than anyone around him, Renaud stuck out like a sore thumb, but he stood with a nothing-can-touch-me air of confidence that came from power and money. Lots of both. Usually obtained illegally.

"Six months ago," Barnes said, "Hamilton received three million dollars, routed through a Swiss bank and deposited in a Caymans account Walker tagged."

"Origin?" Aidan asked. "Any more deposits?"

"Origin still unknown. As for additional deposits, three million was deposited on the day of the first hack and another four million was deposited less than an hour ago."

Ten million total.

Aidan would lay even money on the attack occurring today.

And he had sent his best friend and brother in alone.

"We've got a team on-site at the Port," he told Gary. "We'll have them see if they can find anything on Renaud there. In the meantime, we need to get backup, evac, and search teams out there right away. Call Helms, get everyone you can. I'll run it on the ground, you run it here."

"We're on it." Gary grabbed his hat and headed for the door. "Torres, Barnes, with me."

Barnes moved to follow, but Walker grabbed him by the arm. "Were there any payments out of Hamilton's account?"

"Yes, transfers were made out of Hamilton's account to two others. We assume those belong to Terry and Jo Ann, as Hamilton's accomplices. We're running those down."

Walker signaled Aidan to wait and followed Barnes out

the door. He slipped back into the interrogation room and sat across from Jo Ann. Aidan watched from the other side of the glass.

"Jo Ann, just one more question. Did Terry or Eric pay you for helping them?"

Tears filled her eyes again. "They didn't have to. The threats were enough."

Walker covered her hand with his. "Thank you, Jo Ann. You've been a big help to this investigation." She smiled through her tears, the Walker charm working its magic. He waited for two officers to arrive to escort her back to holding before he stepped back into the observation room.

"That other account isn't Jo Ann's."

"No, it's not," Aidan agreed. "It's for Hamilton's other inside man. The one here."

TWENTY-ONE

Jamie poked his head out the observation room door and checked that the hallway was clear. Confirmed, he closed the door and turned his attention back to his partner. "Wanted to be sure we didn't have any eavesdroppers or interruptions."

Aidan paced the room's narrow length, his fingers twitching for an invisible pen. "Do you think Torres is the inside man?"

Barely avoiding a collision, Jamie skirted past his partner and collapsed into one of the chairs along the back wall. Elbows resting on his knees, hands hanging loose between them, he considered Aidan's question. All clues pointed to Oscar—the computer skills, the shoddy police work, the waiting private sector job. But in his gut, Jamie didn't think Oscar was their guy.

"I don't think so."

Aidan nodded. "Torres is off the table, then."

"You're just going to accept that?"

"Your instincts are good, Whiskey."

Before Jamie could object to the weight of their investigation resting on his fledgling field instincts, Aidan claimed the seat one over from him and pulled out his phone. He tapped the screen a few times, then laid the phone on the chair between them, speaker on, ringing Cruz.

"What've you got for me?" she answered.

"Are you on-site?" Aidan asked.

"If by on-site you mean watching Don Juan Danny cozy up to some twenty-year-old blond bombshell, then yes."

Aidan chuckled. "He has a type."

"Tú también, hermano."

Aidan's laughter died, and Jamie didn't need four years of college Spanish to know that last bit was about him. Cruz hadn't said a word to him this morning about the Bureau's position on fraternization, despite the mountain of evidence at the condo that that was exactly what he and Aidan had engaged in. Jamie wanted to know what she might have said to Aidan, but there had been no opportunity to ask his partner about that or about where they stood after last night. Aidan had been on the phone with the field office the entire drive in, and it had been nonstop chaos since they'd arrived.

Because there was a bomb at the Port.

That was the bomb Jamie needed to focus on. Not the one that had exploded last night. But Cruz's muttered Spanish had thrown him right back there. To the nagging doubts that had kept him up long after Aidan had drifted off into dreamland. His mind had whirled with the implications of what they had done. Disregarding Bureau policy, complicating their partnership, exposing them to potential scandal, possibly pushing Aidan into something he wasn't ready for. Something Jamie might not be ready for either. Not to mention the injuries they'd ignored.

At the same time, he had known deep down what Aidan had needed last night, same as him. They had needed to feel alive, spared from what could have been another tragedy in both their lives. But what troubled Jamie the most was that they had been so good together—fit so perfectly, moved so seamlessly, felt so right. Did Aidan feel the same way? Or had he been a stand-in for someone Aidan wanted and could no longer have? Someone Jamie shared certain similarities with? Jamie didn't think so. Aidan had called out *his* name in the throes of passion. But there was no denying both he and Gabe were tall, well-built, athletic, good with numbers—Aidan's *type*—and Cruz was in a better position than anyone to recognize it.

But she wasn't lingering on the matter, so neither would he. "Give me something to go on," she said. "I've got a lot of ships and containers and not a lot of help here."

Jamie put aside his internal conflict and turned to the very real one staring them down. "We've got a name," he said. "Pierre Renaud. We're working on specifics."

"Aidan, get that backup down here. Now." Cruz's voice was more commanding than normal, and beneath the order lay the leading edge of alarm. Jamie wondered if that name meant something to her.

"In motion. Gary's coordinating backup, search, and evac as we speak. We're likely dealing with straight-up triggered explosives. Not a bioweapon."

"GNL was a diversion, on both fronts," Jamie added, per their conversation that morning. "They were never after a bioweapon. They've got everything they need at the Port already."

"Shit!" Her one word cracked like a whip, sharp and strident. "Backup, Aidan, now." The pace of her high heels striking metal increased, reverberating over the line. She was running somewhere.

"Mel, take care of my brother," Aidan said, not hiding the fear in his voice.

"I won't let anything happen to him."

"Don't let anything happen to you either."

"Not planning on it."

She hung up and Aidan ran a hand over his face, his chest rising and falling rapidly.

Jamie brushed the backs of his fingers down his arm. He didn't know if this was okay, but the need to comfort won out. "They'll be fine, Irish."

Terrified eyes met his, and Jamie was torn in two. Half of him ached that Aidan was in such turmoil while the other half rejoiced that Aidan had let him see it, let him help carry the burden, even if only for a minute. Warmth flowed between them, through their locked gazes and through cotton and wool, Jamie's hand still on his arm, until Aidan blinked slowly and reopened clear, focused eyes.

It was a masterful demonstration of self-control.

"All right, then," Jamie said as he drew back and stood. "Let's go."

Aidan clasped his wrist. "You're not going anywhere."

"Are you going to the Port?"

Rising next to him, Aidan pocketed the phone with one hand while the other remained wrapped around Jamie's wrist, nothing but heat in his touch and his answer. "Yes."

"I don't follow. I'm your partner. I'm going with you."

"I need you here, Jamie."

Jamie saw red and didn't check his words or his spiteful tone. "Oh, so that's how it's gonna be? Trot out the 'Jamie' whenever you want something?"

Hurt flashed in Aidan's eyes, and on its heels the same terror he had moments ago driven away. Terror for his loved ones caught in the crosshairs, and that was when Jamie got it.

He wrenched his arm free and stepped back. "You want me out of the line of fire."

Aidan's control slipped its leash a little more. "Whiskey," he whispered hoarsely.

"This is my job. I can protect myself and I can protect you. We're partners. Do not leave me behind."

Eyes slipping shut, Aidan turned his face away and Jamie saw the effort it took to gather his control again. He cleared his throat and returned determined eyes to him. "You can do your job, Agent Walker, by finding the missing hacker. They have the potential to disrupt our entire operation. I want you and Torres here with Gary." Aidan closed the distance between them and lowered his voice. "I need someone I trust running point, and right now, that's you and the two people I already have out in the field. No one else."

Aidan's words, his arguments, were belied by the hands he laid over Jamie's beating heart. *Alive,* he had said last night. Aidan needed him alive.

Well, he needed Aidan alive too. "This is bullshit."

"I know you don't like it, but I need you to trust me."

Jamie clenched his jaw, biting back a retort.

Aidan unfastened the gold and emerald cuff links,

reached for Jamie's hand, and dropped them in his palm. "For Katie, if anything happens."

Jamie glanced down at the sparkling clovers in his hand, then back up at his partner, whose autumn eyes hid nothing now. Fear, resolve, desire, and something more Jamie didn't want to put a word to for all the complications those four letters could bring.

More than all those things, though, Aidan regarded him with trust.

Trust that Jamie would cover his back and his heart, and the only way he could do that was to stay at the field office.

"Fuck, Irish." Jamie fisted the cuff links and curled his other hand around Aidan's neck, slamming their mouths and bodies together.

It was desperate, it was messy, and it was the best kiss of Jamie's life.

He memorized Aidan's coffee-infused taste, the rough slide of his tongue, and the silky press of his lips. Aidan's hands tangled in his hair and clenched in his shirt, his lithe, hard body aligned perfectly with his own. And somewhere in the middle of the too brief kiss, Jamie understood Aidan's decision. He'd had this once before and he'd lost it. Jamie couldn't blame him for not wanting to lose the promise of it again.

Reluctantly breaking the kiss, Jamie rested his forehead against Aidan's. "I'll stay."

A gust of warm breath rushed over his lips. "Thank you."

"Come back to me."

Aidan's cuff links weighed heavy in Jamie's pocket as he split his attention three ways between the back trace of yesterday morning's hack, bank account records, and the operation in progress at the Port. Gary was in his office, ordering the cruise ship companies to divert their vessels, while Jamie and Oscar ran comms from the conference room. Not an easy task considering the number of law enforcement teams bearing down on the Port, including Aidan and Todd's mobile command unit.

There were other agents in the conference room as well —recruiting emergency responders from nearby counties, putting local hospitals on alert for explosion victims, harassing Swiss and Cayman bankers for account information. From the speaker on the phone in the center of the conference table, Jamie heard similar activity on his partner's end.

Since they didn't know the exact size of the explosive or its blast radius, certain emergency personnel were held farther back while search teams, including Aidan's, assembled in the well-positioned bank parking lot they had used for their stakeout. All teams would gather and organize there before converging on the Port. By doing so, Aidan was buying Mel and Danny and him and Oscar time to pinpoint the location of the bomb.

"You find anything in those manifests yet?" Jamie asked Oscar.

They were reviewing manifests of docked ships and associated storage lots, searching for connections to Renaud. Anything that might tell them precisely what they were dealing with or where Hamilton might have assembled the explosive.

Oscar made a few quick keystrokes, and a map of the Port and its storage lots appeared on the screen at the end of the conference room. Jamie swiveled in his chair and rolled closer to get a better look. Red crosses marked five different locations dotted the Port's acreage. "I've narrowed it down to these lots," Oscar said. "Containers in these five areas originated from cities where Interpol reports Renaud has a base of operations."

Jamie glanced over his shoulder. "Cities?"

Oscar nodded. "Yes, plural, and this is no guarantee. Renaud could have paid anyone for access to their containers or lots, but he probably has closer contacts in places where he regularly conducts business."

Jamie gave the map a final glance, then spun back around and rolled into place beside Oscar. "Something's better than nothing." He pulled the speakerphone closer, shouting Aidan's name to get his attention on the other end. Together with Oscar, they brought him up to speed on the potential locations.

"Good work," he said. "We'll move on those locations first unless we hear otherwise from Mel. Teams are assembling. Will confirm when we're on the move."

Aidan's voice drifted away, his attention diverted to something Todd was saying about EMS teams. Jamie sank back in his chair, a giant knot forming in his gut. He hated being here while Aidan was out there. Granted, he could monitor all the operation's moving parts from here while continuing to hunt for the missing piece that would foil this entire plot, but it felt like he was supposed to be somewhere else.

As if hearing his thoughts, Oscar asked, "Why aren't you out there?"

"Aidan wanted someone he trusted running point, and I'm more useful doing this." He skimmed his fingers over his keyboard.

Oscar's rapid keystrokes ceased, and he angled toward him. Jamie expected Oscar's knee to rub against his under the table, but no unwanted touch came and their bubble of silence in an ocean of noise grew heavy. So heavy Jamie was forced to look up and meet Oscar's gaze.

"I would have done the same thing," he said.

"Left me behind?"

"Kept you alive." He smiled softly—genuine—not his usual overly flirtatious self. "The world—*his* world—is a better place with you in it, Jamie. I wouldn't risk you either. And he's right; you're far more valuable here."

Raw and exposed, Jamie hunched over his computer and sought comfort in the numbers and lines of code streaming across his screen. It took a few minutes to focus and realize what he was seeing. The simple elegance of the designs Dave Fuller had shown him and Aidan the other day at GNL. The designs Dave used to teach his crypto class at the local community college.

"Excuse me a moment."

In the hallway, he withdrew his phone, scrolled to Dave's number, and dialed. While Dave had been cleared of any wrongdoing, one of his students could be their missing hacker. Oscar, Jamie recalled, had done two years at the community college before transferring to UT.

"Agent Walker," Dave greeted. "I hear we're out of the woods here."

"GNL, yes, the Port, no. There could still be another breach. The persons behind this are attempting to divert emergency responders from the Port, but we don't think anyone's actually trying to take biological agents out of GNL."

"Thank heavens."

"Stay vigilant, though. With the Port operation going on, we won't have extra hands to help you shut down any intrusions."

"I've got Jake and Mike here with me."

"That's good," Jamie said. "Dave, I'm calling about that list of your top crypto students. Did you get clearance to send it over yet?"

"As a matter of fact, I just got off the phone with the dean. Give me a second and I'll email it." The tap of keystrokes was followed by the whoosh of sent email. "On its way."

Jamie checked his inbox, which, after two forced pushes, brought up Dave's email. "I've got it. Thank you. We'll be in touch."

Quickly scanning, he didn't see Oscar's name anywhere on the list. Starting from the top again, he read more slowly, and his breath caught at the fifth name down.

Gary Clark.

Gary Clark, who was absent right now and, thinking back, had been absent during each other breach. Gary Clark, who let Oscar bear the brunt of their suspicion. Gary Clark, SAC of the FBI's Texas City Field Office, who had more than enough juice to threaten Port employees into silence and pressure Terry and Jo Ann into assisting Hamilton.

Jamie closed his email and dialed his partner.

"What've you got?" Aidan answered.

"Step out of the van." Jamie didn't want any of the other agents to overhear their conversation.

"I'll be right back," he heard Aidan tell Todd, followed by the *click* and *thunk* of heavy van doors. The sirens and shouted commands of the staging area filtered over the line before things quieted, indicating Aidan had found someplace relatively private. "What's going on?"

"I'm looking at Dave Fuller's list of his top crypto students."

"That finally came through. Torres on it?"

"No, but Gary Clark is."

"You're kidding me."

"Afraid not." Half a second later, the intrusion alarm on Jamie's phone blared.

"Shit, he's inside the system again." Jamie spun on his heel toward the conference room and was brought up short by the business end of a Glock 22.

"No, I'm right here." Gary stood ten feet away, right arm raised, gun pointed at Jamie, center mass. "You're too late, Agent Walker. It's already in motion. The cruise ships are pulling into dock, EMS is too far away, and the bomb is set to blow. Now, put the phone down."

"I can't do that."

"Then I'll put you down."

Jamie couldn't say which was louder—the gunfire that erupted or Aidan's screams from the phone in his hand.

He twisted just in time, the phone clattering to the floor as Gary's bullet whizzed past his shoulder and lodged in the plastered wall behind him, sending chunks of concrete flying. On its heel, the report of a second shot and more flying plaster. Gun arm wavering, a streak of red bloomed on the outside of Gary's right shoulder, bleeding through his sweat-stained dress shirt. Hunched over, he clasped his arm, and Oscar stood behind him with his weapon raised, his tan face pale and lined in shocked anger. Before he could say anything, though, Gary straightened and lurched forward, lifting his gun arm again and firing off another round.

Jamie ducked his head and narrowly missed the second bullet. "Aim high!" he shouted at Oscar. Gary was a potential source of critical information; they needed to stop him without killing him. Jamie rushed forward, colliding with Gary's midsection. Another shot jolted the older man's upper body, a direct hit to the shoulder, and Jamie rocketed up, sending Gary tumbling over his back. Spinning, Jamie came down on top of Gary, a knee to his back and a forearm across his shoulder blades, but not before Gary managed to get his left arm free and with it, his gun. Despite the awkward grip, Gary moved to lift his arm and Jamie pressed his elbow into his wounded shoulder, causing the raised shooting arm to fall.

"Get his gun," Jamie hollered.

Oscar slammed a booted foot down on Gary's forearm and knocked the gun loose. He kicked the weapon out of reach. "Clear."

Jamie levered up, grabbing Gary's limp arm and yanking it behind him with the other one. He held out a hand as Gary struggled and howled in pain. "Cuffs." One of the other agents who'd flooded into the hallway tossed Jamie a pair. He clicked the metal around Gary's wrists and hauled him up. "Say hello to our missing hacker."

"How could you?" Oscar demanded of his boss.

Jamie spun Gary around and shoved him back against the crumbling plaster. "Where's the bomb?"

"I'm only talking to Cruz," Gary gritted out between clenched teeth.

"No, you're talkin' to me," Jamie said, getting in his face. "Where's the fucking bomb?"

The SAC's lips remained sealed even as the pupils in his milky blue eyes dilated in pain. Out of patience, Jamie shoved the heel of his hand into Gary's bleeding shoulder. The red spot beneath his palm spread wider as Gary's skin turned ghostly pale.

Still no answer.

Jamie pressed harder.

"I don't know!" Gary finally gasped. "I don't know. He never told me."

"He who?"

"Hamilton."

"You took your orders from him?"

"Yes. No one else."

"And you know nothing about the bomb?"

Gary shook his head, eyes growing increasingly hazy. "I was responsible for diverting EMS resources and making sure the ships docked."

"And keeping people quiet?"

"Yes. But that's all, I swear."

Jamie yanked Gary off the wall and shoved him into Oscar's hands, not trusting the turncoat agent to anyone else. "Put him in interrogation. Keep pressure on the wound and get a medic to look at it." Jamie wiped his bloody palm off on his pant leg and patted his pocket to make sure Aidan's cuff links hadn't fallen out in the scuffle. "No communication with anyone else. Two guards on the door. Got it?"

Oscar nodded as another agent handed Jamie his phone. A panicked, tinny "Jamie!" screeched through the speaker.

"So much for keeping you safe," Oscar said, before turning and leading Gary away.

After a deep breath, Jamie lifted the phone to his ear. "I'm here, Irish."

TWENTY-TWO

One gunshot. A second on its heels. Or was that an echo of the first? The crack of Walker's phone hitting the floor. Shouting, a struggle, another gunshot, followed by a jumble of muffled grunts and indistinguishable voices.

Fuck!

Aidan burst around the side of their mobile command center, fear and adrenaline coursing through him. Feet pounding the cement parking lot, he paid no mind to the curious eyes watching him pace or the sirens wailing around their staging area.

"Jamie!" he yelled into the phone. Sweat poured down his face and under his dress shirt and flak jacket. "Goddammit, Whiskey, answer me! Jamie!"

His stomach roiled, his heart hammered, his mind revolted as he waited the longest two minutes of his life. Two minutes in which he cursed himself for leaving his partner behind, thinking it would keep him safe when it might have gotten him killed. Two minutes in which he replayed every smile, touch, and kiss from Jameson Walker over the past three weeks, remembering what it had felt like to be alive again. Two minutes in which he bargained with God and any other deity that would listen to let Walker live.

"Agent Talley?" said an unfamiliar voice.

"Where the fuck is my partner?"

"Subduing SAC Clark."

"Tell me he's all right."

The line went muffled, and Aidan shouted "Jamie!" into the phone, fearing the worst, sure the firefight had erupted again. But then that deep, Southern drawl he had grown so fond of came over the line. "I'm here, Irish."

Knees going weak, Aidan steadied himself with a hand to the side of the van. "Oh, thank God. Are you okay?"

"I'm fine."

Aidan turned his face into his outstretched arm, hiding the emotion there. "Jamie, I thought . . ."

"I know, baby, but we don't have time right now." A soft endearment followed by a firm reminder that today was bigger than the two of them.

Proving his point, Walker's voice faded as he spoke away from the phone. "Get on the horn and tell any EMS crews en route to GNL to reverse and head back to the Port."

When he came back, Walker was all business. "Aidan, everything is in motion, including the docking cruise ships and ticking bomb. Gary doesn't know where the latter is. You need to move on the five locations Oscar provided. I'll be running point from here."

Jamie hung up, leaving Aidan bereft, the brief conversation hardly enough to quell the panic that had consumed him, but then a flare went up over the Port, red and thunderous, and the haze of fear cleared. He had given Mel that flare gun and told her to fire it in the air if she and Danny found the bomb.

"Barnes!" he barked, as he climbed back into the van. "We've got a location. Let's move."

They pulled their vehicles to the Port's main entrance and unloaded, not waiting for their foreman escort. Law enforcement teams fanned out, jogging down the rows of containers and moving into position. Aidan, on point, hustled his team toward the flare's location.

A commotion could be heard several container rows ahead—a crash of metal, the thud of bodies hitting aluminum, grunts and curses, gunfire.

Aidan and his team sprinted the final ten feet, then held on the other side of the corner of the aisle where the noise had come. Once Barnes radioed that his team was in position at the other end of the row, Aidan gave the go-ahead signal, and they rounded the corner, guns drawn.

"FBI!" rang the chorus of shouts.

The aisle was littered with downed bodies, including a writhing Terry, and Mel stood in the middle of them, engaged in hand-to-hand combat with Hamilton. She landed a roundhouse kick to the merc's head that sent him reeling, and Aidan lowered his weapon, thinking the fight was over. Until Hamilton suddenly righted himself with a blade in hand. He swiped it in a sharp, upward motion, slicing through Mel's jacket sleeve before she could jerk out of his reach.

"Hold!" Aidan bellowed, not wanting anyone to take a shot that might hit Mel.

She and Hamilton parried back and forth, jabs and hooks, the knife glinting in the sun, and Aidan struggled to get a lock on Hamilton. Finally, Mel caught Hamilton's arm at the elbow, out of the knife's reach, and swung him so his back was to Aidan. "Fire!" she shouted.

Aidan took the shot, nailing the merc in the middle of his back. The bigger man stumbled forward, knife still slashing, and Mel spun behind him, wrapping both arms around his neck.

"Did you get my picture?" Hamilton said, as he raised the knife again and took deadly aim behind him. Mel wrenched his neck to the side, the crack audible. His lifeless body crumpled to the ground at her feet.

Mel leaned over and pressed two fingers to Hamilton's neck, checking his pulse.

Danny's low whistle drew Aidan's attention to his brother, who had popped out from behind a stack of crates, the flare gun in his hand. "Damn, woman."

Mel ignored him and turned her attention to the officers behind Aidan. "Get these men out of here." She gestured to the confirmed-dead Hamilton and the rest of his injured crew.

"Where's the bomb?" Aidan asked.

Mel pointed at the container behind him. "Hamilton swallowed the key."

"Someone get a set of bolt cutters," Barnes hollered.

"That's my cue." Hopping into action, Danny handed the flare gun to Aidan, shuffled past him, and took a lock pick set out of his jacket pocket. Thirty seconds later, the heavy door swung open to reveal barrels of explosives, intricately wired with C-4 and multiple trigger devices. A laptop sat atop the bomb, attached to a countdown clock displaying three minutes.

Three minutes—180 seconds—wasn't nearly enough

time. Aidan had thought the two minutes on the phone earlier, listening to Walker fight for his life, was the worst his day could get. Now his own mortality, and that of his best friend and brother, and anyone else in the blast radius, was three very short minutes away.

Mel stepped inside the container, using the flashlight on her phone to inspect the deadly contraption. "There are too many redundancies for me to cut in the time we've got."

Aidan's stomach hit the floor and his hand clutched his phone like a lifeline.

A lifeline.

A half-court Hail Mary.

Could one of the best shooters he knew beat the buzzer?

Aidan whipped out his phone.

"Walker," his partner answered.

"I'm looking at a very big bomb that Mel can't defuse in the two minutes forty-five seconds the counter says we have left until we're blown to bits."

"There's an electronic device controlling it?"

"Laptop," he said, then struggled to hear Walker's reply as Mel shouted behind him for everyone to clear out. "What was that?"

"Put me on speaker," Walker said, after which his voice came across loud and clear. "Reach into the front right pocket of your flak jacket."

Aidan yanked up the Velcro flap and pulled out a cable he hadn't put there. Walker, with those better-than-average field instincts, thinking ahead.

"Plug the one end of that cable into your phone and the other into the computer."

Following orders, Aidan gasped, almost dropping the phone, when it took on a life of its own. Or rather, not its own. Someone else had taken it over. Just like with his email.

"Did you hack my phone?"

"Hush, Irish."

Walker's answer was given distractedly—Aidan could hear his fingers flying across a keyboard—but those words, the same ones he had used last night when Aidan had been on desperation's edge, calmed him now as they had then. He set the phone and its dizzying matrix of screens next to the computer and turned to survey the scene. Everyone had followed Mel's orders and cleared out, except the one person who didn't take orders from her. The one person Aidan wanted gone the most.

Danny.

Aidan's tenuous calm snapped.

He grabbed his brother by the lapels of his suit jacket and shoved him against the aluminum side of the container. "Why the fuck are you still here?"

"Because you're here." Danny shrugged as if it was the most obvious answer in the world. And it was. Aidan would have done the same thing, were their roles reversed. "Not leaving you, bro."

Walker's voice called from the phone, and Aidan didn't have time to be angry anymore. He kissed Danny's forehead, then turned back to the computer and phone. "I'm here. I'm here," he said, with a glance at the countdown clock. "It's still counting down. Forty-five seconds left."

Their lives ticking away by the second . . .

"I'm going to give you a code to manually enter, and you need to press Enter at the same time Cruz cuts the redundancy wire that would be last in the sequence. Can she locate that one?"

Mel circled the device and crouched at its right side. "Got it. Danny, you have something in the pick set to cut with?"

Danny tossed her the tool she needed and came to stand next to Aidan.

"All right, Whiskey, go."

He punched in each number and letter as Walker rattled them off, and at the end, with five seconds left, his brother by his side, his boss and sister-in-law waiting for the go-ahead, he gave her a nod and pressed Enter as she sliced through the wire.

They held their breaths.

Four seconds.

Three seconds.

Two—

The clock stopped. The device powered down completely.

Danny collapsed against Aidan's side, Mel sank to her knees, and Aidan ran a hand down his face in relief.

"Aidan! Aidan! What's happening?" Walker called frantically from the phone. "Baby, say something!"

He picked up the lifeline, switched it off speaker, and held it to his ear. "Nice shot."

Sometime between the takedown at the Port and their return to the field office, Mel had changed into a different wrinkle-free suit and wrangled her curls into a bun at her neck. Despite her outward composure, Aidan knew her well enough to realize she had been shaken.

"You want to talk about it?" he asked, low enough that

anyone on the other side of the observation glass wouldn't hear them. They sat next to each other in the interrogation room, waiting for Torres to bring in Gary. Aidan didn't expect they had an audience yet—Walker and Barnes were interrogating Terry, and Torres had texted that the doctor was finishing up with Gary—but Mel showed weakness to only a select few and he wouldn't risk that trust.

"Talk about what?"

"Oh, let's see"—Aidan ticked off their day from hell on his fingers—"our near death by bomb, your near death by mercenary, Walker's near death by SAC, said SAC's betrayal."

Mel laid her phone screen-down on the table and slid back in her seat, one leg crossed over the other. "Not our best day ever." She tapped a manicured nail on her knee, that tell of hers sneaking past her defenses.

"Far from it." Aidan shifted in his chair toward her. "What picture was Hamilton talking about? And why'd you kill him?"

She flinched. So tiny a motion an average person wouldn't notice it. But as accustomed as Aidan was to her grace and deliberate movements, the tiny jerk amounted to an earthquake.

"Mel—"

She held up a hand to silence him. "I killed him because he was cornered. He wouldn't stop until someone took him down."

"Death by cop."

"I chose to minimize any further loss of life. As for the picture . . ." She grabbed her phone off the table, tapped it a few times, then handed it over. Onscreen was a black-and-white photo of him and Walker on the condo balcony, lips locked and bodies tangled.

Aidan handed the phone back and kept his posture casual and his voice level. "There's nothing here you hadn't guessed at already." From the clothes scattered around the condo that morning, to the bite mark on Walker's chest, to the shouted *Jamie* and *baby* on the phone that afternoon, Hamilton's picture could not have been news to her.

She turned the display off and set the phone back down on the table. "I still don't want the confirmation."

"I know it flies in the face of Bureau recommendations."

Dark eyes pinned him and silenced his further explanation. "This isn't about Bureau policy." Her voice hadn't risen, and her dismissal hadn't been delivered in condemnation or anger. Rather, her gaze and words were concerned and sympathetic.

"Is it about Gabe?"

She turned her face away, taking a long, deep breath, and Aidan was sure that was it. Familiar guilt slammed into him, at Mel having to see that picture and at himself for betraying her brother's memory, but before he could go under completely, she put a hand on his arm, keeping him above water.

"It's not about Gabe. It's about you, Aidan." Her fingers tightened around his arm. "My brother's death was unexpected. Neither of us could have predicted that accident knowing what we knew then. Tom's death hurt too, but he was an FBI agent. It was always a possibility. And Jamie is an FBI agent too. A damn good one who, after this week, I have no reservations promoting to full field agent status."

Aidan sucked in a choked breath. "Which means his life will be in danger every time we go out there." He braced his elbows on his knees and hung his head, running his hands over his face and into his hair. He knew all this, had been including it in his litany of reasons why not to start something with Walker, but hearing it spoken aloud by his best friend, by his boss who understood the daily dangers they faced better than anyone, brought it into startling focus.

Mel rubbed his shoulder. "I couldn't pick a better man for you. Jamie's smart, loyal, decent, but he's got a target on his back, same as you."

Aidan tilted his head to meet her gaze. "But you partnered us."

"For those very same reasons. He'll make a terrific partner, and he gives us an advantage in our other investigation. But before this thing with you and him becomes anything more than that"—she nodded at the phone—"you need to think long and hard about how much you're willing to risk, and possibly lose, again."

Before he could respond, two firm knocks sounded against the door. Aidan straightened and, with a sharp shake of his head, focused on the man Torres led into the room. The former SAC appeared pale and deflated, a larger-than-life figure reduced to a tired old man with his casted arm in a sling.

"Leave us," Mel ordered Torres as Gary took the seat across from them.

"Agent Cruz—"

"SAC Cruz," she corrected. "And I said leave us."

Torres had the good sense to listen to her the second time and left the room without further protest. Gary fidgeted in his chair, bouncing his bad arm in its cradle against his chest and swiping the other across his forehead. Mel waited for him to settle then asked, "Why?"

Gary's bloodshot eyes darted from Mel to Aidan, then back to Mel. "I only want to talk to you."

Aidan had expected this. Walker had told them about Gary's demand when they had debriefed after returning from the Port. Walker had managed to get some additional information out of Gary right after their skirmish, but since being put in custody, the SAC hadn't said a word to anyone.

Mel, however, was not in the mood to do him any favors. "Aidan's my number two and lead on this investigation. You'll talk to both of us."

He hesitated, eyes locked with Mel's, then his gaze dropped, and he seemed to shrink in on himself, looking utterly defeated. "Addy's dying," he said hoarsely.

"Addy?" Aidan asked.

"Addison, his wife." Mel uncrossed her legs and tilted forward. She didn't reach for Gary's hands, but the instinct was there. They were friends, and she must have also met and liked Addy. "Since when, Gary?"

He swallowed hard and looked up, tears pooling in his eyes. "She was diagnosed four months ago. Cancer, the aggressive kind. They gave her nine months, a year at most."

"And Hamilton knew about your wife's condition?" Aidan asked.

He nodded.

"It can't have been the hospital bills." Mel shot down the leverage Aidan's mind had instantly conjured. "Between the salary and pension here and your share of the profits from your family's ranch, you make plenty."

"Not enough for the experimental treatment we found. We're mortgaged to the hilt and still came up short."

"Until Hamilton offered you a few million," Aidan said, and Gary nodded again. "Did you ever have contact with Renaud?"

Mel opened the file folder she had brought in, removed the picture of Renaud, and pushed it in front of Gary. He'd already seen it when Barnes had first briefed them on the suspected terrorist, but Gary picked it up again and examined it at length. "I've never seen him. Hamilton was my only point of contact."

"And the full extent of your orders?" Aidan asked.

"As I told Walker, to keep Jo Ann in line and provide backup on the breaches, to make sure the cruise ships docked and the EMS crews were diverted, and to keep the Port crews silent, though Hamilton took care of most of the Port stuff himself. I just showed up and rattled cages from time to time."

Mel took the photo back and tucked it in the file. "All those lives almost lost, for one."

Gary shrugged, resigned and beaten. "She's my wife. Forty years. I'd do anything to save her."

Aidan knew that feeling all too well. If there'd been a way he could have prevented Gabe's death—his murder—he would have given it serious consideration. Before his mind went down the rabbit hole of what-ifs, two taps sounded on the one-way mirror behind him. He and Mel excused themselves and entered the observation room where Walker waited.

"When did you get here?" Aidan asked, momentarily panicked that Walker might have overheard his and Mel's conversation before Gary entered.

"I stepped in after Oscar stepped out. I take it you didn't know about his wife being sick?"

Mel stared through the two-way glass at her friend and colleague who had conspired with terrorists and nearly succeeded in killing thousands of people. "Last time I saw Addison was six months ago at a conference. She seemed fine." She turned and rested against the window ledge. "When he called to request you, he didn't mention it."

"Explains the erratic bank account." Walker handed them both copies of a bank account ledger, then claimed one of the chairs.

Aidan removed his coat and took the seat next to him, reading over the ledger, immediately struck by the large sums going in and out. "Did you ask him about this before?"

"I only found this account an hour ago. Don't forget, Gary was on Dave's list of top crypto students. He'd hid this slush account pretty deep."

Something else on the ledger caught Aidan's attention. "These transactions date back before Gary's involvement with Hamilton."

Walker hesitated, and Aidan looked up to see his blue eyes on their boss.

"Go ahead and say it," she replied to his silent question.

"Gary's been on the take for years, turning a blind eye to illegal activities at the Port. He kept his hush money in this account. It was just shy of a million when Hamilton's first deposit hit. He transferred out most of it the next day."

"Expensive treatment." Mel glanced over her shoulder and Aidan's gaze followed, seeing Torres lead Gary away by his good arm. "But he loved her more than anything."

A chill raced up Aidan's spine. "Can you tie the deposits

from Hamilton back to Renaud?" he asked, ignoring the disquieting unease.

Walker rested his elbows on his knees. "Eventually, but it's going to take time and some not-so-nice conversations with bankers to follow it all back to the source, assuming I keep it on the up-and-up."

"Priority one when you get back to San Francisco," Mel ordered. "And don't tell me how you get the answers. Just get them."

"So I guess I'm not getting reassigned to Texas City?"

Aidan tried and failed to hide his grin.

"I have no plans to let you go, Agent Walker."

"Why did Gary request us on this case?"

"He knew about you," she said to Walker. "Most of the FBI higher-ups do. He had Jo Ann under his thumb, but if he expected her to crack, he needed another door into GNL's security network."

Walker hung his head. "And I gave it to him."

"No." Mel pushed off the wall and took the seat on the other side of Walker. "You gave it to Torres, who didn't think twice when his boss asked for the security protocols to make sure you weren't the inside man."

Aidan reclined with a groan, letting his head fall back and staring up at the ceiling. "So Torres suspected Walker, while we suspected him."

"Gary played everyone, including me, and I'm sorry for involving you two." After a moment, Mel asked Walker, "How was Terry involved?"

"He was in it for the money. And to get back at his father. Hamilton had convinced him they would pin it on his old man. Of course, he was never given any specifics and didn't ask for them either. He seemed as surprised as we were about the bomb already on-site. He thought they were going to take one of the toxins out of GNL for a dirty bomb."

"Hamilton covered his bases. Everyone had a different story, he had leverage on them all, and he took the truth with him to his grave."

"We're back to square one, then," Walker said.

Aidan laid a hand on his arm. "You stopped a bomb from blowing up two ships full of people. I'd say that's better than square one."

The smile on his partner's face did not reach his tired blue eyes.

"We're done here," Mel said, and the three of them stood. "Go home, take the rest of the week off, and we'll reconvene on Monday."

"Should we book a ticket for you?" Aidan asked.

"No, I'm going to be a few days. I need to finish processing Gary. I don't trust anyone else here with it. And I've got a lift already."

"Oh, that's my cue again." Danny appeared in the doorway with a lascivious smile.

"How come you get to ride home on the private jet?" Aidan huffed at her.

She winked as Danny slung an arm over his shoulders. "Don't ask questions you don't want the answers to, big bro."

Everyone laughed, including Aidan. While he didn't want to think about what his brother and Mel would get up to on the plane, he couldn't help but be thankful for a night off before traveling.

Handshakes between Danny and Walker were exchanged, and his partner mentioned finishing paperwork to process Terry before following Mel out, leaving Aidan and Danny in the observation room alone.

Aidan crossed his arms and leaned a shoulder against one side of the glass frame. "You want to tell me what's going on with you and my sister-in-law?"

Danny mirrored his position on the other side. "It's just a wee bit o' fun."

"That didn't look like 'just a wee bit o' fun' to me."

"You and I have different definitions of *fun*, bro. Maybe you should try mine out again, *baby*," he added with a smirk.

Of course Danny hadn't missed that agonized shout from Walker over the phone. Gary, Torres, and half of Galveston's EMS responders had also heard him screaming Walker's name in terror. He didn't think anything could have been worse than that gut drop in the car accident yesterday morning but waiting helplessly on the other end of the line, knowing he might have sent Walker to his death, beat it, hands down. And then his own brush with death . . . Mel was right to caution him.

He ran a hand over the back of his neck, eyes slipping shut. "When I listened over the line to my partner almost get killed, it felt like losing Gabe all over again. That terror, being helpless to stop it . . . We were lucky today, Danny. We might not be so lucky in the future, and I can't go through that again."

"*Fun.*" Danny dropped the keys to the Benz in his palm. "Just think about it."

Aidan couldn't deny the past eight months had been miserable, and he was no good at being lonely. He had a liquor cabinet full of half-empties and a memory full of fairy tales to prove it. Could he have a bit of fun and avoid the fear of loss that came with attachment?

"Don't think too hard." Laughing, Danny kissed the side of his head and headed out.

Grabbing his coat from the chair, Aidan turned to do the same when Barnes and Torres crowded the doorway.

Barnes stepped forward, hand extended. "Agent Talley, it was a pleasure working with you."

Aidan took the offered hand, smiling. Agent Hipster was all right. "Same, Todd." Barnes's perpetually worried look gave way to a bright smile. "Sorry I was so hard on you."

"I was happy for the opportunity to learn from the best."

From anyone else, Aidan would have written off the brownnosed comment, but from Barnes, it was genuine. "You find yourself in San Francisco, be sure to stop by and visit us."

"Thank you, sir."

"I think Walker wanted to run a few follow-up matters by you," Aidan said, and Barnes nodded, scurrying out the door after another round of handshakes.

Torres remained, leaned back against the wall.

"Agent Torres," Aidan said. "I'm sorry we were unwittingly on the other side of this thing the past week. I hope you understand why the ruse was necessary on our end."

Torres looked contemplative, not angry, as he considered him with assessing eyes. "I understand, but just so *you* know, I didn't buy it for a second."

"That Walker was somehow involved?"

"That you and Walker were fighting and that he had any real interest in me."

"Well then, you played your part much better than us."

"My interest wasn't a ruse. I genuinely wanted to sleep with your partner. Still do. But it's obvious he has no interest in me."

Had it really been obvious? It sure as hell hadn't felt that way at times, the jealousy sinister and choking on more than one occasion.

"He's all yours, Agent Talley." No handshakes, no back pats, only a nod of acknowledgement before he left the room.

And left Aidan's head spinning.

TWENTY-THREE

They should have taken the last flight out instead of waiting until morning. Jamie would gladly surrender the past hour he had spent soaking in the oversize tub or the California king bed calling his name if it meant escaping the suffocating tension between him and Aidan. It couldn't be cut, not by the condo walls or the blinding light of the gleaming bathroom. His partner's dark mood surrounded Jamie, as if the summer sea breeze had carried it through the open balcony doors and into his room. Under the heavy weight of it, Jamie sank further into the swirling, lukewarm bathwater.

The past thirty-six hours had been hell, but both times on the phone that morning—once with his life in danger, the other Aidan's—there had been something there. Something they hadn't put words to but had been said all the same. Jamie had begun to hope. Maybe the warning signs had been wrong. Maybe this thing with Aidan *could* be something more. But then Aidan had shut down, saying exactly fifteen words to him since they had left the field office.

"We'll fly out tomorrow morning," as Jamie had merged the convertible, top down, onto the interstate, the roar of rush hour traffic making further conversation impossible.

"Dinner's in the fridge," after they had returned to the condo.

"Be packed and ready at six," before Aidan had disappeared into his room with half a bottle of Maker's Mark.

Since then, not another word or glimpse of Aidan, just the sound of the shower running several hours ago. Jamie had padded around the condo for a while, popping his pain pills and eating two of the sandwiches the concierge had stocked in the refrigerator. Hoping to draw out his partner, he had loudly ripped into a package of Oreos, played a few games of *Destiny* on the Xbox, and opened the balcony doors to the living area and his bedroom.

Aidan's door remained closed.

After packing up their scattered files and notepads, the computers, and his suitcase, Jamie had finally succumbed to the lure of the whirlpool tub. The jetted soak was long overdue—sleepless nights, injuries and long days in the Texas sun had worn his body down—but ten shriveled fingers and toes later, he was no closer to relaxed.

He lifted an arm out of the water to remove the washcloth from his eyes when suddenly the light filtering through it vanished. On alert after a week of surprises, he snatched the cloth off his face and grabbed the bar of soap from the holder, ready to hurl it if necessary.

"Easy, Whiskey." Aidan stood in the shaft of moonlight streaming through the skylights, his shoulder against the doorjamb, dressed in tattered jeans and a thin white undershirt. Judging by the curled ends of his hair and the quarter bottle of whiskey dangling from his fingertips, he had been drinking outside on the balcony awhile before wandering down to Jamie's open door.

Jamie placed the bar of soap back in its resting spot and slapped the button to turn off the whirlpool jets. He resumed his reclined position—legs outstretched, knees barely breaking the water's surface—and extended an arm. "I'll take a shot of that."

Surprise flashed in Aidan's eyes. "You don't drink."

"I do."

Aidan raised a brow.

"On special occasions. This is one of them."

A hint of a smile turned up the corners of Aidan's mouth as he pushed off the door and ambled forward. He passed the bottle to Jamie, toed over the thick woven bath-mat, and sat with his back against the tub and his arms spread along the marble's edge.

Jamie nearly drowned in the overwhelming desire to run his fingers through the curls at Aidan's neck or over the freckled skin that was a shade darker than the marble. He settled for drowning in bourbon instead, taking a healthy swallow from the bottle. Liquid fire hit his tongue, then mellowed into something sweet and smooth. It warmed his insides, calmed him, but the peace was short-lived.

Aidan began bouncing one knee and tapping out a matching rhythm with his thumbs. Jamie leaned forward and placed a hand over Aidan's, stilling its motion. Aidan whipped his head to the side, gaze clashing with his, a strange mix of guilt and anxiety swirling in his night-dark-ened eyes. Tension rushed back in between them, and Jamie retreated, giving him space.

"What's got you so worked up?"

Aidan gave a short, humorless laugh. "You lived the same horrible day I did, right?"

"The special occasion I mentioned earlier." He took another swig of the bourbon and passed the bottle back.

Aidan turned it over in his hands. "For some reason, the whiskey's not doing the trick tonight." He set the bottle aside and rotated more fully around, folding his arms on the tub's edge. The look on his tired, drawn face said he was waiting for Jamie to work out the obvious.

Jamie just wanted a straight answer. No more doublespeak. "Why not?"

Eyes darkening, Aidan tilted toward him. "What would you do," he said, voice rough and rumbling, "if you'd already lost the love of your life, only to find a second chance at something—maybe love, you're not sure yet—and before you can even wrap your head around the idea, that second chance is almost snatched away? Not once but twice."

Jamie drew unsteady breaths, the full meaning of Aidan's words sinking in. He had never imagined Aidan's feelings were so close to his own. Given the past year's losses, Aidan had to be hanging on by a razor-thin thread after the accident yesterday and today's near misses.

"I'm sorry this is so hard," he whispered.

Aidan held his gaze a moment longer, then picked up the bottle, swallowed the rest of the whiskey in one gulp, and shot to his feet. Jamie feared he was going to leave, but he tossed the empty in the trashcan and crossed to the vanity instead. He palmed the gold and emerald cuff links Jamie had left there, turning them over several times before setting them back on the vanity. He braced his hands against the counter, straightened his arms and hung his head between them. "It is what it is."

Jamie rose, not thinking twice about his actions or his state of dripping undress. Needing to comfort this tortured man and fully prepared to drown, he stepped out of the tub and laid his wet hands on Aidan's back. "Irish," he said, imparting the nickname with all the need and longing Aidan's *Whiskey* had carried last night.

Aidan was on him the next instant. Spinning, he slammed them against the wall at the end of the vanity, trapping Jamie between smooth, cold marble and a hard, hot body. "Fucking hell, Whiskey," he gritted out between clenched teeth. "What are you doing to me?"

Jamie saw in Aidan's stormy gaze the battle his heart and mind were waging, but his partner's taut, vibrating body indicated victory was there for the taking. Jamie entered the war. He ducked his head beneath Aidan's chin and inhaled the combined scents of whiskey and salt, tasting the same heady mixture as he blazed a line of open-mouthed kisses up his neck, returning the sensory overload Aidan had bestowed on him last night.

Aidan shivered, his arms tensing where they were braced on either side of Jamie's head. Gliding his hands down Aidan's torso, Jamie snuck them under his damp shirt, seeking the warm skin underneath. "I need . . ."

Aidan's breath grew shallow. "What do you need?"

So many things. But right then, all he wanted was Aidan on him, in him, connected, gunfire and bombs be damned. "You remember what you said to me last night?" he murmured behind Aidan's ear, lips dragging over pin-prickled flesh.

"That I needed to feel alive."

Jamie flattened a hand over Aidan's chest. His partner's heart pounded beneath his palm, racing in time with the waking beast in his own chest. "You need that assurance again. So do I."

Aidan tangled in his fingers in Jamie's wet hair and tugged him back, forcing him to meet Aidan's desperate, heated gaze. "I can't promise you anything. I can't get attached."

"I'm not looking for promises. I don't need commitments." Jamie lowered a hand between them, palming Aidan's erection through his jeans. "I just need you."

Whatever had been holding his partner back evaporated.

Aidan's lips crashed onto his, and Jamie was pulled under, just like he had been on the balcony last night. Moaning, he opened his mouth and Aidan's tongue darted inside, tangling with his own. Jamie welcomed the invasion. There was nothing like Aidan's taste—complicated layers of light and dark, just like the man himself.

His legs went weak at the onslaught of sensation, and Aidan caught him, sliding hands over his bare behind, fingers leaving bruises as he hauled him up against his straining erection. Aidan's growl reverberated against his lips and echoed off the marble walls, sending all Jamie's blood rushing straight to his dick.

In a very Cruz-like move, Aidan had him off the wall and on the floor in the blink of an eye. It was a much gentler descent, his face-up landing cushioned by the plush bathmat at his back. Jamie laughed nonetheless. "There's a perfectly good bed right out there." He tilted his head toward the bedroom, even as he worked furiously on undoing Aidan's fly.

Straddling his hips, Aidan reached both hands behind his head, grabbed the back collar of his shirt, and yanked it off. Unable to resist the temptation of skin, Jamie ran his hands up the hot, taut muscles that had tortured him for the better part of three years, none worse than the past twenty-four hours of remembering the smooth, hard expanse of them.

Aidan smirked and pushed him back to the floor with his hands and mouth. "And there's a perfectly good rug right here."

Jamie grinned against his lips, and Aidan answered with a sharp thrust of his hips, the rough denim wreaking havoc on Jamie's already frayed control. Craving more, he raced his hands down Aidan's back and inside the waistband of his boxers. He raked his short nails up the backs of Aidan's thighs and over his ass, leaving one hand behind to tease his crack and dragging the other forward to grasp his erection. He was so entranced by the feel of Aidan in his hand, by the taste of his lips, by the rocking motion of his hips, that he could have kept going right there until they came.

Two strokes later, though, Aidan wrenched out of the intimate hold and stood. Jamie's heart crashed into his chest, and his stomach plummeted. He darted his gaze to Aidan's, expecting to see guilt and regret painted there, but all he saw was hunger. The same hunger raging inside him.

He shifted to get up. "Bed now?"

A size twelve foot came down on his chest, holding him in place. "What've you got against the floor?"

If Aidan wanted to play this game, Jamie was more than happy to give him a run for his money. Wrapping his fingers around Aidan's ankle, he gave it a slow caress before sliding his hand inside denim and stroking Aidan's firm calf. "You're not on it with me anymore."

Goosebumps rippled under Jamie's hand, and Aidan groaned, his eyes slipping shut as his head fell back. "Ten seconds, Whiskey." His voice was tortured and full of that Irish brogue Jamie couldn't get enough of. "Give me ten seconds to get rid of these goddamn pants and grab a condom and lube."

Jamie swiped his fingers over the back of Aidan's knee, provoking a full body shudder. "Why didn't you say so?"

Growling, Aidan didn't give him time to pull his hand out before dropping his boxers and jeans, leaving Jamie tangled in silk and denim. He tossed them aside as Aidan riffled through his kit on the vanity.

It was closer to fifteen seconds by the time Aidan returned to the floor, kneeling between Jamie's legs. Repaying the earlier torture, Aidan stroked his cock, long and slow, circling his thumb over the head, before diving lower and cradling his balls. Bending, he teased his nipples with teeth and tongue, and Jamie, out of his mind with frustrated need, let loose a string of curses that would make a sailor blush. He yanked Aidan up by the neck, smashing their lips together once more. Aidan's free hand climbed his torso, nails digging in where the tattoo was inked across his pec.

"I need you, Irish," Jamie breathed against his lips. Truer words had never been spoken. He had never wanted anyone this badly in his life. "Now," he pleaded.

"I want a taste first."

"A taste?"

He lost Aidan's mouth, the warm wetness rambling down his neck and his chest. When those kiss-swollen lips closed around his cock, Jamie flailed, scrabbling for purchase on sheets that weren't there, fingertips slipping instead on cold, hard marble. He finally caught the lip of the tub with one hand, Aidan's hair with the other, and anchored himself against the building waves.

His own groans reverberated off the walls, echoing in his ears, an erratic counter rhythm to his galloping heart, as Aidan blissfully tormented him to within an inch of climax. In control where he hadn't been last night, Aidan was masterful, his tongue doing mind-blowing things to his cock, his fingers teasing everywhere else. By the time Aidan slapped his thigh with a grunted, "Over," Jamie was primed, hard as a rock, and beyond ready to take him inside.

Front pressed to the bathroom rug, he lifted his ass in invitation as Aidan's hands skirted down his sides, hot and branding, and Jamie wanted to be owned, completely. Aidan seated his cock against him, steel sliding along his crease as their bodies rutted together, an imitation of things to come.

"Inside, baby," Jamie begged.

The heat at his back disappeared and he glanced over his shoulder. Aidan sat on his haunches, tearing into the condom, rolling it on, and coating his cock with lube.

Jamie licked his lips. "You are the sexiest thing I've ever seen."

Aidan crawled over him, placing one hand on the rug next to his and palming his ass with the other. "You're not so bad yourself." He draped himself over his back, impossibly hotter, impossibly slicker. "You want it slow and sweet or fast and hard?"

Even stretched and lubed, the latter option would hurt

as it'd been months, but Jamie was too worked up to care. Fast and hard sounded perfect. "Give it to me, Talley." He lifted his ass higher and rammed back, making his choice clear.

His partner obliged, lining up and thrusting into him. Jamie stifled his cry with his fist, biting into his knuckles until the pain gave way to pleasure, the exquisite clench of taut muscles around Aidan's cock. Their bodies settled into the intimate embrace, fitting seamlessly together again. They rocked back and forth, their rhythm in sync, just as they had been the past few weeks.

They hadn't needed to find this. It simply existed.

Jamie reached an arm back to grasp Aidan's hip, keeping him close and the strokes rough, short, and hard. He rocked his hips counter to Aidan's, building friction as he drove inside him. As their movements quickened, the strokes becoming erratic, Aidan reached around and fisted his cock, pumping in time with their pitching hips.

Stimulated inside and out, surrounded by everything he could want and need, Jamie's release washed over him, spiking when Aidan bit the nape of his neck and planted himself deep inside, coming with a muffled growl. He tightened his fingers on Aidan's side, holding him buried as they splayed out on the floor, panting together, the smell of sweat and come with a hint of the ocean everywhere around them. Jamie didn't think he had ever felt anything so right before.

A minute, five, maybe fifteen later—Jamie wasn't sure—Aidan pulled out and rolled off him. Flopping over, Jamie lay on his back and watched his partner move around the bathroom—pitching the condom, washing up, and pulling on his boxers. It was some view, and by the leer on Aidan's face, he knew it.

"Bed now." Aidan held out a hand. "I think we've had enough of the bathroom floor for one evening."

"Now who's the hater," Jamie grumbled in mock protest as Aidan pulled him up. He was barely vertical when Aidan snaked a hand around his neck and brought their mouths together for another searing kiss.

And then he was gone, leaving Jamie alone in the bathroom, dizzy and breathless. He steadied himself against the vanity, then splashed cold water on his face, cleaned up, and dragged on his boxer briefs. He waited by the bed for Aidan, who returned from the living area with a glass of whiskey and a glass of water. Jamie grabbed the water and downed it in one gulp. Aidan drained the other, took the glass out of Jamie's hand, and set both tumblers on the bedside table.

Jamie gracelessly fell into bed, a mass of tired, sated limbs, while Aidan shut the balcony doors and turned off lights. A moment later, the bed dipped, and he eased in beside him, throwing an arm around his chest and a leg over his thigh. Jamie laid a hand over Aidan's where it rested on his tattoo.

Warm breath tickled his neck. "No promises, Whiskey. We have fun, we enjoy each other, we keep it casual and quiet," Aidan whispered, voice low and seductive. He punctuated his proposal with a kiss just below Jamie's ear, his tongue darting out to tease skin ever so briefly. Jamie's body shuddered, hard. "Can you do that?"

"Yeah," he gasped breathlessly. "I can do that."

Aidan grinned against his neck and relaxed into his side, his breaths evening out in sleep. Jamie struggled to do the same, his body on board with slumber but his mind and heart disobliging. This didn't feel casual. This didn't feel unattached. This felt like something a whole lot more. Closing his eyes, his stomach knotted, his chest clenched, and he couldn't help but wonder if he'd told Aidan a lie.

TWENTY-FOUR

Aidan had hoped the late summer heat would break by the time he returned from Texas. No such luck. Early morning and it was eighty already. They'd be pushing triple digits by midafternoon.

Leaving his sunglasses on, he carefully lifted the stack of prickly roses off the passenger seat, checked the side-view mirror for passing vehicles; seeing none, he shoved open the car door. He hustled across the street and between the stone pillars that marked the entrance of the grounds. The brown-hued grass crunched beneath his feet, the lawn having been watered enough for maintenance and fire safety but not enough to keep it green this late in the season. Except where Aidan was headed, beneath the large oak tree in the far corner, its dense foliage filtering the sun's rays and keeping the grass a little greener.

"I'm sorry I missed our date last weekend." He knelt and brushed aside the hearty lantana that drew butterflies to the man who had loved them so, who had filled their own yard with flowering plants that attracted and nurtured the delicate creatures. Aidan ran his hand over the simple bronze headstone that marked his husband's final resting place.

Gabriel Cruz
Beloved Husband, Brother, Son
El amor sigue con vida
Love lives on

The Talleys had made sure of it, welcoming Gabe here too, next to the headstone that marked Sean's memorial, among what would eventually be more Talleys, including Aidan. He leaned to the left and passed a hand over his brother's headstone. "Thanks for that secret, big bro. Saved mine and Danny's ass." He lay one of the roses atop Sean's memorial before angling back toward Gabe's. For the catch-up he had missed while in Galveston. Missed because he was back at work.

"I know, I know," he said, imagining Gabe's dark eyes rolling at what should have been a nonevent but which to Aidan had felt like an insurmountable challenge eight months ago. "Back to the regularly scheduled program."

He dipped his chin, nose drawn by the sweet-smelling roses. "Your babies are blooming." When they'd bought the house in Redwood City, the bed of roses out front had been in a sad state of affairs. Three stumps of dead bushes and one lone purple floribunda struggling to survive. Gabe had nursed and babied that one bush back to health; she was now the tallest among others in white, peach, pink, and red that Gabe had planted and cared for, which Aidan now babied in his stead. "They're almost as tall as Mom now." He laid the colorful bouquet on Gabe's grave. All except the purple rose, which Aidan kept to twirl in the absence of his pens. He shifted to sitting, his back to the tree and his legs out in front of him, his usual position for these gossip fests.

More like a confessional today. "Fair warning," he said, "I might have rewound a little far in the program. You're probably not going to like what you see."

He winced at the *You're better than that* in Gabe's voice in his head.

"Yes, yes, I know." Hell, he hated what he'd said already. He had also typed then erased cancellation texts half a dozen times for the dates with others he had lined up for this week, but the alternative—ditching those dates and spending all his time with a certain blue-eyed baller turned Cyber agent—was terrifying.

Why? phantom Gabe asked.

"Running scared about covers it." He twirled the rose between his fingers, smiling as he remembered Walker picking up his habits and doing the same with his pens in Galveston. Remembered watching his partner's brilliant brain work as he had sorted through evidence and pieced together theories. "He's amazing, Gabe. Smart, funny, gorgeous, tenacious, a protective streak a mile wide. This accent that just . . ." He bit his lip, recalling too that honeyed Southern drawl in all its variations. Rough with lust was Aidan's favorite, followed closely by gentle and patient, the voice Walker had used to coax him back from the edge of anxiety on the balcony that night after the accident and from the edge of despair at the Tavern the night before they'd left for Galveston. In those moments, when Aidan was mired in fear and past heartache, Walker's voice was like the best cup of hot coffee on the foggiest San Francisco morning. "Makes me weak in the knees."

He smiled. "Yes, I know, I've still got a marshmallow center."

Gabe used to lovingly pick at him for being a softy under the three-piece suits, never more so than when they were with Katie. It was Gabe's favorite taunt when they were on the court together. "He played ball too," Aidan told him as he closed his eyes and relaxed against the tree. "You'd like him. Probably better than you like me."

The mental image of Gabe, arms crossed, brow raised, a smirk he was fighting, flashed behind Aidan's eyelids. "No, I don't like him better than you." He shook his head and muttered in exasperation, "Fucking competitive athletes. I like him different."

The other brow raised, and Aidan's eyes popped open at the word that flitted through his head in both their voices.

"Love." His harsh laugh startled a butterfly that had landed on the delicate peach polka. The painted lady flew aerials a couple times before relighting on the lantana. "Little early for that."

He closed his eyes again and confessed the truth, something he had never been able to keep from Gabe. "But I could. When I thought I'd lost him after that accident . . ." His chest ached as the film reel replayed in his head—blood trickling down the side of Walker's head, the seat belt snapping and his big body collapsing, the hazy blues that had struggled to focus. Aidan lifted the rose to his nose and inhaled deep, recentering himself in the here and now.

"I like him different, but I can't let it be love." He swallowed hard around the truth lumped in his throat. "Because if I lost him, it would hurt like it did when I lost you."

They sat in silence, in the truth, for several long minutes

until Aidan's vibrating phone reminded him of one of those dates he was going to be late for if he didn't get a move on. "Danny said to have fun, so that's what I'm going to do. I'm gonna be like a s'more, all burned and crusty on the outside."

He laughed, knowing what Gabe's response would be.

"Yes, I'll probably fail at keeping the marshmallow from leaking out, but I'm going to try." He breathed in the floribunda's sweet fragrance one more time, then moved back beside the headstone. "Maybe don't watch this part."

Tears pricked the corners of his eyes as he laid the last rose—Gabe's favorite—with the others. "I could never look away from you either. Love you, baby."

He spread his fingers over the name of the last man he had loved. Of the only man he could let himself love because living without that man, without the love of his life . . . Fuck, it still hurt. He wouldn't survive that loss a second time.

TWENTY-FIVE

Jamie barely escaped a paper airplane to the forehead, spinning left in his office chair as the folded paper sailed between his computer monitors. Glancing the direction the distraction had come, he spied a bigger one at the opening of the cave's bullpen. Dressed in a navy three-piece and silver tie, Aidan leaned against a server rack, a file folder tucked under his arm, a smirk hitching up one corner of his mouth. His gaze swept the otherwise empty room before landing back on him. "You being antisocial again?"

Three days without that devilish smile, without those autumn eyes, and Jamie felt his partner's absence all the way to his balls. He tried not to let the longing show, unsure how Aidan wanted to play this. *Casual* was how they'd left it, right before falling asleep tangled with each other Thursday night. Jamie's arms had been empty when his alarm went off Friday morning. He'd felt a pang of loss, then a spike of panic once he'd realized his phone was set for work hours, not flight hours. He had started the day behind and stayed that way for all of it. Behind in packing, behind in making it to the airport, behind in reconnecting with Aidan, behind in sorting how he felt about *casual*, and still behind, three days later, in getting his case report to SAC Cruz.

He sank back in his chair and scrubbed his hands over his face. "Trying to get this report done. I don't think I've ever had this much post-case paperwork in my three years here."

"Welcome to being my partner." Aidan didn't sound the least bit sorry about that. A good sign. So too was his smile as he dropped into the visitor chair across from Jamie. "You're a field agent now. You're responsible for the entire report, not just the cyber portion."

He raked a hand through his hair. "Cruz wants this by end of day. I just want it to be right."

"I'm sure it'll be perfect, Walker."

Walker, not *Jamie*. Because they were at the office or because Aidan was pulling back? Further back than casual, even? He had been perfectly civil if a little grumpy at Jamie's delay on the way to the airport in Texas, had discussed the post-case follow-up with him before sleeping the rest of the flight, then had insisted on taking a cab to his place instead of having Jamie drive in the opposite direction to drop him off. Radio silence since then, other than Aidan sending him his notes for the case report. Had Jamie lost his shot at more with Aidan, at *casual* even, because he had been too damn tired and too damn busy to pick up the phone?

"Hey, Earth to Whiskey." Aidan's softer voice and waving hand snapped Jamie out of his spiral.

"Sorry, and I'm sorry I didn't call. I've just been caught up in this"—he gestured at the monitors—"all weekend."

"It's fine, Whiskey. I had a packed weekend too."

"Family stuff?"

Aidan's gaze flitted away. "Mostly."

"How's Katie?"

Then back, eyes brightening, same as his smile. "Better now that I'm home."

"That's good."

Aidan stood, and the same pang of loss from Friday morning pierced Jamie's chest again. He hadn't had enough time back in Aidan's presence. A desk apart, a perfectly polite too-short conversation, a *Walker* and a *Whiskey*, a smile, a smirk, and a flitting autumn gaze. Not enough.

But then Aidan circled the desk, shoved a stack of papers and a soda can out of the way, and leaned a hip against the corner. He dropped the folder that had been under his arm in Jamie's lap. "Once you finish the write-up on Galveston, we have a new case to dig into."

Stifling his sigh of relief, Jamie opened the file and flipped through the first few pages to get a sense of the case. A series of possibly connected ransomware attacks on multinational corporations in Silicon Valley. He glanced up at Aidan. "Local?"

"Most of them will be. Galveston was an aberration."

Jamie looked away before Aidan saw the loss and doubt creep back into his gaze. An aberration. Back to business as usual. How wrong had he read everything in Texas? Over the past month?

"We'll alternate who takes the lead on closing reports," Aidan continued. "I wanted you to write up this first one to learn." He reached into his pocket, pulled something out in his fist, then flattened the same hand on the desk, palm over the object as he slid it in front of Jamie. "And I needed time to pull this together for you."

Jamie rolled closer to the desk and snuck his hand under Aidan's—and over a flash drive. "A full copy of the one Mel gave me, plus everything else I thought you might need from my own records, official and otherwise."

At least Jamie hadn't read this wrong—the trust, the partnership he and Aidan had solidified over the past month. He met Aidan's gaze again, hoping his partner saw in his eyes the appreciation, the promise to handle this gift with care. "Thank you."

Aidan shifted his hand to the side of Jamie's resting on the desk, except for his pinky that lingered there. "You're gonna want to keep that on you so Building Services doesn't misplace it."

It took Jamie an extra few moments for the words to register, entranced as he was by Aidan drawing random designs—no, not random, the *N* and *C* of his chest tattoo—on the back of his hand. "Building Services?"

"There's a desk across from mine waiting for my partner on the main floor." He tangled their fingers. "If you want to claim it . . ."

Jamie's gaze shot back to his, and the autumn staring down at him was molten. There was an invitation there, to share an office and more, and Jamie was sure he wasn't reading that wrong. "I do."

"Good." Smirking, Aidan gave his fingers a playful squeeze, then pushed off the desk, turning for the door and tossing a promise of his own over his shoulder. "We'll celebrate after work."

Jamie couldn't wait.

Files, check.

Crypto tomes, check.

Personal items, aside from the one in his hand, check.

Jamie folded the last piece of tissue paper around the framed picture of his family and placed it gently inside the open box on his desk. Impromptu moving day had turned his little corner of the cave into even more of a disaster area than it usually was—dangling cables, stray pens, towering stacks of boxes. He was amazed how much clutter he had amassed in three years.

IT had already taken his monitors and phone. Building Services would move the boxes after hours. By tomorrow morning, he would be set up in his new workspace, at the other desk in Aidan's office. Jamie wasn't entirely comfortable leaving the cave behind for a glassed-in office on the main floor, but he didn't want to condemn Aidan to the vampiric Cyber surroundings he so clearly disfavored. Jamie wouldn't mind the view either—of San Francisco or of his partner.

Smiling, he remembered the view during their last night together in Galveston. Aidan standing over him in the moonlit bathroom—lips swollen, hair tousled, pants undone, his head and eyes rolled back in tortured ecstasy.

He looked forward to seeing that view again tonight, Aidan's promise to "celebrate" on the road to reality, judging by his text from fifteen minutes ago asking Jamie's choice of champagne and the whereabouts of a liquor store close to his house. A thirty-minute commute was all that stood between Jamie and the man he wanted in his arms again.

Or so he thought, until the staccato *tap-tap-tap* of high heels on linoleum wiped the smile off his face. Jamie recognized the rhythm of those steps. He had been waiting for this particular rock-studded shoe to drop the entire weekend. His boss glided through the server racks toward him like the deadliest supermodel he'd ever seen. She stopped at the opening of the cave bullpen and lowered her arms in front of her, index finger tapping against a slim manila file folder in her hands. Jamie could guess its contents.

A call transcript from the morning of the bomb scare—Aidan's shouted *Jamie* and his hollered *baby*. Security camera shots of them inside the observation room or outside on the condo balcony, wrapped in each other's arms, bodies and mouths locked together. Accounts from Oscar and Todd as to the heated interactions they had witnessed last week.

"Give us the room, please." Cruz waited for the other agents to clear out and lowered herself into a visitor chair. "Sit down, Jamie."

Startled into action, he moved the box on his desk to the floor, pushed aside the loose cables, and swiped the rest of the detritus into an empty desk drawer.

"SAC Cruz, I can explain," he started, though he didn't have a good explanation ready to follow. He had slept with his partner, his mentor—Cruz's brother-in-law—and he intended to do it again. Telling her anything different would be a lie.

She held up a hand and nodded at his chair. "Sit down," she repeated more gently. "After saving my life last week, you've earned the right to call me Mel. And don't say anything else about what may or may not be going on with you and Aidan. I'm walking a razor-thin line of plausible deniability as it is."

He clamped his mouth shut and took his seat.

Cruz—*Mel*—crossed one leg over the other and balanced the file folder on her knee. "Do you know why you were assigned to Agent Talley?"

"You wanted him to assess whether I'm ready for fieldwork."

"I think Galveston proves you're more than capable in the field."

"Thank you, but—"

She cut off his would-be confession of relative inexperience. "You have a new assignment, Agent Walker."

Opening the file, she pulled out a photo and pushed it across the desk. Similar to the one Todd showed them last week, it was a color shot of Renaud standing in a North African or Middle Eastern bazaar. In this photo, however, by his side stood a towering man with warm brown skin, broad shoulders, and eyes the same shape and color as those of the woman sitting across from Jamie.

His mind reeled, recalling Mel's demand for backup once Renaud had been connected to their case and Gary's surprised reaction to the incident Wednesday morning. The former Texas City SAC had nudged Jamie for more details on the drivers of the SUVs. Because Gary hadn't sent them. They were unknown variables at play in a scenario he thought he'd had under control.

A scenario Mel understood better than any of them.

"The accident Wednesday morning had nothing to do with the attack on the Port, did it?"

"No, I don't believe it did."

Jamie's gut knotted at the myriad implications. "It was connected with Aidan's accident eight months ago."

Mel leaned forward. "Neither incident was an *accident*."

If he thought his heart hurt for Aidan before, this was a whole new level of pain. "How much of this does Aidan know?"

"Aidan knows I suspect the crash that killed Gabe and Tom was not an accident. I told him as much when I partnered you two. I told Aidan I was giving him what he needed to solve Gabe and Tom's murders. I was giving him *you*."

"And the flash drive," Jamie said.

She nodded. "Aidan doesn't know Gabe had ties to a suspected terrorist. And he doesn't know my brother may have set a chain of events in motion that resulted in his and Tom's deaths."

Jamie tapped his finger on the photo. "So Aidan doesn't know about this?"

Mel pulled it toward her, gaze riveted on the damning piece of evidence. "No, he doesn't, and you won't tell him."

"I won't—"

She raised her cold, hard eyes to him, and Jamie's protest died. He'd seen what she could do to a man, and he didn't want to make himself a target.

"I received this"—she lifted the photo off the desk—"on the day I was promoted to SAC. It arrived in an envelope with the flash drive, with no return address, postmarked Houston. Right before he died, Hamilton indicated he'd sent me a picture."

All the pieces clicked into place. "You didn't owe Gary a favor, did you?"

Mel slid back in her chair, laid the photo in her lap, and

folded her hands over it. "Gary did request you. I granted his request because I suspected Renaud might be involved." Her eyes flicked down to the picture, then back up. "If I'd known Gary had been flipped, I wouldn't have risked you or Aidan. That said, we're one step closer to the truth."

"Are you sure neither Tom nor Aidan were involved?" It felt like a betrayal to ask such a question, but after the week they'd had, he had to.

"I don't believe so. But I was wrong about Gary, and about Gabe, so yes, you should look into Tom. As for Aidan, you know his family's history with the IRA?" He nodded, and she carried on. "Given that, he's the last person I'd suspect of terrorism. And his grief over Tom and Gabe was real, as was the shock on his face when I told him my suspicions about the accident."

Jamie breathed a little easier. This woman seemed to know Aidan better than anyone, and she was right about his personal history with terrorism. But she'd said it herself; Mel had been wrong, twice so far. He would still have to investigate Aidan and Tom, and he would also investigate her. "You want me to look into Gabe's involvement with Renaud's organization?" He didn't let on how deep he intended to dig.

"Yes, and I want you to find out what really happened that night eight months ago."

He nodded and moved to sit back in his chair.

Mel tilted forward and caught his trailing hand. "More importantly, Jamie, I need you to keep Aidan alive."

Her eyes weren't cold and hard anymore. They blazed with loyalty and determination, and Jamie breathed another sigh of relief, assured she was as invested in Aidan Talley's life as he was coming to be.

"You did a hell of a job this past week." She squeezed his hand. "Can I count on you to keep doing that?"

It was a heavy burden to bear—a man's past, present, and future in his hands—but Jamie wouldn't trust Aidan's life to anyone else. Protectiveness surged through him for this man whose fate seemed inexorably tangled with his own.

This time he didn't lie or question the truth of his answer.

"Yes."

Reviews are an invaluable tool when it comes to spreading the word about great reads. Please consider leaving an honest review for *Single Malt* on your favorite review site.

Thank you for reading!

ACKNOWLEDGMENTS

First Edition Acknowledgments:

I would not have been able to bring this book to life without four very important people. My best friend, Tera, who read an early draft, told me to keep writing, then read all the drafts to come. My freelance editor, Kristi Yanta, who focused my thoughts and words. My Carina editor, Deb Nemeth, who lived up to every expectation I had for a wonderful collaboration. My agent, Laura Bradford, who agented on the run (through airports) like nobody's business. Thank you all so much for your invaluable assistance.

Thanks also to D.M., for the technical advice, to T.C. and S.W., for the LEO tidbits, to my critique partners—D'Ann, Peggy and Julie—for the craft input, and to my family, for encouraging my writing and entrepreneurial spirit.

Last but not least, all the whiskey, wine and coffee to my beta readers—Sandra, Chelley, Jaya, Morgan, Mirna, Jess, Val, Jennifer, Beth, Michelle and Victoria. Many of you had never before read m/m romance when I dropped this book in your inboxes. You've hung with me for years, in one writing form or another, and your feedback, friendship and unwavering support mean the world to me. Cheers and all my love!

Second Edition Acknowledgments:

The paperbacks are finally here! And aren't they gorgeous! Many thanks to Cate Ashwood, Wander Aguiar, and Robbin for making this second edition of *Single Malt* so smoking hot, to Adam and Sandy for the editing polish, to Kim and Rachel for beta reading the new scenes, and to Nina and the VPR Team for getting the word out. Finally, dear readers, thank you, thank you, thank you for loving this series, these characters, and this world for over six years. What a ride!

ALSO BY LAYLA REYNE

For the most up-to-date list of titles and a helpful reading order, please visit www.laylareyne.com.

Agents Irish and Whiskey:

Single Malt

Cask Strength

Barrel Proof

Tequila Sunrise

Blended Whiskey

Angel's Share (2024)

Trouble Brewing:

Imperial Stout

Craft Brew

Noble Hops

Final Gravity

Fog City:

Prince of Killers

King Slayer

A New Empire

Queen's Ransom

Silent Knight

Perfect Play:

Dead Draw

Bad Bishop

King Hunt

Soul to Find:

Icarus and the Devil

Changing Lanes:

Relay

Medley

Freestyle

Table for Two:

The Last Drop

Blue Plate Special

Over a Barrel

Standalone Titles:

Dine With Me

Variable Onset

Sweater Weather

What We May Be

ABOUT THE AUTHOR

Layla Reyne is the author of *What We May Be* and the *Agents Irish and Whiskey, Fog City,* and *Perfect Play* series. A Carolina Tar Heel who spent fifteen years in California, Layla enjoys weaving her bicoastal experiences into her stories, along with adrenaline-fueled suspense and heart pounding romance.

You can find Layla at laylareyne.com, in her reader group on Facebook—Layla's Lushes, and at the following sites:

BB bookbub.com / authors / layla-reyne

facebook.com / laylareyne

instagram.com / laylareyne

tiktok.com / @laylareyne

www.ingramcontent.com/pod-product-compliance
Lightning Source LLC
Chambersburg PA
CBHW071415200726
48294CB00002B/401

* 9 7 8 1 9 6 2 0 1 0 0 1 6 *